HOW TO FAKE DATE A VAMPIRE

THE CHARMING COVE SERIES

LINSEY HALL

CHAPTER
ONE

Emma

"I don't know about you, but I feel like a stalker," I said to my friend Holly.

"Just drink your beer and wait." She leaned forward to look out the window of the pub. "I think the duke will be here any minute, and I heard he's *hot.*"

I rolled my eyes and took a sip of my beer. Around us, the pub bustled with activity. The Drunken Clam was new to Charming Cove, the seaside village in Cornwall where I lived. Like Holly and me, many of the locals had come to check it out.

But that wasn't the only thing they'd come for. There were three paparazzi standing across the street, which meant that the Duke of Blackthorn must have come into town. Yes, *that* Duke of Blackthorn, the reclusive, sinfully handsome vampire who owned a massive estate outside of

1

the village. He'd spent years away, but now he was *back*, and everyone was dying to get a peek.

"I don't know what the fuss is all about," I said as I looked down at my beer.

Holly shot me an exasperated look. "It's the *Duke of Blackthorn,* you muppet. That's what the big deal is. Handsome, wealthy, powerful, famous."

"Eh." I waved my hand, unimpressed. Someone with that much going for them had to have a terrible personality. And it wasn't like he'd earned any of that. I'd learned from experience how awful dukes could be.

Still, I craned my neck to see if I could spot him because I was just as nosy as everyone else when it came down to it. There was no way he was as hot as the gossip suggested, and I wanted a glimpse of the weak chin to prove it.

"Why did he come back to Blackthorn Hall?" I asked. "Shouldn't he be out jet-setting or something?"

Everyone knew about Blackthorn Hall, the magnificent estate outside of town that wasn't open to visitors like so many of the old country estates were. Of course we were all curious, but the duke was notoriously private. There were articles about him in the papers occasionally, but never photos.

"No idea, but I've been hearing people say that he's been at his country house for the last month."

"What, living like a hermit?"

Holly shrugged. "I'd keep him company."

From the sound of the whispers around me, she wasn't the only one. Flora, who was a hundred if she was a day, sat at the table next to us, a martini glass clutched in her hand.

"Well, I'm just saying"—she pointed at her companion with a ruby-red nail—"we well-preserved ladies know our way around the bedroom. Experience, and all. The duke could benefit from that."

I grinned. *Get it, Flora.*

She caught me looking at her, and I tilted my glass in salute, grinning.

Flora nodded at me. "See, the new girl knows what I'm talking about, even if she's just a spring chicken, barely toddling around the coop."

I frowned, then mouthed at Holly, *Barely toddling around the coop?*

Holly shrugged. "If the shoe fits."

I rolled my eyes. Flora was right about me being the new girl, though. I'd been in town only two years, and in a place like Charming Cove, that made me very new indeed. Charming Cove was an old fishing village built right on the sea in Cornwall. Regular humans, who had no idea that magic existed, lived on the east side around the cute little harbor. Magical beings lived on Foxglove Lane, a pretty street on the west side of town that sat on a small cliff overlooking the sea. We had all our own shops and restaurants and even a little cinema.

Thanks to magic, humans knew nothing about our neighborhood, and it was a divine place.

The duke was one of us, a vampire who also mixed with human society due to the fact that his title had been given by some long-ago human regent. There weren't many supernaturals among the nobility since humans didn't know we existed and we tended to avoid them to keep it that way.

Unlike the vampires of myth, real vampires died just like the rest of us. His family had held the title for centuries and passed it down generation after generation. Humans knew him as a duke, but we knew him as the *vampire* duke.

Of course, all around me, people talked about him.

"I've heard he's a billionaire," Mike said.

"Well, I heard he's donated most of his money to charity," a woman added.

"No, he's starting a business that will take tourists to space," Mike said.

"He's a cage fighter on the weekends," Flora added. "I'm sure of it." The lascivious gleam in her eye made me think she wanted to get in the cage with him.

I rolled my eyes. I knew what he was—a jerk, just like his father. The former Duke of Blackthorn had pulled funding from Eventide Children's Home, where I'd spent the first few years after my parent's death. I'd had pretty poor opinions of the nobility ever since, especially the Blackthorns. I'd never told anyone in town about it, though.

"How long do you think he'll be back?" I asked, hoping he'd leave soon and I could stop being reminded of bad memories.

"No idea, but what do you say to visiting his place later tonight to find out?"

A laugh exploded out of me. "Creep up on the Duke of Blackthorn's notoriously private estate? Sure, count me in." *As if.*

"Really?" Her eyes gleamed with excitement.

"No, you ninny." I bumped her shoulder with mine, which turned out to be a very bad idea. I somehow managed to tip my beer glass toward my lap, and the cold splash of liquid made me yelp.

Holly jumped up and stared at my crotch with a horrified expression. "You look like you—"

"I know what I look like." I groaned. My new burnt orange trousers were meant to be cool, but that had gone to hell. The liquid had turned the fabric super dark, and it I looked like I'd wet myself. Embarrassing as hell, which was very on brand for me. "I'll be back."

"Good luck." She grimaced as I turned and slipped through the crowd.

The area around the toilets was blocked by a group of lads shouting at a football match on the TV over the bar.

"Hey, New Girl!" A blond bloke with a barrel chest tried to catch my attention, but I ignored him and hurried into the loo.

Not only wasn't I interested in him, but I hated being called "New Girl." What would it take to belong here, damn it?

The loo was a quiet oasis, and I headed straight for the sinks and grabbed a paper towel. Immediately, I began blotting at the stain, trying to dry it.

A door creaked open, and I looked up into the mirror to see who had entered.

Of course it was the hottest man I'd ever seen. He entered through a different door than I had, one that appeared to come from a quiet hallway. Our eyes met in the mirror above the sink, and my brain frizzed out. Who could blame me, though?

First of all, he was super tall. *And* broad, with shoulders that shouldn't be possible on someone who wasn't a professional athlete. Which he probably was. He had the kind of body that made something primal light up inside me, like I was a damned alley cat who'd just spotted the hottest tom on the block.

But his face...oh, Lord, his face. Strong jaw, full lips, and emerald eyes that were far too beautiful to belong to anyone but an angel. His warm, mahogany-colored hair gleamed, and I wondered how the hell he got it to shine as it did. I'd tried every spell I could muster and I still didn't have hair like that.

"Are you all right?" he asked, his voice so deep and impossibly posh that it fried my brain for a moment. I'd grown up in the north and then moved immediately to rural Cornwall. I hadn't even realized people could sound so...well, rich. And fancy.

It was a serious contrast to my working-class roots, and I suddenly realized how I must look, with my wet pants and slack jaw. My hands took on a life of their own and flashed up to try to cover the stain on my crotch, which just made it more obvious.

"I didn't wet myself," I blurted as I whirled around to face him.

Oh, shit.

I sounded beyond stupid.

"Ah..." He clearly was at a loss for words, which was no surprise, since I was a total muppet.

"Isn't it cool that this place has gender-neutral loos?" I said, desperately searching for a change of topic.

"They're not gender-neutral."

I frowned. "Yes, they are."

"I'm afraid not." He made an apologetic face, as if it were his fault. "And this is the gents'."

No.

This could not be happening.

I looked around, seeing the place with new eyes. Was that a urinal in the corner?

Oh, my fates, it was. There was a urinal in here, making it super obvious that it was the men's. And I was still covering my crotch with my hands.

There was only one thing to do—I ran for it. A demon took over my body and forced me from the little room. I didn't even say goodbye or try to explain myself, because there was no good explanation other than *I'm an idiot.*

I pushed my way through the crowd of lads who were still shouting at the television and made my way back to my table. I threw myself onto the stool and buried my face in my hands, mortified. "You won't believe what I just did."

"What did you do?" Unease sounded in Holly's voice. She was familiar with the seriously dumb stuff I got into, but this one took the cake.

"The loo isn't gender-neutral."

"Duh."

"Well, *I* thought it was."

She winced. "Dare I ask how you figured out the truth?"

"The hard way." I filled her in on every excruciating detail, watching as her face went from horror to delight and back to horror.

When I finished, she asked, "Do you know who it was?"

"No, just that he was the hottest man I've ever seen and

that I panicked and ran for it before I could get his name." Not that he'd want to give it to a weirdo like me.

She gave one of her signature snort-laughs. "Okay, my sincerest apologies, but that is absolutely hilarious."

"Ugh." I threw a little pretzel at her, then turned to look out the window, searching for any kind of distraction. Tonight was supposed to be about getting *away* from the crap in my life, not creating more of it.

My gaze landed on three men with massive cameras. "They're still there. Hasn't the duke showed?"

"Not yet." She nodded her head toward Flora. "But I think she's planning her attack."

I grinned, liking the image of Flora taking down the duke like a lion going after a gazelle on the savannah.

My humor was short-lived, though. The cold beer soaking through my trousers was an unavoidable reminder of what had just happened. "I think I'm going to head out."

"Come on, Em." She shortened my name in the way that I loved. All I wanted was to belong, and the nickname was proof that I did. With her, at least. "Let's have another. You said your day was shit, and that was before the loo incident."

"Ehhh."

"Come on." She slung an arm around my shoulders. "I haven't seen you at work lately, and I'm sure Lily has done something horrible we need to discuss."

Complaining about my fellow novice witch in the Aurora Coven was always a surefire way to let off some steam. Maybe she had a point. "All right. One more."

"Excellent!" Holly jumped up and went to the bar to get us another round of beers, then sat down next to me and said, "Now, spill." She looked down at my trousers. "Not literally, though."

"Ha, ha." I took a long drink of my beer and said, "It's just the usual stuff. She's always making comments about the spells I screw up. She said she'd seen hedgehogs with better spells than me. I just know she'll be chosen to be the next Official Witch, and then she'll make my life hell."

"Emma!" Holly gripped my arm. "Look, I think the duke might be outside!"

I leaned closer to see where she was pointing, unable to help myself. I spotted the dark-haired man exiting the alley to the side of the pub.

"That's not him," I said. "That's the guy I saw in the loo."

Holly's head whipped toward me. "Really?"

"Yeah."

The paparazzi went wild, jostling to get close to him. "Well, bad news, friend. That's the duke."

Of course it was. Fantastic. I groaned as I again buried my face in my hands. "He did have a nice accent. I should have realized."

"Don't beat yourself up."

"Yeah, yeah." Heat flushed my cheeks.

What did it matter, anyway? It wasn't like I'd see him again.

CHAPTER
TWO

Emma

THIS COULD *NOT* BE HAPPENING.

But it was, and it was so horrifying that it went in slow motion while I stood on a patch of grass behind the Starlight Café, the sun shining down like it was a normal day.

I stared, frozen, as a very pissed-off goat slammed his head into the arse of the Duke of Blackthorn.

I thought I'd never see him again.

Instead, I'd just assaulted him with my goat.

The duke stumbled, dropping the large cardboard box he was carrying. The sound of shattering glass made me wince.

As part of the Aurora Coven, it was my job to fix problems brought to us by members of the magical community. When a local farmer had asked me to improve the temperament of his ornery goat, it would have been an easy job for any other witch.

And yet, I'd screwed it up.

Majorly.

I ran toward the duke, who had turned around to glare at the goat. He wore a dark sweater and sturdy work trousers, along with dark leather boots. It was obviously his outdoor labor look, but everything was perfectly fitted and definitely expensive.

Which just annoyed me. Any reminder of what he was poked at the wound I'd done my best to forget.

Not to mention it was annoying that he was even more attractive that I'd remembered.

His green gaze flicked up to mine, and I stilled. He seemed to pay far closer attention to me than anyone I'd ever met, and it felt like being under a spotlight. He was far taller than I was, and even though I stood about a meter away, I had to tilt my head up to meet his gaze.

"You again." There was something soft in his voice that I had to be imagining. Something almost...interested.

"Yep...Your Grace." I barely avoided wincing.

"Is this your goat?"

"Um, no," I said, looking at the goat, who had begun to chew on the cardboard box at his feet. "Not exactly."

"How could a goat be 'not exactly' yours?"

I grimaced, not wanting to admit that it had been my job to improve the goat's temperament, since I'd so drastically failed with the spell to do so. "He's part of my job."

"You're a goat wrangler?"

Heat flushed my cheeks. "Maybe." I raised my chin. *Be polite, you numpty.* "I'm sorry about your boxes, though. Can I replace the contents?"

He looked down, then sighed. "No. But thank you for the offer."

"Maybe some of the bottles didn't break." I knelt and shooed the goat away, hoping I'd find most of them okay.

The ornery beast snapped out to chomp on my hair, but the duke moved with lighting reflexes, blocking the goat from taking a bite before shoving him gently away.

I looked up at him, realizing that he was far closer than I'd expected. His scent wrapped around me, sandalwood and pine. I frowned at him.

"What is it?" he asked.

"You smell good. Like, too good," I blurted.

Then I wanted to die.

I'd actually said that...*out loud.*

I shot upright. I needed to get my goat and get the heck out of there. If he wouldn't let me replace the broken bottles, there was nothing I could do, and I needed to remove myself from whatever future embarrassment I was sure to create.

"I'm sorry again." I grabbed the goat by the collar, praying he wouldn't turn around and bite me. "Are you sure there's nothing I can do to replace what was broken?"

"No, but thank you." He looked at me like I was an alien, or at least some kind of creature he'd never seen before.

"Right. Sorry again." I whirled around and hurried off, dragging the goat along.

I was halfway across the lawn when his voice stopped me. "Wait. What's your name?"

I turned back. "Um, it's Emma. Emma Willowby."

He nodded, his expression unreadable. Was that interest in his eyes?

No, it couldn't be. And even if it was, I didn't want there to be.

He turned to the crumpled box and picked it up.

I tilted my head back and looked up at the sky. How was this my life?

The goat bleated.

LATER THAT DAY, I finally managed to get the goat to chill out and be nice.

Kind of.

He stood next to me in the coven meeting room, where we sat alone as he chewed on the piece of taffy I'd given him. It was the extra-tough kind made by the little shop down the road, so it would keep him busy for a while. As a seaside village in Cornwall and a top vacation destination for supernaturals from all over Britain, we had an excellent assortment of ice cream parlors, candy shops, and pubs.

My spell to make the goat behave only worked about ninety percent of the time, so I'd decided to hedge my bets and get him something to distract him.

Our coven owned a shopfront on Foxglove Lane, which meant that the front room overlooked the road and the sea beyond. That was the public-facing room where people came to get our help. The meeting room was located behind that. It was a cozy space that we used for socializing and coven meetings, filled with squashy armchairs, plants, and books. The large window had a view of the colorful back garden, which was surrounded on all sides by tall stone walls.

I caught a flash of movement as someone passed by the window to reach the exterior door. It opened silently, and Lily stepped in.

It took everything I had to keep from showing my stink face. That's what Penny called it, and I'd caught sight of it in a mirror once. Unfortunately, she wasn't wrong.

Lily was one of four other apprentice witches in the coven, and we were at odds as often as we weren't. But that was her fault, not mine.

Mostly.

"Emma!" She smiled widely at me. "How's it going with the goat?"

"Good, yeah." I patted him, hoping he wouldn't nip at me.

She arched a brow. "I heard there was a little run-in with the Duke of Blackthorn?"

"Oh? Where'd you hear that?" I tried to play it cool, but inside, I was cursing up a storm.

"From Coraline, who was sitting in the Starlight Café. She saw it happen right through the window."

I resisted dropping my head back and groaning, but it took a real effort.

She sat in the chair next to mine, her perfectly fitted sundress flaring around her as if she were in an advert. "Well, *my* task went phenomenally well, thank you for asking."

"Fantastic. What was it, again?" But I already knew. She'd been assigned her job at the same time I'd been assigned mine, and it had seemed like a more difficult task, which I'd thought meant the senior witches trusted her more. When it came time to choose the newest official member of the coven, she was most likely to get the spot.

"Oh, you know, silly." She batted my arm playfully, and I gritted my teeth. "I had to get rid of the pixies at the Cupcake Cauldron. They kept destroying the newest cakes."

"It sounds like you managed it."

"*Of course* I managed it." She flipped her hair over her shoulder. "It's all perfect now."

"I'm sure it is." I gave her the sweetest smile I could manage and reminded myself that I wouldn't accomplish my lifelong goal if I decked her in the face right then.

It wasn't that my lifelong goal was to join the Aurora Coven as an official member, although that was part of it. No, my goal was to find somewhere I belonged. Like, *really* belonged. I'd read enough self-help books in my early twenties that I knew, as an orphan, it's what I was lacking. I didn't mean to sound clinical about it, but it was a simple truth.

In the two years since I'd moved to Charming Cove when I was twenty-five, I'd been working toward full membership in the Aurora Coven. A coven was a bit like a law firm where becoming an official member was like making partner—it meant you were truly official. That you were *chosen*. I'd never been chosen for anything in my life. Nothing that mattered, anyway. After the Eventide Children's Home had been shut down, I'd been shuffled from foster family to foster family, not one had decided to keep me. This was my chance to make my own family.

I wanted that *Official Member* designation badly enough that I could taste it.

So I didn't deck Lily, and I gave the goat at my side a little pat, hoping he would behave himself when the senior witches arrived.

The three other apprentices appeared—Holly, Cleo, and Elle—and each gave a little wave as they sat. I glared at Holly, a look that was meant to convey *You're late, and you left me with Lily.*

Holly grimaced and quickly mouthed *Sorry.*

Cleo, one of the friendlier apprentices, swept her dark hair off her shoulder and leaned forward to speak. Before she could get a word out, the door swung open and Hazel walked in.

The five of us straightened and gave her our best *serious witch* faces. At least, I did. Lily always seemed so much more comfortable in these scenarios, and I couldn't help the tiniest twinge of jealousy. I shoved it down and reached out to give the goat another pat.

"Is he your emotional support goat?" Lily whispered.

I snatched my hand back from him and glared at her.

She just smiled.

I turned to Hazel, who'd taken the wide pink armchair near the fire. Hazel was in her late thirties, with a sharp black bob and brilliant green eyes. Every witch had a specialty, and hers was divination. I'd wondered if that meant she knew who the next official witch would be, but she'd said it didn't work like that.

The last four official witches filed in—Ember, Willow, Luna, and Stella. Though there were five official witches and five apprentices, we didn't study directly under one witch. The younger witches often became close with one of the older witches, though.

Willow was my witch big sister, as I liked to think of her, and she gave me a hopeful glance when she saw the goat standing placidly next to me. From the look on her face, whatever expression my face made back at her wasn't a smile. Probably a grimace, with Lily sitting so close.

"All right." Hazel's voice rang out over the small crowd of witches clustered onto every cushioned surface in the room. "It's time to begin. Apprentices, check in with your progress." She pointed to Elle, who nodded.

"I've had great luck with the haunting at Pinny Pond. All sorted, and the ghost is on his way."

"Excellent." Hazel nodded, then turned her attention to Cleo.

One by one, the others reported their progress until it was my turn. I sucked in a breath and said a quick prayer to Hecate before saying, "Cliff is doing fantastically." I patted his head. "Behavior problems all fixed."

"But not before he headbutted the Duke of Blackthorn," Lily murmured.

"What was that, Lily?" Hazel asked.

"She said, not before he headbutted the Duke of Black-thorn," repeated Luna, who sat closer.

"That was *before* I'd finished with him," I said. "Just a little mishap."

"Hmmm." Hazel's brows rose. "Well, if you're sure."

The goat chose that moment to turn his head and take an enormous bite out of the cushioned arm of the chair that I sat in. He must have had teeth like a tiger, because he tore the fabric away.

I closed my eyes. *Hecate, take me now.*

There was dead silence.

"I'll keep working on him," I said, glancing at Willow, the witch who had a particularly close connection with animals. I was probably going to have to go to her for help.

"You should probably just give up," Lily whispered, so quietly that only I could hear. "It's clearly not going well for you."

If only my damned goat would bite *her*.

"We have some exciting news," Hazel said, and I turned to her. "It's time to start planning the Beltane Ball."

A frisson of excitement went through me. The Beltane Ball was the biggest event of the year. Our coven hosted an enormous party for the townspeople and the visitors who came to town specifically for the event. The goal was to make people as happy as possible—to delight them and thrill them—so that we could collect that joy and use it in our spells for the upcoming year.

Everyone who attended the party knew that we were collecting their joy, so it wasn't shady. And they benefitted because it was the same townspeople who came to us to solve their problems. We used some of that joy and delight in our spells, so it was a win-win for everyone.

"Normally, one of the senior witches would plan the party," Hazel said. "But we think that you apprentices have been with us long enough that if any of you want to attempt it, you may do so."

A low gasp echoed through the little crowd of apprentices. She couldn't be serious. Plan the entire Beltane Ball?

"Obviously, if you succeed at such a monumental task, you will be made an official witch."

My head began to buzz. This was it.

Her face turned serious. "But if you fail, we'll have to reassess your membership with the coven. One of the most important parts of being a witch is knowing what you're capable of. It's important not to bite off more than you can chew, or you could hurt someone with a spell gone wrong or a potion poorly mixed. Not to mention we wouldn't have enough joy for all our spells for the upcoming year, so we wouldn't have enough work to go around, anyway."

Oh, shit.

Reassess your membership.

That meant *get kicked out*—no question.

Was I willing to take that risk?

"I'll do it." Lily's voice rang out clearly. She shot me a pitying look, then looked at the goat at my side.

It lit a fire within me, one that burned with the heat of a thousand insane suns, because the next thing I said was, "Me, too."

Hazel's brows rose. "Two volunteers?"

We both nodded.

"Are you sure you're both up to the task?" she asked.

"Of course." Lily smiled calmly.

I nodded, feeling a bubbling hysteria rising within me. What was I doing?

But then Lily shot me another look, and I nodded more emphatically.

"Well, there should only be one, so why don't you both come up with a venue for the ball and report back? We'll make a final decision on who it will be then."

I blew out a breath.

Okay, maybe that was an out. If I didn't have a great venue, I could return to the safe space of being an apprentice.

But then Lily would win. She'd be an official witch and make my life hell. She might even find a way to boot me from the coven.

CHAPTER
THREE

Emma

"You are officially insane," Holly said when she walked into my flat later that night.

"I know, but I can't face that right now." I held up the bottle of wine and the remote control. "What do you say we forget our problems for forty-two minutes with the most recent episode of *Love Island*, and then, as soon as it's over, we brainstorm venues?"

The truth was, I needed to *not* talk about it for a little while. My brain was still going a mile a minute over the craziness of what I'd done, and I needed it to chill out. *Love Island* was a surefire way to distract Holly, who loved the show as much as I did.

She sighed and rolled her eyes. "I'm not sure that delaying it is a great idea, but I *am* desperate to know if Katia hooks up with that businessman who looks like a loaf of white bread." She pointed at me. "But as soon as the credits roll, we're discussing it."

"Excellent." I grinned as I tossed her the remote, then poured her a glass of wine.

I wasn't proud of my addiction to human reality TV, but I also didn't try to fight it. After a long day of trying to fix magical problems, it was nice to disappear into something silly.

It didn't hurt that my little flat was on Foxglove Lane. It was the best location, and the cozy living room had double doors that opened onto a patio overlooking the gardens across the road, and the sea beyond that. I handed Holly her glass, then walked over to the doors and pushed them open to let the warm spring breeze rush in.

Holly sighed with delight. "You know how much I love those doors."

I grinned at her. No matter the weather, I would open them to get the sound and smell of the sea air. With a glass of wine—or hot chocolate, if it was cold—my living room was the perfect place to enjoy some downtime.

Except this particular downtime was filled with thoughts of the upcoming Beltane Ball. As Holly watched Katia try to win the heart of a sentient loaf of bread named Chad, my mind spun. I couldn't even enjoy the hot air balloon ride where Katia almost fell out after drinking one too many Kir Royales.

Where the hell was I going to host this ball? It had to be the most spectacular and awe-inspiring venue in Charming Cove, which was...what?

As the TV hummed in the background, the idea came to me.

The Duke of Blackthorn.

True, he probably didn't like me much right now, and I certainly didn't like him, but he *did* have the most spectacular estate in the area. I'd never been, but I'd heard enough to know how great it was.

"What's that expression for?" Holly asked.

I looked up at her, surprised to see that the show had ended.

"I've got it." I drew in a deep breath. "We'll host the ball at the Duke of Blackthorn's estate."

She burst out laughing, then sobered. "Wait, are you serious?"

"As an overboiling cauldron."

She blew out a breath. "You sure?"

"You've heard how spectacular it is. Tommy, the shifter in the building next door, dated the head gardener for a while. He told us stories of the grounds that night we were playing darts at The Sea Shanty."

"Oh, yeah. He'd had a few too many Jail Ales and started to talk like a poet. Said the flower garden was the thing of dreams and that the pond had a mermaid who sang like an angel."

"Don't forget the enchanted woodland and the hedge maze filled with statues and faerie lights. It sounded glorious." I could see it now, with everyone awed to be going into a place they'd never been allowed to visit.

"You'd have people lining up to attend the party if you hosted it there. Everyone has been dying to get a look."

"I bet they'd come from miles around." I was already imagining my glorious success.

"I'll be honest, it is a good idea. But are you sure you can pull it off?"

"If I can host it there? Then, yes. The venue will do most of the work for me."

"Good point." She nodded. "I think maybe this isn't such a bad idea after all."

I grinned. "I think you're right."

THE NEXT MORNING, I wasn't feeling quite so confident. Of course the Duke of Blackthorn's estate would be an amazing place to host the party, but how the heck was I going to convince him?

I needed a very strong coffee to even start thinking about that. Holly and I had drunk one too many glasses of wine the night before as we'd rhapsodized about how glorious the party would be, but the result was a head that was both foggy and pounding.

After a shower, I put on a cream top and yellow skirt, finishing off the look with my biggest, darkest pair of sunglasses. Once dressed, I headed out into the bright morning sunlight. Charming Cove was the sunniest place in England, thanks to the skills of previous Aurora Coven members. They'd enchanted the weather to be pleasant for most of the year, and normally I loved it.

That day, I wanted to hiss at the sun like a vampire out of

human movies. Real vampires had no trouble with the sun, though, and I tried to pretend that I didn't, either.

I squinted as I headed down the street to Margo's coffee shop. On the other side of the road, a team of local volunteers tended to the flowers that filled the long, narrow garden between the road and the ocean cliffs. The sea sparkled bright and blue beyond the garden, the breeze blowing their lovely scent toward me.

As pretty as it was, I was grateful to duck into Margot's café. The cozy space smelled gloriously of fresh pastries and coffee. There was no line, thank Hecate, and Margot bustled out of the back as I stepped up to the counter. She was a pretty woman in her mid-sixties with wild gray curls and bright eyes.

She wiped her hands on her apron and smiled. "What'll it be, darling? Rocket Fuel?"

"Yes, please." Margot always knew when I needed one of her hangover cures.

"Coming right up, lamb." She turned and got to work with the espresso machine.

I admired the pastry case as she worked, trying to pick the best one.

"I thought I might find you here." Willow's familiar voice sounded from behind me, and I turned.

"How'd you know?"

"I saw the look in your eyes right after you threw your hat in the ring." She shrugged. "Then I heard you and Holly laughing like hyenas around midnight as I was walking home from the pub."

I winced. "We were that loud, were we?"

"Could have heard you out at sea."

"Fantastic." I winced. "So, what do you think?"

"I think you can do it." She gave me a serious look. "But it's not a given. It'll be tough. There's a lot that goes into planning the Beltane Ball—more than you apprentices have seen. It's not just the guests' joy that we preserve to use in our spells—it's their awe and wonder. Creating that kind of awe and wonder takes a lot of skill. If you don't manage it, we won't reach our quota. And if we don't reach our quota..."

She didn't need to finish. Without the preserved positive emotions from the Beltane Ball, we wouldn't be able to take on as many clients in the upcoming year.

"We're in trouble," I finished her sentence for her.

"Yes, *we'd* be in trouble. But you'd be in the most trouble."

I drew in a shuddery breath. "Are you trying to scare me?"

"A little, yes. Although I don't think it would look good to back out now. Very flaky."

"No one wants a flaky official witch." I squeezed my eyes shut.

"You just have to make it work," Willow said. "I believe in you."

Her words warmed me and made me want to become an official member of the coven even more.

But they also scared me.

"I'm assuming you already have an idea for the venue?"

I nodded. "The Duke of Blackthorn's estate."

Her eyebrows rose. "That would be impressive. Do you think you can get it?"

"I've got no idea."

"Well, I saw Lily headed out of town toward the Garden of Enchantment. The only place that could possibly beat that is the duke's estate." She grinned. "So you've got to get it."

I nodded, sucking in a deep breath. "I can."

"Good. Now don't disappoint me."

Right. No pressure.

CHAPTER
FOUR

Emma

I WAS ABOUT HALFWAY to the duke's estate when I realized that sneaking through the woods had not been the best idea. I'd already torn the sleeve of my blouse and had a suspicious-looking brown stain on the side of my skirt. Worse, I was pretty sure a bird had created a nest in my hair.

In my defense, I'd had my reasons for this dumb idea. As I'd pulled up to the gate that blocked the road to the duke's estate, I'd seen half a dozen cars, two of which had borne the emblems of local news agencies. There was no way I wanted to run into the paparazzi, so I'd turned my own car onto a country lane that I'd hoped would approach the estate from the back.

It hadn't, but according to the GPS on my phone, the main house should be right past the woods that looked like a reasonable shortcut.

Breaking news: they weren't.

At least I was almost to the edge of the woods. I was pretty sure the trees were thinning out up ahead, and I'd be at the duke's estate in no time. I'd done a bit of internet stalking that morning to see what I could learn about him, and I hadn't liked what I'd found. There hadn't been much written before that month, but a few articles had come out recently. One talked about him withdrawing funding from an orphanage in South London.

Just like his damned father.

What did these men have against needy children? It was almost comedically villainous.

To my left, something rustled through the bushes.

I froze solid.

Were there bears in England? No, there was only Paddington, right? And he wasn't even real.

A tiny black and white creature scampered out of the bushes and stopped in front of me, tilting its head as it blinked dark eyes. Horror shot through me, and I stumbled back.

A skunk. I couldn't ask the duke for a favor if I smelled like a skunk.

Rude.

I blinked at the skunk. "Did you speak?"

Yes. And you're staring. With quite the stink face, I might add.

"Um, I'm sorry." I stared down at the skunk. "You're really talking and I'm not hallucinating?"

I'm really talking.

Oh, she really was. Her lips weren't moving, but I could

hear her in my head. And that meant only one thing—she was my familiar.

I dropped my head back and stared up at the sky. My luck was on fire lately. First the embarrassing run-ins with the duke, and now Hecate had given me a skunk for a familiar. Not a cat or dog or something more normal, but a skunk.

You should be happier right now. The skunk stood up on her hind legs and glared at me. *Presumably, you've been waiting years for your familiar. You probably thought you weren't going to get one at all.*

She was right about that, and I realized I'd been a jerk. Only the most powerful witches got familiars, and this was a big deal for me, skunk or not. It had to mean I was on the right path with my life and my magic if my familiar had shown up.

You don't look impressed, the skunk said.

"I am! I really am. I just—"

Wasn't expecting a skunk. She shook her head. *Anti-skunk bias is just out of control in the UK. I know we're not native here and there aren't many of us, but we are delightful!*

"I'm sure you are! I was just surprised. I never expected to get a familiar."

She tsked. *Poor dear. Low self-esteem.*

"It's not that." Maybe it was? But I didn't like the pity in the skunk's voice. "I just haven't figured out my magical talent yet, and things aren't going super great at work, and it's all just a lot, you know?"

The skunk nodded. *Well, I'm here to help.*

"Thank you. And please forgive me. I'm really glad to meet you, and I'm not biased against skunks." I actually kind of was, but I'd have to work on that, clearly. I didn't want to be that kind of person. "What's your name?"

Penelope.

"It suits you."

She preened, raising a little paw to fluff at her ear. *I know. Now, what are you doing in these woods? You're creeping around like a stalker.* Penelope gasped. *Tell me you're not one of those horrible paparazzi.*

"I'm not. I'm trying to avoid them. But you're right, I *am* sneaking around. I need to see the duke."

She grimaced. *Well, that's going to be difficult. The journalists are parked on his doorstep.*

I cursed. "They must have left their cars at the gate and walked."

Some of them ran.

"Of course they did. Will you show me?"

She nodded, then scampered off. I followed, moving as quickly as I could. When we reached the edge of the woods, I stuck close to the shadows of one of the big oak trees. Penelope pointed to the huge house across the lawn, and I spotted the six men standing on the front steps, cameras at the ready.

They were dwarfed against the size of the building. Built of white stone, it had two massive wings that extended out from either side. A wide flight of steps led up to the main door, and rose vines climbed up the walls. Pink blooms unfurled in the sun, making the austere front of the house into something beautiful.

I didn't want to like the house, so I turned my attention

to the paparazzi. "What do they think he's going to do? Come out and pose?"

Not the sharpest knives in the drawer.

"Or they're desperate." And desperate men were dangerous ones. "I need to get them off that doorstep. Unless there's a way to sneak to the back?" I searched the entire lawn, but there wasn't a convenient row of bushes to hide my approach from the side. The garden was all in the back. "Looks like I'll have to go all the way around through the woods."

I wouldn't suggest it. I felt some pretty strong magical wards back there.

"Oh, drat." I looked at Penelope, then smiled. "Could you help me?"

We've just met, and you're already asking for help?

"I'm desperate. And isn't that what familiars are for?"

Maybe, but its mutual. I'm going to call in the debt sometime.

She sounded like a mini furry mobster, but I didn't have many options. "All right. No problem, I'll owe you one if you can clear out those paparazzi."

How do you propose I do that?

"Well..." What was the proper term for it?

She seemed to know what I wanted because she shook her little head. *You want me to stink bomb them, don't you?*

"Please?"

She scoffed. *The indignity.*

"What indignity? You're a skunk. It's like your superpower. I wish *I* had a superpower."

Hmmm. She sat back on her haunches and tapped her

chin. *I suppose when you put it like that, I'm not entirely opposed. Having a superpower is quite impressive.*

Excellent. If flattery was the way to my familiar's heart, I could manage that. "Thank you! You're the absolute best."

I am, and don't you forget it. She heaved a deep sigh. *Wait here and watch a master at work. I probably won't even have to bomb them, though I might. Just for fun.*

I did as she commanded, watching as she waddled off across the grass. She moved at her own pace, and there was something regal about it. Penelope was a skunk who rushed for no one.

The paparazzi didn't seem to notice her approaching. She climbed the stairs behind them, then skirted around to the side of the little huddle of men and sneaked between them and the door before standing up on her back legs.

They saw her, and all hell broke lose. The men shrieked, each of them joining a chorus of panicked angst as they jostled to escape. They turned tail and ran, cameras bouncing against their chests and clutched in their hands.

Penelope chased them down the road back to their cars, and I was a little jealous of her. Sure, she probably had a hard time entering a party without receiving some side-eye, but nobody messed with her. I'd love to be able to scare a group of grown men into doing what I wanted.

There was no time for fantasies, though. The paparazzi had disappeared around a curve in the road and the path was clear.

I hurried across the immaculate lawn, ridiculously worried that I was leaving mud marks on the grass. I felt too dirty and disheveled to be even walking on the duke's grass —what was I going to do when he opened the door?

As I climbed the stairs, I lifted my feet to brush away some leaves that had got caught in the laces of my short-heeled boots, then adjusted my shirt to hide the rip. When I reached the top step, I looked down to try to swivel my skirt so the brown mystery stain wasn't visible. How the heck had I even got it?

I was still struggling with the damned thing when the door opened. I froze, then looked up to see the duke standing in front of me. He looked as perfect as ever, with his mahogany hair swept off his forehead and his thin navy sweater pushed up his forearms.

I did the first idiot thing I could think of and blurted, "It's not poo." I closed my eyes, horrified. "On my skirt, I mean. Your Grace."

The corner of his mouth tilted up in a devastating smile, and he said, "We really need to stop meeting like this."

A small, delighted laugh escaped me, but it didn't stop the blush of embarrassment that rose into my cheeks. I wasn't supposed to like him, especially not when I was humiliating myself like this. And *especially* not after what I'd learned from my research the previous night. "Could you give me a moment while I go die of embarrassment, then I'll resurrect myself so I can return and we can continue this?"

Interest lit his eyes. "Can you do that?"

"Um, no. Not that kind of witch."

"Pity. I've got a very nice grandfather I'd like to have back."

"Oh, that's actually..." I searched for the right word. "Quite sad. I'm sorry you've lost him."

He smiled. "Thank you. And see? You're not the only one who can make things awkward."

This wasn't what I'd expected at all. He was supposed to be a jerk, like his father before him. He *was* a jerk, given what I'd read about him in the papers. So this was entirely unexpected.

"What can I do for you?" he asked. "Surely I owe you if you managed to scare away the press."

Wow, so far, this was much easier than I'd expected. "Actually, there is something I came to ask you about. I was hoping you could loan me the use of your estate grounds for the Beltane Ball."

His face hardened, and a frown tugged at his lips. When he spoke, his voice was granite. "Absolutely not."

Aaaand there it was. The jerk duke. My heart fell. "Really? It's just a party, and it will benefit the community."

"No. I've been asked before, and I refused then, too. There's not a chance in hell that I'll allow people all over my house." It shouldn't be possible, but somehow his voice had hardened even more. Any friendliness had eased away from him.

"Not the house, just the grounds." Desperation flooded me. This was my best shot, and it was going horribly. How had I messed this up so badly?

"Whatever the case, the answer is still no. We are incredibly private here, and we'd like to remain that way. We don't want people from town running all over the place."

"We?" I'd thought he was alone out here.

"That's none of your business." His tone was sharp.

I'd stepped out of line. Of course I had. It wasn't my business who *we* was. Of course he probably had a girlfriend with him. A man like him would always have a girlfriend with him. With enough money, there were plenty of people who didn't care if you were a jerk. "Right, sorry. Forget I asked that, I'm sorry. Just please let me tell you about the party and why it's important."

"No, and that's my final answer." From his tone, I definitely believed him.

The sound of a car rumbling down the drive made me turn, and I spotted the fanciest, oldest looking automobile I'd ever seen. No one had *ever* called that thing something as simple as a car. It was an *automobile*, and even that term should only be uttered in a posh accent. It looked like something Cruella de Vil would drive.

The vehicle was so impressive that it held me enraptured as it stopped in front of the steps. The door swung open, and an elegantly dressed older woman slid out. She appeared to be in her late seventies and wore a cream-colored wool suit that looked positively divine. Red jewels sparkled at her neck, and I had to believe they were real.

Despite her incredible appearance, she looked tired, with shadows under her eyes and the faintest pinch to her lips. Was she ill?

I glanced at the duke and saw worry on his face.

A dog's bark sounded from the car, and I turned back to see a massive creature bound from the open door behind the woman. She reached out and grabbed his collar, stopping him in mid-jump. He jerked her forward, but she didn't fall.

It was an impressive feat, actually. The dog was a gray Great Dane at least as big as she was. Maybe she wasn't ill?

I looked back at the duke, who still looked worried.

"Darling!" the woman said. "Is this her?" The excitement in the woman's voice was matched by the sudden glow to her face. All of the exhaustion seemed wiped away. She hurried toward me. "This must be why all the paparazzi are here!"

"Hello, Granny." He leaned forward and kissed her cheek. The warmth in his voice was a sharp contrast to the way he'd turned down my request to use his estate for the party, and he clearly loved his grandmother.

She gave him a big kiss on the cheek, then turned around and looked at me, the excitement gleaming in her eyes. "You must be his special friend."

"Ah—" I looked up at him.

He stood behind her where she couldn't see him, and to my shock, he took the opportunity to mouth the word *Please*.

Oh, holy Hecate. Did the duke want me to pretend to be his special friend?

The look in his eyes was remarkably close to pleading.

He did.

I looked back down at his grandmother, who seemed so hopeful that it hurt my heart. For the briefest moment, I'd do anything to keep that look on her face.

But what happened when she discovered the truth? She'd be even more hurt. There was no way I could keep this charade up, and I didn't want to hurt her.

I looked to the side, then back at her. "Um, why don't I let you two get caught up?"

"No, stay! I insist, darling." She put a gentle hand on my arm, and I wanted to lean into her.

I'd never had a grandmother, and fates, did I want one.

Nope!

She wasn't mine, and I needed to get the heck out of there before I created a situation I couldn't fix.

"I really should give you time to catch up." I stepped backward, nearly falling off the top step. At the last moment, I managed to right myself and hurried down. I looked back, knowing I needed to say something else to avoid looking like a total numpty. "I'll leave you to it. Lovely to meet you."

Without another word, I hurried away from the house.

CHAPTER
FIVE

ALARIC

I STARED AFTER EMMA, realizing that I'd lost my damned mind. There was just something about her that scrambled my thoughts. She was beautiful, with hair of spun gold and huge brown eyes. Full lips that made wicked thoughts run through my mind. But that wasn't the true source of her allure. Maybe it was the way she talked with no artifice at all, or the way she hadn't been impressed by my title. I loathed the attention I received for being a duke, and she didn't give it. She made me feel like a person.

But I'd been a right bastard to her. Katrina had done a number on me, but there was no excuse for being so rude.

My grandmother turned and gripped my arm, smiling up at me with a beaming grin. "Oh, darling, she's wonderful."

Ah, shite.

And this was where it got complicated. My grandmother

had come here expecting to meet the woman to whom I planned to propose. However, that relationship had exploded in a ball of flames for severely dire reasons, but I hadn't had the heart to tell her. I'd hoped to break it to her in person.

And then *this* had happened.

"She is wonderful," my grandmother said, her face glowing with happiness as she stared after Emma's retreating back. "There's just something about her that is so kind. And clever. She's very intelligent, I can tell. You know how I've got a sense for these things."

"You do."

"You chose a good one." A wide smile stretched across her face.

"You have hardly spoken to her." Panic began to twist through me.

"It doesn't matter. I sense it. She's perfect for you, and I haven't been so happy in decades."

Oh, bloody hell. I loved the life I was seeing in my grandmother's eyes, but it was based on something totally untrue. My grandmother had been on me to start a family for ages. Ever since the accident that had taken my parents, she'd hoped our family would grow. Her daughter Madeline had never wanted to settle down into that life, so my grandmother had pinned her hopes on me.

It was why I'd been so pleased to tell her about Katrina, which I definitely should not have done.

I resisted shutting my eyes and put a smile on my face. "How are you, Granny? Well?"

I wanted her to say yes. She did, of course. But I couldn't

banish the image of her stepping from the car. She'd looked so tired, reflecting the exhaustion I'd heard in her voice on the phone over the last few months. It was why I hadn't told her about Katrina.

"Have you given any thought about moving back to Blackthorn Hall?" I asked, hoping she would say yes. Her recent frailty made me want to have her close so I could keep an eye on her, and then there was the little problem with the journalist. I wanted her close if that news story broke, which I was trying to prevent.

"I hadn't, but now that I've met your lovely girl, I just might consider it."

Oh, no. She couldn't be basing it on that, could she? How the hell would I tell her it wasn't a thing?

"Stop worrying about me," she said. "Why don't you go after her, dear? I insist." She nodded down the road, and I could still see Emma walking away as quickly as she could. I imagined she'd break into a sprint if she'd thought she could get away with it. "I'll take Milo in and get him settled."

I looked down at her massive Great Dane, who smiled up at me with a lolling tongue. "I'll come with you and help."

"No, you go after your girl. I came here specifically to meet her, and if she's not here, then I can just turn around and go home."

"I can't promise I can get her to come back immediately." *Or ever.*

"Tomorrow, then. But you need to go finish saying goodbye to her or she'll think you're rude."

She already thought that, but that was the last thing I

could tell my grandmother. She was really boxing me into a corner.

I looked down at her dog. "You're sure he's not too big for you?"

"Never." She patted Milo's head, then shoved my arm. "And if you keep insisting, *I'll* think you're being rude. Now go get her, or I'll be disappointed."

I resisted wincing, but it was close. Guilt was a specialty of my grandmother's, but she employed it so sparingly that it worked every time. For the last twenty-five years, after my parents' tragic death when I'd been seven, we'd been all each other had had.

"I'll give it my best," I said, wanting to add some malarky about Emma being shy and that's why she wouldn't come back, but I resisted.

My grandmother disappeared inside the house as I hurried down the path. My mind raced as I tried to catch up with Emma. What the hell was I going to do when I reached her? Ask her to pretend to date me so that my grandmother would stick around to get to know her?

Actually, it wasn't a bad idea. I wanted my grandmother close in the event that the journalist published the horrible story about my family. Before we'd broken up, Katrina sold several of my family's secrets to the press. The journalist to whom she'd sold them had published some, but he'd held on to the big one. Instead of releasing it, he'd chosen to blackmail me, and I was paying. Not for myself, because I didn't give a damn, but to save my grandmother from finding out what my father had done. She didn't deserve to know something so terrible about her son, especially since he was gone and we could all forget what a bastard he'd been.

I still didn't know if the journalist would reveal that secret after he'd got sick of trying to bleed me dry, but I had a plan for that—I just needed time. A month, max, according to the witch I'd hired to create a spell to silence him. It was one of the most notoriously difficult spells to create, so she'd said it would take time. I just needed to get her that time.

It was just a month, maybe less.

"Stop," I called out to Emma's retreating back. "Please."

She halted abruptly, then turned to look at me. Her brows rose. Fates, she was beautiful in the sunlight, with a scattering of freckles across her nose. Her hair gleamed, and I wanted to see if it felt as soft as it looked. I'd been struck dumb the last two times I'd seen her, and this was no different. It took a conscious effort to get my tongue to work when she asked, "You followed me?"

"Yes. I, ah...wanted to apologize for how abrupt I was earlier."

"Yeah, you were pretty intense." She frowned. "Is your grandmother all right? She looked tired."

The fact that even Emma had noticed made my heart twist. I definitely needed to convince her to stay here where I could keep an eye on her. "She's fine. I think. She's getting Milo settled."

"You think?"

I sighed, not wanting to discuss it with her. "Yes."

"Is that all you came to say, then?"

"No, actually. I was hoping that I could convince you to help me."

She laughed, and I didn't blame her. I'd been a right bastard when she'd asked to use the estate, but I was wary of letting anyone close after what Katrina had done. And my grandmother had never liked having too many people over. That was no excuse for my rudeness, though.

"I was rude earlier, and I apologize."

"You've already said that."

"Right." I pushed a hand through my hair. I was a damned duke, for fates' sake, with more money than God. As a result, I was rarely in a position where I felt awkward. And yet, she managed to bring it out in me.

I kind of liked it, though that was ridiculous. "Pretend to be my girlfriend."

Her jaw slackened. "No. Definitely not."

"We can be hazy with the details."

"Why?" She sounded exasperated, and I couldn't blame her.

"It's complicated." Granny's illness, the issue with the press. I didn't want to explain all that.

"Inheritance?" she asked.

"No." I glared at her. "I wouldn't use my grandmother like that. And I've already inherited."

"Hmmm. Must be nice." She looked me up and down. "So you have a super-secret reason for wanting to pull one over on your grandmother, and you want me to help you?"

"I do. And I promise, it's not a bad reason." I could tell her. I should. It was just that after Katrina's betrayal, I'd become gun-shy about telling anyone anything about me or my family. My grandmother would hate it if the press published that her grandson was worried because she looked unwell, so I wouldn't tell Emma that unless I absolutely had to. "I'd like her to spend more time here. I miss her. And she likes you. She's more likely to stay if you're around occasionally."

Her face softened, but only for the briefest moment. "My answer is still no. She seemed like a really sweet lady, and I'm not going to lie to her."

Damn it, I liked that about her. Not that it mattered—it would be a long time before I trusted anyone again.

"I'll let you use the estate for your party," I said, shocking myself. But I was full in on this plan, and nothing was stopping me.

She hesitated just long enough to show how badly she wanted to use the estate, then shook her head. "Still no. I'm not tricking your lovely grandmother."

"I promise, I'm doing this to protect her." I put as much sincerity into my voice as I could, and she studied me.

"I believe you, actually. You're rude, and you're definitely entitled, but I can tell you care for your grandmother." She shook her head. "All the same, I'm not doing it. I don't even know how to be in a relationship."

That was unexpected, and I wanted to know more. I wanted to know everything about her. "Why not?"

"I've been busy, and my relationship status is none of your business. But I can't fake it. I'm a terrible liar and I definitely can't lie to your grandmother. I won't be responsible for her getting hurt. And she *will* be hurt when she realizes what's going on."

This really wasn't going well, but as crazy as the idea was, I was hooked on it. "Just think about it, all right?"

She frowned. "No. You're bonkers."

"Bonkers?" I frowned. No one had ever called me *bonkers* before. My life was mostly filled with people bowing and scraping to me—whether it was because of the peerage, my money, or my involvement in various nonprofits—but not this woman.

And I liked it.

No. I wasn't supposed to like anyone right now, especially after what Katrina had done.

"Just think about it, please. I'll ensure you have the best Beltane Ball"—whatever that was—"that ever existed. I just need your help with my grandmother." I gave her what I hoped was a winning smile. "Think on it and get back to me, all right?" Before she could respond, I turned and left. I didn't want her to have an opportunity to say no again.

Still, I could feel her eyes on me as I walked away.

Emma

I watched the duke walk down the path back to his estate, my head spinning. He was bonkers. Trick his grandmother into thinking we were in a relationship?

There was no way I could do that. Not only was I a terrible actor, but I couldn't think of a single way it could be in her best interest. I did believe him, though, when he said that it wasn't for a bad reason. At least, *he* believed it. He'd been a jerk to me, but he clearly loved his grandmother.

It was too wild of an idea, though. And potentially risky. Real vampires weren't like the monsters of myth, but they were still dangerous. True, they didn't make a point of drinking blood straight from the source, but they were predators by nature. Just because they'd become more civilized with the modern advent of blood distribution services didn't mean they *wouldn't* bite another person. Dating a vampire was like having a lion for a house pet.

"Whatever!" I threw my hands up and continued down the road, wanting to get as far away from the duke as possible. This had been a major bust, and I needed to figure out my next steps.

Unfortunately, I couldn't go back across the lawn toward my car, or he might notice, so I had to take the long way up to the gate house and down the narrow road to where I'd parked. Penelope and the paparazzi were nowhere to be seen, thank Hecate.

It took another thirty minutes to reach my car, and I couldn't stop thinking about the duke's offer. It was a mad idea. If I'd been even slightly considering accepting, the idea of dealing with the paparazzi would have scared me away. They were vicious to the girlfriends of famous men.

But where else would I find a place?

By the time I walked into our headquarters on Foxglove Lane, I still didn't have an answer. Apparently, I also looked like I'd crawled out of a woodland ditch, because when Holly looked up from her book, her jaw dropped. "Whoa. What have you been doing? Cavorting with forest gnomes?"

I shook my head. "You know they party too hard for me."

She laughed. "Seriously, though. Where have you been?"

"Doing something stupid, of course." I buried my face in my hands and resisted screaming.

"Oh, boy, code red." Her book thumped as she set it down. "You go out to the garden. I'll be there in a minute with supplies."

"What about the desk?" We didn't technically have a desk in the front room of our shop, but Holly was currently doing a job that we called *manning the desk*. During business hours, we had to have at least one witch—always an apprentice—sitting in our front room in case a customer came by for a spell. We'd decorated it to be cozy, with several large chairs around the fire and a few shelves of books and plants. It was actually a pretty good job since you were able to relax with a book and tea when you did it.

She waved her hand. "Don't worry about the desk. I'll put up a sign directing them to the back garden."

I dropped my head back and looked at the ceiling. "You are the best. Truly."

"Oh, I know."

She gave me a quick hug as I passed her on my way to the back door.

The day was still bright and sunny as I stepped out into the pretty walled space. I drew in a deep breath, letting the garden soothe me. Like many of the properties on Foxglove Lane, this building had a large garden behind it. The walls that surrounded it were rough stone that had been laid hundreds of years ago, and they extended a good four meters above the ground, providing privacy that was very welcome indeed. Beautiful flowering vines climbed up the stone, spilling pink, purple, and yellow flowers in a profusion that smelled divine. The rest of the garden was filled with plants that we grew for our spells, though we often bought supplies from Seaside Spells, the local potion shop at the end of the road.

There were a number of benches and tables positioned throughout the garden, and I took the table closest to the door in case a customer were to come in while I talked to Holly.

As soon as I sat, a flash of movement drew my eye to the top of the stone wall on the far side of the garden.

Penelope.

She scampered down and ran over, hopping up on the chair next to me and looking at me expectantly.

"How did you find me?" I asked.

I can always find you. Also, I have a sense for when snacks are about to appear.

"A sense?"

She nodded. *Like a superpower. More valuable than my ability to stink out a situation, if you ask me.*

I actually couldn't argue with that. I, too, liked snacks. I'd love the ability to show up whenever they were about to be served.

"How did it go with the paparazzi?" I asked.

She grinned, revealing tiny white fangs. *Wonderfully. I scared them into their cars and then hopped around on the bonnets until they decided to give up and drive away.*

"Nice work." If I took the duke's offer, she could keep them away from us. I shook my head. There was no way I was taking that offer. I had to be insane to even think of it.

"Snacks!" Holly's voice rang out as she stepped through

the door. I turned just in time to see her eyes widen as she screeched, "Skunk!"

She nearly bobbled the tray of tea and cake that she carried. I lunged upright, reaching for the tray. "Hang on! Penelope is fine. She's my familiar."

Holly's jaw snapped shut, and she looked at me, eyes wide. "Your familiar?"

I grinned. "Yep. Just got one."

She squealed in excitement. "That's amazing!"

It really was. I shot Penelope a smile, and she grinned back.

Then Holly frowned. "You're going to need to put a bow on her or something so that people know she's not wild."

Oh, I'm wild, baby. Penelope grinned.

"Behave." I waved a hand at her. "A bow is a great idea. Don't you think, Penelope?"

Actually, yes. One with diamonds?

"Okay, that's above my pay grade, but we'll see what we can do."

"What did she say?" Holly asked.

"That she'd like a bow with diamonds."

Holly shot Penelope a look. "Wouldn't we all?"

Penelope grinned. *I like her.*

"I'll tell her." I was still gripping the other side of the tray that Holly held, and I gave it a slight tug. "Let's sit."

"Of course." She relinquished the tray so that I could set it on the table and took a seat. I did the same and reached for the cake knife while she picked up the teapot.

We had a ritual whenever one of us had a bad day: tea

and cake during work hours, wine and cake at night. Whoever was having the crisis got to cut the cake.

Excuse me, but I don't see a third cup or plate.

I looked up at Penelope. "Right, sorry. Holly? Could you do us another plate and cup?"

"Sure thing." She smiled and murmured a few words, waving her hand over the table. A teacup and plate appeared.

Holly had a gift for conjuring, and I'd be lying if I said I wasn't a little bit jealous since I had no gift at all.

I looked at Penelope and smiled. I *did* have a familiar now, so maybe things were looking up.

CHAPTER
SIX

Emma

HOLLY HANDED me a cup of tea. "Now spill."

I blew out a breath. "I need a bite of cake first."

"Of course." She gestured to my cake. "How silly of me."

I felt a smile tug at my face as I cut into the slice of orange marmalade cake. It was one of my favorites, dense and sticky and divine. It took a few bites for me feel up to the task of talking.

"Where to start?" I asked.

"The juicy bit."

"All right. The duke wants me to pretend to date him."

Holly just stared at me. "What?"

"Yeah. Exactly that."

Her eyes lit up. "Oh, Hecate! That's... a lot. Do you think it's safe?"

"Because he's a vampire?"

She nodded, then winced. "Sorry. I know I shouldn't make assumptions. Most vampires are civilized."

"He's one of them."

She smiled. "If you're sure of it, then you have to do it."

"Absolutely not."

"Why?"

"A lot of reasons."

"I can't think of one."

She groaned. "How about you tell me the story, and I'll decide?"

"First, I'm the one doing the deciding. But I will tell you the story."

Since she was my best friend, I started with the worst bit —the moment I declared, "It's not poo."

She winced. "Very on-brand for you."

"Tragically, yes." I told her about this refusal to let me host the ball at his estate, his rudeness, and the arrival of his grandmother. She sat enraptured as I finished with the story of him chasing after me to make his proposition.

When I was done, she leaned back and blew out a breath. "Yeah, that's a lot to process."

"Right?"

She nodded. "I can see why you're hesitating. Tangling it up with hosting the Beltane Ball is iffy. You know how the coven prides honesty, and are you willing to tell them you're fake dating the duke so he'll let you host the ball at his place?"

"I don't think it's a great idea." I thought of the duke's grandmother. "If Lily found out what I was doing, she would tell the grandmother. I'm sure of it, and I can't bear to hurt her."

Holly nodded. "I agree. Lily is a snake, and she would definitely rat you out to the gran. She'd rat you out to everyone, actually. Especially if it ruined things with the duke for you. She's been obsessed with him ever since he got back to town."

I frowned. "Really?"

"Well, most of us have been obsessed with him, so yeah. He's hot, wealthy, titled. What's not to love?"

"The titled part. Those paparazzi were everywhere." Not to mention his father was the worst of the lot, and the apple never fell far from the titled tree.

Holly frowned. "Good point. They'd make it hard to keep up the charade, too. It would suck to have them hounding you."

Penelope spoke for the first time, crumbs of orange cake quivering on her whiskers. *I can help with that.*

"Thank you, Penelope."

"Did she offer to spray them?" Holly asked.

"How did you know?"

"It's what I would do if I were a skunk. It's a real superpower."

Penelope preened, and I silently thanked Holly for saying the exact right thing to my familiar.

"This is a tough one," Holly said. "Have you got any other ideas for where to host the party?"

"Nope. Nothing as good as the Enchanted Garden, at least." The duke's estate was the *only* place within fifty miles that could compete with the newly renovated garden.

Willow appeared at the door, her gaze going to the cake and tea in the middle. "Oh, no. What happened?"

"Nothing." I smiled, trying to give off super chill vibes. "Just having a snack to celebrate my new familiar."

Willow's eyes lit up. "You got a familiar?"

I nodded toward Penelope, and Willow grinned widely at her. "Oh, how lucky! A skunk!"

That's what I loved about Willow. Always able to see the bright side.

Hazel appeared beside her, and I stiffened slightly. I loved the head witch—I loved all the witches in the coven—but right now, when I was in a sticky spot, she made me nervous.

"What's this I heard about a familiar?" Hazel said, her eyes landing on Penelope.

"She's mine," I replied, unable to help feeling a bit proud.

"Oh, excellent." Hazel smiled. "She'll help you with the ball."

"Um, about that..." My voice trailed off, making my discomfort clear.

Her gaze shot to me, and her voice was sharp when she spoke. "You're not thinking of quitting, are you?"

"Uh—" Could I? Was this an out?

"You'd better not be," Hazel said. "We need witches who stick by their guns and who do what it takes to get the job done. No quitters."

Well, that settled that. I smiled. "Of course. I'm just debating where to hold it."

Hazel arched a brow. "Well, it had better be good,

because I hear Lily has something up her sleeve that will be pretty impressive."

Lily. Just hearing her name made me want to growl. "It will be."

"Excellent." Hazel clapped twice, a gesture that was both celebratory and final. "I look forward to hearing what it is tomorrow. I'm counting on you, Emma. I really think you could do this."

Her words warmed me as much as they scared me. Maybe I wasn't as much of a magical disappointment as I'd thought, but I still had to prove myself.

"Let's go and leave these girls to their cake," Hazel said to Willow.

The two senior witches left, and I leaned back in my chair, my muscles feeling like gelatin.

"Well, that settles that," Holly said.

"Yep." I was going to have to try.

"You need get the duke to agree to let you use his estate," Holly said. "There's nothing else nearly as good, and if you propose anything sub-par, the senior witches will think you're copping out because you don't want to try."

She was totally right, and that meant there was only one thing to do.

～

ALARIC

. . .

LATER THAT AFTERNOON, I found my grandmother in the bee garden. All of the flowers were already in bloom due to the unusually favorable weather in Charming Cove and the fact that our garden had been enchanted to bloom both early and late. We had flowers for months before normal places in the United Kingdom.

My mother had established the bee garden, her favorite spot, at the west side of the house before I'd been born. I'd always thought of it as her place. I'd adored her, as most seven-year-olds adored their mothers, but as an adult, I respected her. She'd worked tirelessly to protect the environment, and part of that had been advocating for the bees.

I'd done my best to keep up her work, not only as an homage to her, but because I believed in it. It was the one thing my father had never taken from her. He wouldn't manage it, even in death, if I had anything to say about it.

The scent of honeysuckle and lavender filled the air as I entered the wildest part of the estate's gardens. I let the flowers bloom rampantly every spring and summer. The rest of the garden was managed by staff, but now that I was back, I'd decided to take care of this part.

Tiny tan pebbles crunched underfoot as I followed the path through the wildly colorful bushes all around me. Bees hummed lazily in the air, their song reminding me of my mother.

I found my grandmother at the bench in the center of the garden, watching contentedly as her enormous beast of a dog ate the honeysuckle bush next to her.

"Granny, really?" I looked at the dog, raising my brows.

The creature looked up at me, one massive branch hanging from his mouth.

"What?" she asked, her voice the picture of innocence. "Milo needs his greens."

"Then tell the cook. These plants are for the bees. You know that."

Her face softened. "Of course. I know how you cherish this place. I do, too."

I sat next to her, my heart heavy. My grandmother had loved her daughter-in-law. Maybe more than she'd loved her own son, even though she didn't know the worst of his crimes. My father had been a difficult man to love. Impossible, even. I know I had never managed it and never would.

Fortunately, he was dead.

I shook the thought away and looked at my grandmother, focusing on her. She was the only remaining family that I had, and I adored her. "How have you been, Granny?"

"Wonderful, dear."

"Really?" She still looked tired to me. "You look as though you could use some rest."

Her head whipped toward me. "Rude young man."

"I say it with love." I wrapped an arm around her.

She leaned into me, a smile in her voice when she spoke. "All I need is a proper cocktail and some time with my favorite grandchild."

"I'm your only grandchild."

"Shhh, don't ruin this lovely moment I've created."

I laughed softly. "How long will you stay?"

"I'm not sure. I'd like to get to know this lady of yours a bit better. Ever since you mentioned her on the phone, I've been dying to meet her. I dragged my old bones all the way here for that, and I'm expecting more than a quick greeting on the front step."

"Ah, right."

"Will she come for dinner?"

"Perhaps." I closed my eyes, wishing that I'd handled things better with Emma. I wasn't sure that a fake relationship was the best idea, but right now, I wished that she was here.

Because my grandmother *was* looking pale. And tired. My mind ran rampant with what could be wrong. Vampires lived roughly the same amount of time as humans, and my grandmother should have a good number of years ahead of her. I wouldn't be worried about her if she weren't looking so off.

"Are you sure you're well, Granny?"

She pulled out of my arms and glared at me. "Yes, and it's rude of you to ask twice."

I nodded, chagrinned. After my parents' death, she'd raised me. There had been plenty of opportunity for that tone when I'd been a teenager, and I'd learned to respect it.

"My apologies. Shall we go have a drink before dinner?"

"I would love that." She nodded to me, and I took the cue to rise and offer her my hand. "A drop of the red stuff would do me good."

She stood, a bit too slowly for my liking, then I escorted her down the path. Milo galloped ahead, looking for all the world like a horse as he pelted down the path between the bushes.

CHAPTER
SEVEN

EMMA

"You're insane," I said to myself as I walked up the steps to the duke's house that evening.

Penelope had insisted on coming along, and she hopped up each stair beside me. A big pink bow flopped around her neck, and I hoped it convinced people to chill out around her if they thought she was a pet.

Two massive planters full of ferns sat on either side of the big double doors. I nodded toward one.

Seriously? Penelope frowned at me. *You really want me to hide?*

"For now, yes. Let's keep you a secret in case we need your superpower."

She gave a little shimmy of delight, then walked off to sit behind the planter. I didn't know what scenario here would require me to use my secret word with her—she had insisted

I say *koala* if I wanted her to spray someone—but I wanted the option.

I drew in a deep breath and knocked on the door. Hardly a moment passed before it swung open, and the duke's grandmother stood before me, delight on her face.

Suddenly, I was very grateful that nothing was amiss with the summer dress I'd put on. The dowager duchess looked like perfection in her immaculate white suit and rubies, and I wouldn't have survived another encounter with her where I was covered in leaves and mysterious brown stains.

A wide smile spread across her face. "Emma! How delightful, my girl."

"Hello, Your Grace." I smiled at her, my heart racing like mad. The stress of the subterfuge was already getting to me, and I wanted to wimp out. Hazel's voice was the only thing that kept me rooted to the spot.

A moment later, the dowager duchess's massive dog was in front of me, paws on my shoulders as he dragged a huge tongue over my face. I squealed, unable to help myself, and stumbled backward.

"Milo! Behave yourself." The dowager duchess's sharp voice made the dog drop to all fours and stare at me with a ridiculous grin.

I tried to discreetly pat the slobber away from my face, but I wasn't sure it worked.

"My apologies, dear." She said the words, but I wasn't sure she meant them. "It's lovely to see Milo take to someone, though. He's usually so selective."

I looked down at the dog, who continued to grin up at

me. He didn't look selective. He looked like he'd lick anything that moved. I kept the thought to myself and said, "I'm honored."

She smiled approvingly. "Why don't you come inside, and we can fix you up with a nice, strong drink."

"Um—" I had to speak to the duke before I went in. There had to be rules.

"You're here to see my grandson, I suppose?" Excitement twinkled in her eyes, and guilt stabbed me.

I already liked the dowager duchess. In fact, I wished I had a grandmother like her. Not that I knew her well, but I was good at reading people, and she was an excellent gran.

"I am. And you, of course." I hoped it was the right thing to say. I didn't yet know how to walk the fine line of keeping up the charade and also not hurting her when it was all over, but I was going to have to learn quickly.

"Emma?" The duke's voice sounded from behind his grandmother, and my heart picked up the pace.

The dowager duchess stepped aside, smiling up at her grandson. "It looks like you have a visitor, dear."

"I do." There was warmth to his voice, and I didn't like the way it made me feel. He stopped in front of me, his eyes racing over my face.

His grandmother looked between the two of us, then smiled. "Why don't I give you two a bit of time, and then you can join us for dinner, Emma."

"Ah—" I looked at the duke.

"Perfect," he said. "We'll see you inside, Granny."

"Enjoy yourselves." She grinned broadly, then walked away.

I stared after her, uncertain of what I'd just seen. "Did she just waggle her eyebrows?"

"Probably." He smiled, and it was both exasperated and loving. Then he met my gaze, and the smile dropped from his face in favor of something more serious. "Shall we take a walk?"

I nodded, not wanting his grandmother to overhear our conversation.

"This way." He escorted me down the stairs and toward a path that led around the house.

I followed him into the formal gardens, immediately transported by the beauty of the place. Roses of every shade and shape grew in swoops and swirls around us. The grass beneath my feet was as soft and perfect as an expensive carpet. The scent was enough to make my head spin, and I could already see fireflies starting to appear as the sun set in the distance. Fireflies weren't yet out in the rest of England, but here in Charming Cove, they were. Just like the flowers, and weather they were influenced by the magic here.

This truly was a phenomenal place, and just the thought of hosting the Beltane Ball here made my head spin.

"I'm glad you've come back," he said.

"I'll do it," I blurted, before I could lose my nerve.

A smile pulled at the corner of his too-perfect mouth. "Really?"

I nodded. "Yes. As long as your grandmother never finds out that it's fake and she's not disappointed when it's over." How I was going to make that happen, I had no idea. But I'd find a way.

The smile broadened. "I agree. That is to be avoided at all costs."

"And my coven can never know. About any of it."

He nodded, his smile fading. "All right. We can have our dates at the house."

Dates. I would be going on dates with the Duke of Blackthorn. It was insane.

"*Why*?" I asked. "I still don't get why you need this."

"It's a long story—all of which I don't feel like sharing tonight."

"You're going to have to give me some of it."

"I'm worried about my grandmother's health, and the one thing that has perked her up in the last month was when I mentioned my ex to her. Katrina wasn't my ex at the time, of course, but now she is."

"And you haven't told your grandmother yet?"

"I'd prefer not to—not until I know she's well."

It was reasonable. And maybe the breakup was why he'd returned to his estate. It must have been a nasty one. Maybe she'd learned about him pulling funding from an orphanage. That would make me dump a guy.

"And the paparazzi," I said. "They need to go." I had Penelope to help with that, but I didn't want to have to rely entirely on a skunk. The paparazzi who stalked him in Charming Cove worked for magical news outlets since humans couldn't find our village. But I didn't want *any* paparazzi associating me with the duke. I'd never have any privacy.

"I'm working on that," he said.

"How? By hiding?"

He shrugged. "It's part of the plan, yes. If I don't give them anything to photograph, they'll go away."

"But *we'd* be something to photograph."

"True. And I've made an appointment with a coven in London to come out tomorrow and place wards on the house that will repel them."

"A London coven?" I glared at him. "Don't you know there's an incredibly skilled coven here in Charming Cove?"

"Yours, I presume?"

"Yes. *Mine.* The Aurora Coven is highly skilled and could whip up a spell in no time."

"I'm sure they could. But it's a small town, and I was hoping to avoid gossip."

I laughed. "Oh, Your Grace, I assure you that everyone already knows you are here and is already gossiping. Hiring the local coven wouldn't add to that."

"I suppose you have a point." He tilted his head in acknowledgment. "I was operating on autopilot. Generally, I avoid anything associated with town."

"So why did we run into each other in the restroom at the Drunken Clam? I can't imagine you were there to check out the new place like the rest of us."

He hesitated, clearly trying to think about what he would say next. "I'll share that information once our relationship has progressed a little."

"Fine." Maybe I didn't need to know all his secrets. Honestly, it was probably best I didn't.

"Then there's one other thing," I said. "The, um, touching."

"Touching?"

"Yes. We'll be in a relationship. We need rules around that."

"Rules for fake dating?"

"Exactly. Like, how to fake date a vampire. Or a witch."

"Of course." He frowned. "You aren't worried I'll bite you, are you?"

"Um, no. Not really."

He shook his head. "Of course I wouldn't. I would never hurt you, Emma."

The intensity in his voice sent a shiver through me, but I was glad to have the question of biting out of the way.

"Good, thank you," I said. "I was thinking more along the lines of dating rules. Like touching."

"Touching?" Something lit in his eyes, though I couldn't tell what. "Where *can* I touch you?"

The words sent a shiver of heat through me. Everywhere?

No, that was a terrible idea. Also, I didn't like him. I knew all about him, and he wasn't my type. I liked decent guys. Anyway, we had to keep this professional. I couldn't lose focus on my goals.

My cheeks heated as I said, "Waist, back, shoulders."

"And kissing?"

"Right, of course. On the cheek is fine."

He nodded. "The cheek it is."

"No flirting."

"Definitely not."

"No emotion."

"I would never." He gave me a horrified look, and I thought he might be joking but was too tense to ask.

I met his gaze, and a frisson passed between us. Finally, I blurted it out. "And obviously no sex."

He stilled, almost imperceptibly, and I was reminded that vampires were predators. Not like the ones in human movies, but they were still apex predators.

And I was about to pretend to date one.

I was so out of my depth.

ALARIC

SHE'D AGREED.

The thought rolled over and over in my head as I watched her drive down the lane away from the estate. I almost couldn't believe it.

When I'd seen her on my doorstep, my heart had picked up its pace and hadn't slowed down since. Our conversation in the garden had made dozens of images flash through my mind, none of which were suitable for sharing. But I couldn't get her out of my thoughts.

I'd wanted nothing to do with relationships after Katrina, and yet somehow, this woman filled my head with thoughts that shouldn't be there.

But I couldn't get the image of Emma out of my mind. She'd stood across from me in the garden, her face lit with the golden glow of the setting sun. A constellation of freckles decorated her nose, and I wanted to memorize the placement of each one. I wanted to find out if there were any more.

Instead of coming into the house, we'd decided to postpone the first meal. I'd have to think of something to tell my grandmother, since she was expecting her.

I shoved a hand through my hair and turned to go into the house. I needed to keep my wits about me—as long as that journalist knew the Blackthorn family secrets, my grandmother was at risk. She was too delicate, especially now, to endure learning that her son had been a raging alcoholic who had killed his wife. She'd known he wasn't perfect, but she had no idea the depths of his sins.

I drew in a shuddering breath, hating that the memory had found purchase in my mind. I worked hard to keep it banished.

"Alaric?" My grandmother's voice sounded from behind me, and I turned.

She stood in the open doorway, her massive dog at her size. A martini glass filled with brilliant red liquid was in her hand, and I had a feeling she'd spiked her blood with gin, as she preferred in the evening. I could use my own cocktail, though I preferred mixing with whisky.

"Has she left?" My grandmother asked, a frown on her face.

"She did. Emergency at work."

"Oh? What does she do?"

"She's a witch with a local coven." I should have spent more time learning about her. We'd have to make that a priority.

"Oh? Is she in the coven that will place wards on the estate tomorrow to keep the paparazzi away?"

"No, that's a London coven."

She frowned at me. "Dear, you should use local contractors."

I smiled at her. "I'm aware of that now. Next time. But come, let's go to the family room."

She smiled. "As long as your lovely girl comes back tomorrow."

"I'll see what I can do." I held out an arm for her, and she took it. Together, we walked through the house, our footsteps echoing on the gleaming stone floor whenever we stepped off the thick rugs.

The house was far too big and ornate for my taste, with sparkling chandeliers and intricately carved wooden furniture that looked like it would break under my weight. The rugs were worth more than some people's houses, as my father had been fond of telling me. In fact, the entire place reminded me of the man—stiff, cold, and prone to breaking under pressure. If my grandmother didn't love it so much, I'd sell it and be done with the entire thing.

When I was here, I spent most of my time in the wing that had been used by my mother. It felt more like a home, and although nothing about being a duke was normal, at least there, I could pretend.

CHAPTER
EIGHT

EMMA

I ARRIVED EARLY to the meeting room, nerves humming through my body. There was no one there, so I began the process of lighting the candles. While there was no ritual significance to the ivory tapers that smelled of flowers and old books, I knew that Hazel liked them. I did, too, honestly.

There were a lot of things to like about being a witch, but it was the small things I found comfort in. So much of my childhood had been chaotic, what with me being passed from foster home to foster home after the Eventide Children's Home had been shut down. As a result, cozy rituals like this were soothing. Lighting two dozen tapers and checking on the vases of fresh flowers that decorated the meeting room was a simple luxury, but one I adored.

When I was done, I took a seat in one of the chairs, which were positioned in a circle so that the witches could face each other. As soon as my butt hit the cushion, Lily walked in. She saw me and grinned like the cat who'd got the cream.

"Fancy your chances?" I asked.

"Oh, yes. In fact, perhaps you should save yourself the embarrassment and opt out now."

I shrugged. "I think I'll stay."

"Your funeral."

Actually, it would be my funeral to quit without even trying. The senior witches would loathe that. But I didn't correct Lily. Instead, I gave her my best *I know something you don't* smile.

As if she'd read my mind, Penelope came bounding into the room. Her pink bow flopped at her neck with every bounce, making her look even more adorable.

Lily shrieked and jumped on her chair.

I looked at her. "You have got to be kidding me. You're a witch. We're not afraid of small animals."

"That's not a rat, Emma. It's a skunk. And I'm afraid of smelling like a sewer, not of her."

Penelope sat up on her back legs and gave Lily an offended look. *Rude.*

"She called you rude," I said.

Lily did a double take between the skunk and me. "You can understand her?"

I smiled and nodded. Lily knew what that meant as well as I did: *I have a familiar.* Lily didn't have one.

But instead of being suitably impressed, she laughed. "Your familiar is a skunk."

"Penelope is amazing."

"Penelope the skunk." Lily clapped, and I wanted to deck her. "It's perfect for you."

"I agree." I gave her a cold smile. "And if you don't stop being rude to Penelope, she'll take matters into her own paws."

Lily shot the skunk a nervous look. "You wouldn't let her. The senior witches would be enraged if your familiar attacked another witch."

I shrugged. "I can't control everything she does. And you wouldn't be hurt. You'd just need a few baths."

She glared at me, then sat in her chair before looking at my familiar. "I apologize, Penelope."

Penelope and I both smiled at her, though Penelope's baring of teeth looked more like a growl. I let it slide because I'd been telling the truth when I'd said I couldn't control her. We were partners, not boss and subordinate.

Fortunately, the other apprentice witches entered the room, including Holly. She shot me a hopeful grin, and I smiled back. I'd texted her the night before to let her know the good news.

Cleo and Elle, the other two apprentices who didn't yet know about Penelope, gave her a curious look, then took their seats. I shot Lily a look as if to say, *See? That's how you behave.*

She glared.

"Who's the skunk?" Cleo asked.

Before I could answer, the senior witches filed in. They made it a point to all appear at once, and it was an impressive procession, if I were being honest. Their magic filled the air. I found it at once soothing and intimidating.

All five grinned broadly when they saw Penelope. "How excellent!" Luna said. "Willow told me about your new familiar, and I'm so pleased."

"Thank you," I replied. "Everyone, this is Penelope." Introducing my familiar was a moment that was both a triumph and a terror. I'd be lying if I said it wasn't great to show the coven that I'd been chosen to have a familiar, but I still hadn't lived up to the promise that suggested. A witch with a familiar was meant to be great.

I wasn't great. Not yet, and maybe not ever. I didn't even have a magical talent, and without one, I'd definitely never be anything special.

I drew in a steadying breath. *I can do this.*

I just had to believe, even though a little voice in the back of my head hissed that I was unworthy.

Hazel clapped her hands twice. "Everyone, take a seat."

The other witches followed her command, and Hazel took the chair at the top of the circle, right in front of the fireplace.

"Today is a big day," she said. "So big that I believe it needs no introduction." She looked from Lily to me. "Who would like to make their proposal first?"

"I will." The confidence in Lily's voice made me nervous. In my head, I knew I had the best location. But in my heart? When I heard her sound so damned self-assured, I doubted myself.

"Go on," Hazel said.

"The Garden of Enchantment." Lily sat back and smiled, satisfied.

The senior witches murmured to each other, and though

I couldn't catch exactly what they said, I heard words like *impressive* and *beautiful*.

"That's an excellent location," Hazel said, smiling broadly. "Especially since the additions were made. It would be an incredible ball."

"Not as good as Emma's location," Holly blurted.

A couple of the senior witches tsked their disapproval at the interruption, and I glared at her.

What? she mouthed back, clearly not chastened.

"Let's hear it then," Hazel said. "Where would you host the ball?"

I drew in a bracing breath. "The Duke of Blackthorn's estate."

The room erupted in a cacophony of surprised exclamations.

"How?" Stella demanded. "I tried for two years to get permission to host there. I even promised them unlimited spells, and they still said no."

"Would you believe it if I said my charms?" I asked.

"No," Lily said, her tone short.

"What is it?" Hazel asked, her eyes glittering with magic. She had the gift of divination, and she could clearly sense that something wasn't as it seemed.

In fairness, I was such a poor liar that maybe they could all sense it, divination or not.

"There's something more here," Hazel said. "You've managed the impossible."

"Not impossible," I said.

But everyone was staring at me like it was. And didn't they have a point? If Stella hadn't managed it for two years in a row, how had I?

They wanted answers, and I needed to give them. My mind raced. But what should I say?

"I'm dating the duke," I said, when I could think of absolutely nothing else.

There was another eruption of surprise.

"Since when?" Lily demanded.

"It's new. But he was nice enough to agree to let me use the estate for the ball." A sick feeling slithered through me as I lied to my coven. I looked at each of them, wanting desperately to confess to the truth.

But then my gaze landed on Lily. Anger glittered in her eyes, and her jaw was tight. I thought of the dowager duchess and how excited she'd been to see me at the estate.

If I told the truth here and now, Lily would tell the duchess. There was no question. If she could get the duke to retract my invitation to host the ball at his estate, then she'd be the one to host it at the Enchanted Garden.

I couldn't let her hurt the dowager duchess like that. And this was just a little lie. We would break it off shortly after the party and his grandmother's return to her own home— no harm done.

"I just didn't want to tell anyone until I was sure it was going to last," I said, improvising. "You've seen the paparazzi around town. I know you guys wouldn't rat me out, but I've just...wanted to keep it quiet in the early stages."

"I don't blame you," Hazel said.

"And I feel better," Stella said. "I just couldn't figure out how you managed it! The duke is shockingly intractable."

"He's not so bad when you get to know him," I said.

"How did you meet?" Lily asked. There was an edge to her voice that the other witches seemed to notice, because everyone in the room shifted uncomfortably, giving each other surprised looks.

"That's a story for another time," Hazel said. "We have more coven business to attend to, so we need to decide who will host the ball and then move on to other matters."

"Agreed." Stella stood, and the other witches joined her.

They went out into the garden to discuss. Through the window, I could see them huddled in a circle.

My heart started to thunder. This was it, the moment of truth. Did I want to win the opportunity to host the ball? On one hand—yes. I'd have the chance become an official witch and achieve my lifelong goal.

On the other hand—no. It was a risk. Just because they were giving me the opportunity to host the ball didn't mean I would meet our joy quota. If I didn't, I'd be out on my ass next year when we didn't have enough juice in the spell tank to meet our clients' needs.

Penelope pressed herself against my leg, and a shot of comfort went through me.

I didn't have long to stew in my worry, fortunately.

The senior witches returned and took their seats.

"You've both offered incredible locations for the ball," Hazel began. "And we hate to tell either of you no. But the winner is Emma."

My head began to hum.

I'd been chosen.

I'd been chosen!

Holy Hecate, I couldn't believe it. I'd known it was likely, but it had been hard to imagine actually being here.

I swallowed hard and met the gazes of the senior witches before I said, "I'll do my best."

"See that you do," Hazel said. "And it had better be good enough. We're counting on you."

CHAPTER
NINE

Emma

LATER THAT AFTERNOON, once the meeting had ended and Holly and I had got lunch at The Crow's Nest, a cliffside café with the best egg and cress sandwiches, I went back to Blackthorn Hall. The ball was in a month, and I would need every minute of that time to prepare.

There were no paparazzi as I drove up to the house, which meant a random London coven must have come by that morning to put wards on the place. No doubt the duke wanted to protect his grandmother. He obviously loved her, and I liked that about him, even though he could be a grumpy jerk with me.

As soon as I parked my car on the beautiful pebble lot in front of the estate, the front door opened. Milo bounded out, tongue lolling as he galloped toward my car. Behind him, the duke's grandmother appeared in the doorway. Her smile was so big I could spot it from there, and it struck me how happy she was to see me.

Clearly, she wanted her grandson to settle down.

I climbed out of the car and waved at her, narrowly avoiding Milo's slobbering tongue as he lunged for my face.

"Down, Milo." The dowager duchess's voice cracked through the afternoon air, and Milo immediately sat, becoming the perfect gentleman.

I patted his big head. "Good boy."

He grinned at me, then escorted me up the stairs to his owner.

Up close, the dowager duchess looked even more tired than she had been the day before.

"Good afternoon, Your Grace. Are you feeling all right?"

She batted a hand. "Oh, I'm fine. Just staying up too late recently watching television. Did you know you can get pretty much anything these days?"

I smiled. "Really?"

"Oh, yes. I've been watching this thrilling program called *Breaking Bad*. My, what that chemistry teacher is getting up to!" She gave me a sharp look. "But don't tell my grandson. He wouldn't approve."

"Oh?"

She shook her head. "He'd be telling me to go to bed earlier, to keep up my strength. But I'm strong as an ox, just a little tired from my late-night shenanigans. But that's my business, not his. And I expect you to keep my secret. I don't want him bothering me—especially since I've got to watch *The Walking Dead* next."

"All right." I grinned. "I can do that." I *really* liked her. "Why don't you watch your shows in the daytime?"

"Not nearly as fun with the sun out. I like it cozy and dark as I binge-watch." She grinned. "I learned that term on the internet."

I laughed.

"You're here to see my grandson, I presume?"

"I am." I smiled, trying to look as if I were excited to see him.

If I were being honest with myself, I was—a little. I shouldn't be, but I was.

She turned around and shouted into the house like she wasn't a dowager duchess. "Alaric! Your lady is here!" Her voice echoed into the huge hall, and she turned to grin back at me. "He'll be here any moment."

As promised, he appeared at the far end of the hall and strode toward me. The smile on his face looked so genuine that it made my heart stop for a moment.

What would it be like to have him really look at me like that? No charade, no ruse—just genuine joy at my presence.

It would probably stop my heart permanently, and then I would die a second time out of guilt over being swept away by a damned duke. I was lucky this was just an act.

"Darling." His smile was broad as he stopped in front of me and gently gripped my shoulders, then pressed a kiss to my cheek.

It was chaste—not even a second long—but time seemed to slow when his lips made contact with my skin. They were soft and perfect, brushing so faintly against me that the lack of contact made me long for more. His sandalwood and pine scent wrapped around me, and I leaned into him, unable to help myself.

When he pulled back, I caught sight of his grandmother looking at us with delight.

"Are you about to break into applause, Granny?" Alaric asked.

"Absolutely not." She gave him a disapproving look. "I only applaud kisses on the lips." She gave us a hard stare. "Go on, then."

I gaped at her. The last thing I'd expected was for the dowager duchess to egg me on to kiss her grandson.

"Later," he said. "For now, Emma and I will take a walk."

She sighed dramatically. "If you must deny an old woman her simple pleasures, then fine." She gave a little wave with her fingers and smiled. "Have a nice time, dears."

We said our goodbyes and left, going down the stairs and into the garden.

"What will she do this afternoon?" I asked.

"Probably practice her pool game. She's been trying to get me to take her to the local pub so she can fleece the lads on a night out."

I laughed, delighted. "Is she good?"

"She's a shark."

"I can't say I'm surprised." I shot him a glance. "I adore her, by the way."

"So do I." He smiled down at me, and I couldn't help the warmth that shot through me. Surely he couldn't be as bad as the papers made him out to be. But his father had been. There was no reason he would be any better.

"Shall I show you around the grounds and the places you can host your ball?" he asked.

I nodded. "That'd be wonderful, thank you."

"Do you want indoor space as well as outdoor?"

Heck, yes. The townspeople would be thrilled to see the gardens, but if they got a peek inside, they would lose their minds. I nodded.

"This way, then. There's a ballroom that opens onto a large patio."

"Sounds perfect."

As he led me around the side of the massive home, I couldn't help but wonder what it was like to live there. It was beautiful, true. The home itself was a gorgeous pale stone with dozens of glittering windows. And the gardens were the stuff of fantasy. With the sun shining brightly overhead, it was incredible.

But it was just *so big*.

"How do you live here?" I asked, the words escaping before I could moderate my tone. It definitely sounded a bit judgy, and I winced.

"What do you mean?"

"It's just so big and cold."

"You haven't even been inside. I'll have you know that our central heating is very powerful."

I shot him a look. "You know that's not what I meant. And I'm aware you're a duke, so you were raised differently and you're probably used to this kind of thing, but look at it." I turned toward the massive building and gestured widely. "It's just so big. So much. So formal, if the foyer is anything to go by." I'd caught a peek inside while I'd been speaking to his grandmother, and I hadn't wanted to even step on the tiles for fear of ruining them.

"I suppose you live in a cottage by a creek, complete with friendly forest creatures?" he asked. "Cozy and delightful, I'm sure. Until you lure children in to be eaten."

"No." I glared at him. "That's a witch stereotype, and I'll thank you not to use it."

He arched a brow. "I won't, if you won't use your duke stereotypes." He winced. "Though I suppose you are correct. It is very big and formal and cold, despite the power of our heating system."

"Why don't you sell it?"

He shot me an astounded look. "Sell it?"

"Yes. No one needs a house this big." Was this really the first conversation I was having with him? I was going after him about his house and my problems with the nobility? Sure, I wasn't getting into the details, but my tone was making it clear how I felt about dukes.

"Not impressed by the title, are you?" There was something in his tone I couldn't identify. It wasn't bad, necessarily. Just confusing.

"No." I looked around. "Though I do appreciate you loaning the estate to me for the ball."

"Only if you keep up your end of the bargain. If my grandmother finds out, the deal is off."

I shot him a surprised look. That would leave me in a seriously bad spot. "You would really do that?"

Of course he would. Why was I asking?

"Absolutely." His tone was firm. "It couldn't go on. My

grandmother would be hurt. I couldn't have a giant ball here that reminded her of our deception."

"Fair point. She won't find out."

"Good."

We'd reached the back of the estate, and he nodded toward the massive set of stairs that led up to a large patio bordered by stone balustrades. On the far side of the stone patio, beautiful glass doors sparkled in the sun.

"They open to the ballroom. Would you like to take a look?"

I nodded, and he escorted me up the stairs and across the patio. It was enormous, and I could already see the band and bar set up on opposite sides of the space. The townspeople would have a blast. If I could pull this off, it would be incredible.

With a graceful movement, he pulled open one of the glass doors and gestured for me to enter. I stepped into a ballroom that immediately made me feel like Cinderella. Glittering chandeliers hung overhead, sparkling like diamonds in the sun. A curved staircase on the far side of the dance floor led up to a balcony that wrapped around the entire ballroom.

"It's beautiful," I said.

He looked at it with an appraising eye. "I suppose it is. I haven't been in here in years."

"No?" I stared up at him, trying to figure out what was in his tone. Sadness? Anger? It was definitely something negative.

"No." *That* tone was easy to identify.

We were done talking about it.

Time to change the conversation. "Well, it's beautiful. Thank you for letting us use it."

He nodded. "Let's go back to the gardens."

"All right."

He turned and stalked from the room, moving more quickly than he had when he'd entered—almost like he was running from something.

I hurried to catch up, following him down the stairs and onto the grass below. When he turned to look at me, his expression was bland once more. "Shall we go look at the maze?"

"Sure. That would be great." There were a lot of things I could do with a maze, and I needed a distraction from wondering what was bothering him. Whatever it was, it was none of my business.

He led me to the maze, which was made of box hedges that formed walls about three meters high. I couldn't tell how far back it went, but it was at least thirty meters across on this side.

I blew out an impressed breath. "That's really something."

He nodded. "Planted over two hundred years ago."

Rose bushes bordered the box hedges, blooming profusely in different shades of pink.

"It will be so perfect for the party. The guests will love it," I said. "I'll have to think of ways to hide surprises inside for them."

"How many guests do you think it will be?" There was a wariness to his voice that suggested he would be disappointed when I told him the final number.

"Oh, quite a few," I hedged.

"How many?"

"Five hundred? Maybe more?"

Shock flashed across his face. Before he could say anything, the rose bushes in front of the hedge wall began to uproot themselves, dirt flying as they tumbled over.

I gasped as a glittering golden light raced along the line of bushes, uprooting every single one. "What's happening?"

"I have no idea." He stared at the flowers. "This has never happened before. Could it be an animal underground?"

"No, there's a spark of magic. Don't you see it?"

He shook his head, shooting me a confused look. "I see nothing out of the ordinary besides the bushes spontaneous uprooting."

"There's something there." I stepped toward it, curiosity tugging at me.

He gripped my arm gently, holding me back. "Be careful."

"I don't feel anything malevolent," I said. "Do you?"

"No, but it's still unusual."

"I'll be fine." I smiled at him. "Witch, remember? I'm not helpless."

"I would never assume you are."

"You just did." I arched a brow.

"No, I was worried for you."

Worried for me. Sure.

The phone in his pocket buzzed, and he pulled it out. "Forgive me, I'm sure this is my grandmother."

He was right, and I could hear her voice on the other end of the line as she asked him to come help her with something. He agreed, then hung up. "Will you come with me?"

I looked at the bushes. "I'd rather stay here and figure out what's going on."

"It may not be safe."

"It's perfectly safe. Now go on." I shooed him away.

He frowned, not moving.

"This isn't a real relationship, Your Lordship. You can't be worried about me."

"It's *Your Grace*, and yes, I can be."

"Well, keep it to yourself. And go help your grandmother." Penelope trotted up to join us, and I pointed to her. "I'll be here with my familiar, perfectly safe. You do think I'm competent, don't you?"

"Of course."

"Then go."

He finally did as I requested, and I turned back to the bushes. They were still uprooting themselves, more slowly this time, like they were having a tantrum that was starting to taper off.

What's causing that? Penelope asked.

"Don't you see it? There's a golden light."

No. She scrambled up the leg of my jeans, little claws digging in.

"Hey!" I pulled her off of me and held her to my chest. "Ask if you want to be picked up."

I just needed a better vantage point.

I harrumphed. "Well? Do you see it now?"

I see a golden light. Sparkles of magic. But I couldn't see them until you held me.

"The duke couldn't see them, either." I shook my head, bewildered. "I've never seen anything like it before."

It's got to be your magic. She sounded pleased. *It's because I'm here. You're able to do more.*

"You're probably right."

She preened. *Of course I am.*

"But what do you think this new power is?"

She shrugged. *I don't know.*

"Whatever is going on, I'll have to figure it out before the party, or it could cause serious problems."

The rosebushes began to uproot more frantically, as if another tantrum were coming on.

They don't like it when you talk about the party.

I frowned. Well, that was bad news.

TEN

Emma

BEFORE I COULD PLAN the party, I needed to figure out what in Hecate's name was going wrong with the garden. All the rose bushes around the maze had uprooted themselves while I'd been able to do nothing but watch.

Then, as Penelope and I had left, the tiny white flowers that had lined the pathway had yanked themselves out of the ground and thrown themselves to the side.

At least, that's what it had looked like.

I had no idea what plants were capable of. We witches used them in our spells and potions, but I wasn't a specialist.

So I needed to find one.

Fortunately, the Enchanted Garden hadn't yet closed for the day. Penelope rode in the passenger seat as I navigated my car down the narrow lane through the field, headed toward the sea on the other side of town.

The Enchanted Garden had been a fixture in Charming Cove life for decades. Once owned by an eccentric old man called Lionel Sparrow, it had been handed over to a witch named Aria. She'd recently returned to town after a long absence, and I didn't know her well.

Please be helpful, I thought. If she'd agreed to work with Lily to host the party here at the garden, she might be a miserable cow.

I parked outside of the ornate iron gates and turned off the car, then looked at Penelope. "Have you been here before?"

She shook her head. *Not much into nature.*

"But you're a skunk."

She shrugged. *And you're descended from cave people, but I don't see you in a cave.*

"Fair point." I tilted my head at her. "Where do you live, then?"

In your house. Or at least, I'm going to. I hope there's a nice en suite for me.

I laughed. "It's a flat, not a house. And there isn't even a nice en suite for me. But we'll figure something out."

Good. I expect only the finest.

"Don't hold your breath." I climbed out of the car, and she followed.

We walked through the gates and down the path to the little office building that I knew was located in the middle of the garden. About halfway there, Penelope veered off to go look more closely at something, and I was alone.

I'd been there several times before, and it was a gorgeous place. There were hundreds of varieties of plants and over a dozen greenhouses. The garden supplied most of the potion ingredients to Seaside Spells, the local potion shop owned by Aria's family. Other people could buy things as well, and my coven had been customers for years. It was the best place to source ingredients we couldn't grow ourselves.

All around me, birds sang and flowers bloomed in a profusion of color. The scent that filled the air was divine and ever-changing, and I looked around for inspiration for the party. If the duke's garden kept uprooting itself, I would have to replace things. I might as well ensure that they smelled divine.

I reached the pretty little cottage that acted as the garden's main office. Aria was outside, painting the trim of one of the windows in a beautiful pale green. She turned, her dark hair piled high on her head in a messy bun, and shot me a smile. "Hi. What can I do for you?"

"I was hoping you could help me diagnose a problem in a garden. I'm Emma, by the way."

She smiled. "I remember. We met once at Margot's coffee shop."

"Cool. Wasn't sure if you did." I smiled. Maybe she wasn't a miserable cow. In fact, I felt guilty for even considering it. "Should I make an appointment or something?"

"Nah, I'm almost done here." She brushed on a few more swipes of paint, then stashed the brush in the bucket and turned to me. "Tell me what's up."

I described the plants and the golden sparkles, and she frowned. "That's strange. Never heard of that happening before."

"Could you come take a look?"

"Now?"

"If you're free?" I gave a hopeful smile. It was getting toward evening, but I needed all the time I could get to prepare for the party, and the sooner I solved this problem, the better.

"Sure. We close soon, and I don't have plans for the evening. At least, not until later."

"Oh, my gosh, thank you so much." Relief rushed through me. "I can't tell you how much this means to me."

"Where are we going?"

"Blackthorn Hall."

Aria's brows rose, and excitement flashed in her eyes. "Really?"

I nodded, unable to help the wide grin that stretched across my face. "We're hosting the Beltane Ball there."

"Nice! I heard that Lily lost the bid to host the ball, and I can see why now. I've been dying to see the gardens at the estate ever since I was a kid. You're going to have the entire town there."

"I hope so."

She rubbed her hands on her dirty work trousers. "Well, let's go diagnose this problem so the ball can go on. I don't want to miss my chance at a party there."

A badger lumbered around from the side of the house, dark eyes twinkling as he chewed on something unidentifiable.

Aria shot him a look. "What did you get into, Boris?"

He looked up at her, and I had to assume that he was speaking to her in the way that Penelope spoke to me.

Aria rolled her eyes and looked at me. "He found my sweets again. Damned badger is clever."

Penelope appeared at my side, having found her way back to me after her explorations in the garden. She gave Boris an interested look, and as soon as he spotted her, he stopped chewing.

"Ooooh!" Aria said, interest clear in her voice. "Is that your familiar?"

"Yes. And I presume that's yours?"

"Yep." She grinned down at Boris, who was still staring at Penelope. "And I think he's very interested in the lady at your side."

I looked between the two familiars, unable to get a read on their vibe. Whatever it was, it was intense.

"You okay, Penelope?" I asked.

Leave me alone, I've got this.

All right. That was clear enough. I didn't know if they would fight or make out, but I trusted her to tell me if she needed help.

Aria picked up her paint bucket. "Let me put my paint way, and then I'll follow you to the estate, okay?"

"Sounds good, thank you."

Boris and Penelope continued to stare at each other as I waited for her, and then we walked back to the car park together, leaving the two familiars behind.

"Lead the way," Aria said, opening the door to her little yellow car.

We pulled up to the duke's estate twenty minutes later. Dark was beginning to fall, and the dozens of windows in the main building glowed golden with light from within. The house was magnificent at that hour, though far too big and grand to ever be considered a home.

I climbed out of the car, and Aria joined me. Together, we stared up at the building.

She whistled low. "Quite the place."

"Horrible," I said. "To live in, at least."

She nodded. "Too big. Too fancy."

I nodded, shooting her a look of agreement.

"What's the duke like?" she asked.

"Dukely, though I know that's not a word. All formal and stiff."

"I can imagine."

The main door to the house opened, and he appeared, silhouetted by light. As he strode down the stairs toward us, the moonlight gleamed on his face.

Aria whistled low. "Not bad looking though."

"No, definitely not."

He smiled as he neared us, belying my statement that he was formal and stiff. There was something easygoing about the smile that I hadn't expected.

"Emma, you're back." He looked toward Aria and held out his hand. "I'm Alaric."

She shook his hand. "Aria. Nice to meet you, Your Grace."

"She's come to diagnose whatever is going wrong with your rose bushes," I said.

"I own the Enchanted Garden," she explained.

"Thank you for coming by." He looked back at me, and the weight of his gaze felt like a warm blanket. "I'll leave you to it. Let me know if you need anything, darling." He cupped my arm and leaned forward, his lips brushing against my cheek, whisper soft.

It lasted less than a second, but it lit up every one of my nerve endings. The warmth of his body and his scent made my head spin. What was it about him that made me lose my mind so easily?

When he pulled back, I caught sight of his grandmother standing in the doorway, a delighted smile on her face.

Ah, right.

It was all for show. I knew that. Of course I did. I preferred it that way. Definitely.

Without a word, he turned and left. I felt Aria's keen interest as I led her around the side of the house. We'd made it about fifty meters before she said, "So, what was that about him being formal and stiff?"

"Right. Um, well, we're dating."

"No way." She grinned. "Wild."

"Really?" I looked at her.

"Yeah. The duke *never* dates anyone local. In fact, he's almost never here. Were you the reason he came back?"

"No, definitely not."

"Well, he's super into you. The way he looked at you!"

"Don't be silly." He was just a good actor. Dukes had to be. They had to pretend to be interested in all sorts of boring things. Unless he was super boring and liked those things, whatever they were.

I had no idea what dukes did.

"It's really new," I said. "Who knows where it will go?"

"You don't sound very enthusiastic about dating a duke."

"Would you be?" I shot her a look.

She shrugged. "Callan isn't that far off."

Oh, of course. I'd forgot that she was with the famous billionaire mage. Though he didn't have a title, he did have all the other trappings of unspeakable wealth.

"Isn't it difficult, being with someone who's used to having so much?" I asked. "Isn't he arrogant?"

"He can be, but that's got nothing to do with the wealth," she said. "And he's actually given away a lot more of it than people realize."

"That's good, at least."

"What are you so afraid of?" she asked as I led her toward the maze.

"I want a normal life."

Aria turned in a circle to take in the magnificent garden. "Yeah, this isn't normal."

I nodded. Not only did I want to stay away from the nobility, I was telling the truth about wanting a normal life. I'd never had one before—not with how many foster homes I'd been shuffled around. Two of them had been owned by super wealthy families, and they had been my least favorite. I knew that not all rich people were jerks, but it just wasn't what I wanted, as crazy as it sounded. Sure, it would be nice not to worry about money. But this level of wealth could be a poison.

"And the press is never nice to the girlfriends of wealthy men," I said. "Especially if there's a breakup."

"That's true. You'd be hounded."

I shuddered. The idea of it sounded horrible. He was a reclusive duke—and a handsome, wealthy one at that. If there were even a hint of a girlfriend, I'd never escape their attention.

"We're here." I stopped and pointed to the tall maze wall. At its base, the rose bushes still lay on their sides, dirt scattered all around.

Aria grimaced. "That doesn't look good."

"Nope. They just uprooted themselves as I watched."

"You said you saw gold sparkles of magic?" she asked as she approached the bushes.

"Yes. Alaric couldn't see them, but my familiar could when I picked her up."

"Hmmm." She bent and pressed her hand to one of the flowers. Her magic flared, smelling like lavender and green grass. After a moment, she looked up at me. "It wasn't the roses that uprooted themselves. Something did this to them."

"A spell?" I frowned.

"Perhaps. But the roses have no residual magic inside the plant that isn't supposed to be there. I'd feel it if they did."

"So they're victims, not the agents of destruction."

She nodded. "It's definitely a person who is doing this, but the plants aren't dead yet, so I can replant them."

"Oh, you don't have to go to all that trouble." Although I hated the idea of trying to do it myself. It would take at least a full day.

"It's no trouble." She smiled and turned back to the roses, pressing her hand to the ground in front of one of the bushes. Her magic flared more strongly, and the plants righted themselves and sank back into the earth, which moved to neatly cover the roots.

"Whoa," I breathed. "That's impressive."

"Plants are my gift." She stood. "It's where I get my power. Not from the ether, but from plants."

"Oh, that's very cool." Most witches, like me, got our magic from the ether around us. It was full of magic, and witches had the ability to draw from it.

I was a mediocre witch at best, though. The fact that I had a familiar was great, but unless I could discover what my specialty was, I would stay mediocre forever.

I shook away the thought. "Thank you so much for fixing that."

"No problem. I'm sorry I couldn't do more."

"I'll figure it out." I nodded back toward the house. "Shall I walk you out?"

She nodded. "I can fix your Candytuft on the way."

I looked down at the little white flowers. "Is that what it's called?"

"Yep."

"Thank you."

She stopped and quickly replanted the little flowers by the path, and I finished walking her to her car.

"Have you got any idea who might want to sabotage the garden?" she asked before climbing into her little yellow VW Bug.

I frowned, looking up at the house. "No idea. You're sure it's a person?"

She nodded. "It's not the plants themselves, so that's all I can think of."

Oh, bum. Could it be Lily? No, she wanted to host the party, but another witch in my own coven wouldn't sabotage me. What about Alaric? Was he getting my help with his grandmother, then making the garden so inhospitable that I called off that part of our deal? If that was really the case, then I *did* have an idea of who could be responsible. And if he was, then my job was going to be a lot harder.

CHAPTER
ELEVEN

ALARIC

EMMA WAS on my doorstep before I'd finished my coffee. It had been a long night of restless sleep, thoughts of her keeping me tossing and turning until the small hours of the night. I'd given her that kiss on instinct, knowing that my grandmother was watching.

But the memory of it had been impossible to banish. Her scent, the softness of her skin...it didn't matter that it had been nothing but a brush of lips against her cheek.

I couldn't get it from my mind.

Nor could I banish the sight of her immediately after that kiss. The way her full lips had been parted, her breathing quick. Her gaze had been unfocused, dreamy.

She'd wanted more.

I wanted to give her more.

No.

It was a terrible idea. This was temporary, and I couldn't afford another relationship. Not after the last one had left me in this situation.

Still, I couldn't stop thinking of her.

"Alaric?" Her questioning tone broke through my distraction and made me realize she was still standing in front of me on the steps of my home. She was beyond beautiful, with her long golden hair and the scattering of freckles across her nose.

"Good morning." I raised my coffee cup to her in greeting. "Would you care to come in?"

"Uh—" The offer seemed to surprise her.

"We are dating, after all."

"Right." She nodded. "Is your grandmother awake?"

"No, still abed." Worry poked at me. She'd been sleeping later in the mornings than she used to, and it had me more concerned than ever. There was something going on with her.

"All right, then. A coffee would be good."

I led her into the house, through the ornate public rooms and toward the private wing. We were nearly there when I looked back to see how she was reacting to the house. The few people whom I'd allowed in over the last decade had worn identical expressions of awe.

Emma's face was slightly wrinkled with dislike, and it surprised me.

"You don't like it?" I asked.

"Oh, no. It's lovely."

"Liar." I smiled, oddly pleased.

"Fine, I hate it."

"Don't let my grandmother hear you say that."

"Wouldn't she want someone who wanted you for you instead of for your estate?"

The words pierced me to the soul, and I stopped to turn and look at her. How was she so insightful after so little time? And all while wearing a wrinkled expression of intense dislike?

"You raise a good point," I said. "But she cherishes the title and the estate." I looked around. "Why, I have no idea."

"So you don't like it, either?"

"I don't think that *like* is a word that can apply to me in this instance. It is what it is." I shrugged. "I'm a steward of my family's title, nothing more."

She looked around pointedly. "Seems like a lot more."

"Feels like it, too, sometimes."

"Then why did you come back?"

I was running. But of course, I couldn't say that. "I need to check on the place occasionally."

"Now who's the liar?"

She was good. Very good. But I wasn't going to respond to that. "Come on, the coffee is getting cold."

I led her into the more welcoming family wing, which was still more old-fashioned than I preferred, but at least it felt like a home.

The kitchen was my favorite, filled with windows that overlooked the bee garden built by my mother. Emma studied it through the window, but I was grateful when she didn't ask about it. I gestured for her to take a seat at the table and poured her a cup of coffee, then joined her.

"What have you come to see me about? I assume it's not a social visit?" Though I found myself wishing that it was.

"Are you sabotaging me?"

Surprise sliced through me. "What?"

"Aria said that the damage to the garden was caused by a person, not by a problem within the plants themselves. And you were there when it first started happening."

"Why would I do that?"

"To keep me from hosting the ball here."

"But that's the reason you've agreed to this charade." I made sure to keep my voice low, though I knew that my grandmother was sleeping in a bedroom quite far away.

"True, but you said you only needed my help for a little while. What if you sort out your problems before the ball and don't need me anymore? Are you trying to drive me away so you don't have to have people on your property?"

I was surprised that her accusations bothered me. They almost...hurt. She shouldn't have that power over me—it made no sense.

And yet, it was the truth.

"No," I said, my voice short. "I plan to keep my end of the bargain."

"But you don't like having people on your estate."

"True. I greatly dislike any attention paid to me because I am a duke." Which was essentially all attention, hence my hermit status. I'd always had a dislike of it, but Katrina's actions had made me far more private. "However, I will uphold my end of the bargain." I could hear the offense in my voice.

"Good." She arched a brow. "Oh, come now, don't be

offended. You're a duke. Your kind does whatever they want. It's in your blood."

I frowned. There was the slightest hint of venom to her voice, and I had no idea where it had come from.

"Excuse me," she said, sounding genuinely chagrined. "That was uncalled for."

"All right." I wanted to get to the bottom of her feelings, because she clearly carried around some baggage, but she spoke before I could ask more.

"Who do you think is sabotaging the garden, then?"

"I genuinely have no idea. I couldn't see what you could see. Perhaps because you are a witch?"

"Possibly. My familiar pointed out that the damage occurred whenever we talked about the party."

"Someone besides me doesn't want you to host a party here." I frowned. "But because there is no one here except for my grandmother and me, that makes no sense."

"It's not her?"

"No. She dislikes the attention, too, but she loves me more. As long as she thinks you're my girlfriend, she'll want whatever makes you happy. And right now, she thinks that hosting the party will do that."

"She's right."

"It's more than just a party, isn't it?"

She nodded. "It's my chance to become an official witch in the coven. An official, permanent member. If I fail"—she drew in a deep breath—"I'm out of a job."

"That seems rather harsh."

"It's not. At least, it's not intended to be. They wouldn't fire me as punishment or to be vindictive. We rely on the party to gather positive mental energy that we use in spells. Joy, excitement, that kind of thing. If the ball fails and we can't gather enough, then we won't have enough for next year's spells. We still have a bit saved from previous years, but we'll be able to take on far fewer contracts. Someone will have to go since there won't be enough work to go around."

"Sounds like quite the risk."

She laughed softly. "You're telling me."

"Why did you take it, then?"

For the briefest moment, I thought she might answer me. Then she shook her head and said, "That's a story for another time. I need to figure out who is sabotaging the garden ASAP."

"What if it's someone who isn't alive?" I asked.

"A ghost?"

"Perhaps. There are several spirits here, though I haven't seen them myself."

"Ever?" Ghosts were slightly different than spirits in that they had the ability to impact the mortal world. They were also more likely to be vindictive, though not always.

"Never."

"So I need to figure out who the heck is doing this and get rid of him. Or her." She frowned. "Is there anyone associated with the estate who might have died with unfinished business?"

I stilled.

My mother.

My father, too, perhaps, but unfinished business implied that he cared about anything other than himself. And it wasn't likely to be my mother—she would never ruin the garden. It was the only part of the estate that she'd liked.

Finally, I said, "Not that I can think of off the top of my head, no."

"Are you sure?"

"Of course. Why do you ask?"

"You took about thirty seconds to respond, and you didn't look particularly happy while you were thinking."

"It's nothing." The last person I'd told had sold my secrets, and I wouldn't be burned twice.

But I didn't believe Emma would do that. Katrina had badgered the information out of me. With Emma, I found that I *wanted* to tell her.

But I wouldn't.

"Sure." She seemed willing to change the subject, thank fates. "The ghost didn't show themself to me yesterday. What if they refuse to?"

"We can get someone who can make them. Or we can entice them into it."

"We?"

"I said I'd help you."

She smiled, and I found that I wanted to make her smile like that every day, forever.

Whoa, boy. Slow down.

"If it's a ghost who cares about the estate and garden, it has to be someone who lived here. Would your gran possibly know?"

Maybe, but I didn't want to talk to her about the dead. Not if I didn't have to. "It's possible, but she's sleeping. Why don't we check the library? The family Bible is there, and it will list birth and death dates of everyone associated with the estate for the last five hundred years."

"Religious vampires?" She asked.

I gave a short laugh. "Hardly. This tradition was started by a great, great, great, great-grand-something. She wasn't a vampire, though I don't think she was particularly religious. But she did value family, and back then, this was how people recorded their family line. We've kept it up since, but you won't find us in church."

Vampires weren't affected by crosses and holy water like humans thought, but they also generally weren't religious. Most supernaturals weren't, since it was often the church leading the charge when it came to witch burning and vampire hunting.

She blew out a breath. "Your family really is old and posh, huh?"

"Too much so, if you ask me." The title had come down through my father, and he had been the worst example of privileged nobility.

I looked toward the clock. It wasn't yet nine, and if my grandmother slept as long as she had the day before, I had a couple hours before she came down. I stood. "Why don't I take you to the library now?"

"Perfect, thank you."

〜

Emma

. . .

ALARIC LED me out of the family wing, and it was obvious when we entered the public part of the house. I felt like I'd been transported into a Jane Austen novel. It was really very pretty, but it would be terrifying at night, all empty and dark and echoing with ghosts of the past.

Literally, it seemed.

The library itself was absolutely magnificent, though. As soon as I stepped inside, I felt my breath rush out of me.

The room was located on the far side of the house in the other wing. It was two stories tall on the inside, and soaring bookshelves surrounded me, filled to the brim with books.

I spun in a circle. "I feel like Belle in *Beauty and the Beast*."

"That would make me the Beast, then?"

I looked at him, surprised to see the genuine smile on his face. "Exactly."

He shrugged. "If the shoe fits."

He wasn't supposed to be so easygoing and charming. This was not what I'd expected after all my research. He'd removed money from an orphanage, just like his father had. What was he going to do? Take it to hell with him?

"It's this way." He led me toward an ornate table on the far side of the room. A huge old book laid on top of it, and *The Holy Bible* was scrolled on top in golden lettering.

He opened the Bible, being careful with the delicate leather cover. It had once been a very sturdy book, from the look of it, but time had taken its toll.

At the back, there was a list of names and dates in various types of handwriting. Next to several of the dates were causes of death, and I pulled out my phone to take notes.

"Tell me about anyone who died young," I said. "Or if it mentions a violent death."

"All right." He skimmed the writing, finally announcing, "Anthony Lane died at twenty-five from tuberculosis. Belinda Richmond at thirty-two. She was trampled by her horse."

I winced as I typed it into my phone. This was going to be unpleasant.

By the time he'd finished looking through the book, we had four possibilities. And yet, none of the names stood out to me.

Silly thought. Why would they?

"I'm going to the garden to see if using the ghost's name helps call them out," I said.

"I'll come with you." He hesitated briefly. "In case you need help, I mean."

"To protect me?"

He shot me a smile that was next-level charming. "Knight in shining armor, at your service."

"I think I like that." My tone was flirty, and I felt my cheeks heat. I spun and headed to the door.

He followed, and we made our way outside into the midmorning sunshine. Fluffy clouds floated across a perfectly blue sky, and I thanked my lucky stars that I'd moved to Charming Cove. You really couldn't beat the weather.

Birds sang as we walked across the grass toward the maze.

"Do you like living in such a big place?" I couldn't help but ask.

"I'm used to it," he said, glancing back over his shoulder at the enormous house. "But if I could cut off eighty percent of the house, I might."

I laughed. "It would still be enormous."

"Yes, but I wouldn't feel like I was haunted by the ghosts of my ancestors."

"Well, we're about to find one of those ghosts. Maybe we can ask them to clear out."

"I'm not sure that will do it." His voice had roughened, going slightly softer. It was clear that there was more to his statement than just those simple words, but when I looked at him, his face was wiped clean.

I bit my lip. I found that I wanted to know more about him. Like, desperately. But I didn't dare ask. This was all meant to be a ruse. I couldn't go falling for him.

Finally, we reached the maze. The rose bushes and little white flowers had recovered from their trauma, thanks to Aria and her magic, but I hoped no more damage would be done.

"Hello!" I called out. "We just want to talk, Calvin."

There was no response. I looked at Alaric, who shrugged.

"Margery? Are you there?" he called out. "We're hoping for a quick word."

No response.

Names had power, but if we weren't calling for the right ghost, then they wouldn't work. And it wasn't like this was a genie we were talking about. They wouldn't come on command. The name would just help us, not ensure our success.

"Violet? Are you there?" I asked, using the name of the woman who'd fallen from her horse in the garden.

Nothing.

I gave Alaric a look. "You try the last one."

"Morris?" he called. "Would you come out and speak to us?"

Still nothing. Not even the faintest glimmer of magic in the air.

"Whoever you are, please," I begged. "This ball is important, and I just want to talk to you about it. I can prove it will be a good thing, I swear. Whether you are Calvin, Margery, Violet, or Morris, I promise you'll like the sound of this ball."

Using their names one last time didn't seem to help. And my mention of the ball hadn't been a good idea.

Once again, the golden sparkles appeared near a bed of brilliant yellow and orange tulips. One by one, the bulbs uprooted themselves and flew across the lawn.

"Stop that!" I cried. "You're ruining the garden!"

The carnage continued, going faster and faster.

"We should get out of here," Alaric said. "We're just angering them more."

"You're right." But it hurt to leave while they were still causing damage. All the same, it was the only option.

"We're leaving!" I called out, turning to go.

Together, we hurried away. I chanced a glance over my shoulder, noticing that the destruction had slowed remarkably. At least something was working.

We made it back to the house and stopped on the front patio. I looked up at him. "I'm not sure that any of our names matched the ghost. Or if one of them did, we need to know something more personal about them to see if we can entice them out."

"The ghost we're looking for won't show himself, but what if another would? Aren't spirits easier to see?" he asked.

"Oh, I like where you're going with this. Spirits aren't as strong as ghosts, but they can usually see each other. If we can just find a spirit willing to talk, they could narrow down our choices to the ghost we're looking for and maybe even give us info that could help us draw the ghost out."

"There's a full moon in two nights," he said. "Doesn't that help?"

I nodded. "It does. We can go to your family cemetery, where there are more likely to be spirits lingering. If I can bring a spell that is meant to help us see them, our chances of success will be higher. "

"It sounds like we have a plan."

"We have a plan." I grinned, feeling a sense of camaraderie with him that lit me up inside. I tried to banish it. Falling for him was just plain risky. Problem was, I seemed unable to help myself.

TWELVE

Emma

Alaric and I parted ways after developing our plan, and I headed straight to the coven's shop on Foxglove Lane. I had an idea for a spell that would reveal the spirits in the graveyard, and the shop would have the resources I'd need to implement it.

Failure was not an option. I had to get rid of the damned ghost so that I could start properly setting up for the party.

Fortunately, it was Elle's day to run the front of the shop. I didn't think I could handle seeing Lily. I waved at her as I hurried to the stairs that led to our second-floor workshop.

"How's it going with the duke?" she called out as I put my foot on the first stair.

"Um, good." I turned and smiled at her.

She gave a dreamy sigh. "You're dating, like, *the* wealthiest and handsomest man in the entire county. The entire country!"

Not really, but I couldn't tell her that.

"Come on, spill some fun details," she said, grinning impishly. "Let a girl live vicariously."

I laughed. Elle might be poking for info, but she was so charming about it that it was hard to mind.

"Nope! Not telling you a thing," I said. "It's too new. I don't want to jinx it."

She made the sign of the cross over her chest. "Amen, Hecate. I wouldn't risk it, either." She pointed at me. "But when there's a wedding, I want front-row seats. Because I'm calling it now, you two will be walking down the aisle."

"You have absolutely no way of knowing that!"

"Fine, true." She threw up her hands. "I'm not blessed with divination. *But* I do believe in manifesting, and I would love for you to be a duchess. I could be one of your ladies-in-waiting!"

"That is *so* not a thing for duchesses." I turned and waved at her. "Bye, Elle!"

"Bye, Your Grace!"

I rolled my eyes as I climbed the stairs, but her words sent a shiver down my spine. It was a strange, conflicting feeling. The last thing I wanted was for people to treat me differently because of my status. Elle was already being nicer to me. She'd never been mean, of course. Not like Lily. But she was friendlier now that I was fake dating the duke, and I didn't like it.

Actually, that wasn't true. I believe in being brutally

honest with myself—I wanted friends and I wanted to fit in. But not like this. I wanted it to be honest.

I blew out a breath and banished the thoughts as I reached the top of the stairs. I had work to do, and it was vital that I focus.

The workshop was a long room that ran from the front of the building to the back, with views out over the sea and gardens. It was a glorious room, filled with books, cauldrons, and spell ingredients stacked deep on the shelves. The scent of herbs filled the air, and I drew in a deep breath.

There were many kinds of witches, and most of us had specialties like divination or the ability to bond with animals. It was important for a witch to be able to accomplish all kinds of magic, however, and that often required creating a spell. That was where this room came in handy.

We used our power to develop spells that could help us achieve our goals. Sometimes, it was as simple as brewing a potion—though that was never as easy as it seemed—and other times, it was coming up with the right combination of powerful phrases and intention to craft a verbal spell. Still other times, we enchanted objects to help us a achieve our desires.

It was one of the reasons I loved being a witch. There was something almost...flexible about it. Like we could use the power we drew from the ether and our own creativity to manifest whatever we wanted, as long as we were clever enough and strong enough.

I liked a bit of music while I crafted spells, so I turned on the speakers and got to work finding the books that might help me craft the desired spell. It only took a couple hours to get an idea of what I had to do, and I was lucky that we had all the ingredients in stock on the shelves.

I laid them out and began to cut abraca root and ferria leaf. As I worked, it was impossible to get the duke out of my head. He was a mystery to me, and it was driving me mad.

"Well, now, what have we here?" Lily's voice cut in through my absorption in my work, and I looked up to see her enter the room.

She looked perfect, as always, in a pale pink sundress and wedge sandals. Her sunglasses were parked on top of her glorious dark curls, and I really wished she didn't have such amazing hair. The last thing I wanted was to be jealous of her.

"Just a little prep work for the ball." I tried to give her a relaxed smile, but she didn't seem to notice.

Instead, she walked around to my side of the table and looked down at the spell book that I had open to a page about summoning spirits.

"Spirits?" The excitement in her tone made me grit my teeth. "A little trouble in paradise?"

"Just finishing up a job I was assigned before I was given the party to plan," I lied.

"Hmmm." She shot me a look, and it was clear she saw through my bullshit.

"Did you need something in here?" I asked.

"Yes, in fact." She turned and strode to a shelf across the room and began searching for a book.

I did my damndest to ignore her as I worked on the spell. It took precision to develop something that would work instead of blow up in your face, and I needed to nail this.

Fortunately, Lily left shortly after she arrived, and some of the tension drained from my shoulders.

Penelope hopped up on the table in front of my work area. *You really need to sort out your issues with her.*

I looked up at her. "Where did you come from?"

I sneaked in behind her. She looked like she was up to something shifty.

"She always is." I scowled.

Seriously, though. You shouldn't let her get under your skin.

"She makes it a point to try to get under my skin."

And that's her business, not yours.

"Of course it's my business if she's a jerk to me."

Not really. Penelope shrugged. *Lily is a jerk because she's got her own issues. We all do. They have nothing to do with you— you're just her outlet. As long as she's not going behind your back to make you look bad, you shouldn't worry about it.*

"Hmm." I stared at her, rolling her words around in her head. "Maybe you've got a point. She doesn't do stuff behind my back, which I respect. She's just miserable to me when she sees me."

Probably because she thinks you're her competition.

"Nah. No way."

See? Low self-esteem, just like I thought.

"I do not have low self-esteem."

Eh, I call it like I see it. You are going to be a great witch, even if you don't know what your specific talent is yet. And anyone can see that, even Lily. It's probably what's got her being so prickly around you.

"A great witch?" I smiled. "When did you get so nice?"

Ha. Nice? I'm just a truth teller, baby. Of course you're going to be a great witch—you've got me.

"There's the Penelope I know and love."

She fluffed the little bow at her neck and preened. *So you're going to stop worrying about Lily?*

"Yeah, I'll work on it. Thanks, friend. And therapist."

Anytime.

I turned back to the spell I was working on and put the finishing touches on the bundle of herbs that I'd bound together with string and sap from a young pine. The spell book called it a revelation stick, and when it was burned, it would encourage the spirits to show themselves. It wouldn't work as well on ghosts, since they were stronger, but we were only interested in spirits for this step of the plan.

Which would work, I told myself.

If I'd done it right.

Footsteps sounded on the stairs, and I looked up to see Willow enter. She held a big book in her hands and grinned at me. "I was hoping I'd find you here."

"Just working on a little something for the party."

"Excellent." She approached and put the book down on the table in front of me. "This is the guide book for hosting the Beltane Ball. It's got some rules you must follow, along with a record of past balls."

"A record? Like all the cool stuff the balls featured?"

"Exactly. We don't want to repeat ourselves too frequently, so we keep track."

I reached for the book, which had to weigh five kilograms. "Thank you."

"Of course." She smiled. "I want you to succeed." Her gaze dropped to the open box in front of me and the bundle of herbs inside. "Is that a revelation stick?"

Oh, bum. I should have shut the box. "Yeah. I'd like some spirits at the estate to show themselves to me."

"Why?"

"A little problem with a ghost."

Willow grimaced. "Enough of a problem to impact the ball?"

"Maybe."

She whistled. "Let me know if you need any help."

"You can do that?" I wasn't sure if the official witches were allowed to interfere and didn't want to get Willow in trouble. Although I wasn't sure if official witches could even *get* in trouble.

"Of course. The whole coven can help you if you need it. This event is too important for us to make you do it on your own." She gave me a serious look. "With that said, don't lean too heavily on help if you want to become an official member of the coven. You need to use this opportunity to prove your skills."

"So it's a fine line to walk, you're saying. Do enough to prove my skills, but ask for help when I need it to keep from biffing the whole thing."

"Exactly."

I blew out a breath. "Sounds easy enough."

She laughed and turned to go. "Let me know if you need anything."

I grinned. "Not if I can help it."

She chuckled as she departed, and I closed the box

containing the revelation stick and carried the book to one of the squishy chairs by the window. The fresh sea breeze washed over me as I took a seat across from Penelope, who had curled up on the opposite chair.

I started on page one, reading as quickly as I could. I had a couple days until the full moon, when I could use the revelation stick to reveal the spirits, and I should knock as many things off the list as I could.

An hour later, I had my next task.

"Penelope, wake up. We're going to count the joy batteries. We need to make sure we have enough."

She raised her head and blinked at me. *Joy batteries?*

I nodded. "When we collect all the awe and wonder and joy at the ball, we need a place to store it for the upcoming year." I pointed to a spot on the shelf behind her, where glowing glass orbs were lined up in rows. "Those batteries are full. We use them in many of our spells. We need to go check the empty ones and see how many there are. I'm hoping that the party will be such a hit, we'll need extras, but I need to find out how many we've got to make."

And you need me for this? She stretched and glared at me.

"Maybe I just want your lovely company." It was true, though. I liked having her around.

Oh, all right. That's something I can understand.

"Excellent." I rose and put the book on a high shelf where I could find it later, then headed out of the room. "The batteries are supposed to be in the garden shed. Maybe you can pull the wagon where we'll put any broken ones we find?"

Penelope, who had just hopped off the chair and was

following alongside me, stopped dead in her tracks. She stood upright on her haunches and pressed a paw to her chest. *Moi? You want* moi *to pull a wagon?*

I laughed. "Okay, you can ride in it."

That's more like it.

The shop had closed for the evening, which meant that the bottom floor of our building was empty. I made my way to the garden, where butterflies and bees flitted amongst the flowers. Penelope scampered ahead of me, bounding across the brilliant green grass, her pink bow flopping.

I followed her toward the shed at the back of the garden, which was covered in ivy. Penelope stopped in front of it and sat back on her haunches, inspecting the little building. *You call this a garden shed?*

"We do, though I see your point." It was quite a bit sturdier than a normal garden shed, with walls built of stone and a heavy iron door that had been locked tight. We didn't worry too much about thieves in our village, but the joy batteries were important.

I'd memorized the spell to get into the shed while reading the book, and I recited the words as I pressed my hand to the lock. Magic sparked under my palm, and the lock clicked.

I pushed open the door, flooding the interior with light.

At the sight within, I stopped dead in my tracks.

"No." The air rushed out of me. "What happened here?" The joy batteries were no longer on the shelves. Instead, almost all of them had crashed to the ground and shattered. Glass glittered in the beam of sunlight, and my heart fell.

Penelope stopped beside me, staring at the carnage. *This is bad.*

"Only a witch in our coven can get in here," I said, horrified. "There's no way one of them sabotaged these, though. Not even Lily."

Penelope entered the shed, gingerly tiptoeing around the shattered glass. The contents of the joy batteries lay scattered amongst the glass. Though they had been empty of joy, they still contained the magical ingredients that helped preserve the emotions within. Now, those ingredients were ruined, many of them turned to dust after contact with the air.

I don't think it was a person. Penelope's voice sounded from a far corner, and I squinted to see back into the gloom.

"What do you mean?"

Come look at this.

I carefully picked my way over to her, avoiding crushing any more of the glass. Cleanup was going to be a nightmare.

In the corner of the shed, one of the flat paving stones had been pushed up out of its position. Dirt spilled out of a hole that had been dug into the ground. It was too small for a human, though.

Moles. Penelope's voice echoed with darkness. *You can never trust moles.*

"Wait, what?" I stared stunned. "*Moles* did this?"

Yep.

"You're telling me that furry little creatures came in here and destroyed all of this?"

Looks like it. She pointed to the disturbed earth. *See the prints? And the place reeks of them.*

"But why?"

For fun. They are chaos agents.

"This cannot be happening."

Oh, it is. I'm surprised you didn't know how destructive moles can be.

"Sure, to a garden or a lawn. But this is next-level."

Not really. They probably dug up, found this place, and then had a joy ride smashing the batteries.

I rubbed my head. "A joy ride, literally. There would have been residual joy in the batteries. When they broke, they'd have released it, and it would have acted as a drug." I sighed. "They might not have even intended to break the first one, but as soon as it smashed, they'd have thought it was thrilling fun."

Oh, they meant to break the first one. Penelope's left lip was raised in a snarl.

"Chill, there. This is sounding a lot like prejudice."

You meet some moles and then tell me I'm wrong.

I rolled my eyes. "Either way, it doesn't matter if they intended to break the batteries or they just got swept up in the joy of it—the batteries are broken."

What are you going to do?

"That's the million-dollar question. I'm going to have to build more, but is it a big enough problem that I should ask for help with it?"

Penelope shrugged.

"Yeah, you're right. Let's wait and see." I added the job to my mental to-do list, trying not to cringe at the list's length.

Do we have to clean this up now? Penelope asked.

"Yes." The idea exhausted me, but I couldn't leave the shed like this.

She groaned dramatically. *I guess we really will need that wagon.*

CHAPTER
THIRTEEN

Emma

By THE TIME Penelope and I had finished cleaning up the broken joy batteries, it was nearly dark.

We locked the shed door behind us, not that it mattered anymore, and headed through the building and onto Foxglove Lane.

As soon as I stepped out onto the pavement, I nearly bumped into Alaric.

He stood next to a sturdy old Range Rover, the kind that had probably been driving over his family land for decades.

"Emma." He smiled. "I was hoping to find you here."

"Hi." I looked around, hoping there were no paparazzi.

There weren't, but there were a few gawkers. The gardeners across the street—all retired pensioners who were passionate about out-gardening their bridge buddies—had stood up from their weeding to watch us. The lads at an outdoor pub table had also stopped drinking their beer to watch.

"Is this what it's always like to be you?" I whispered.

He tried to smile, but it came out as a bit of a grimace. "For the most part. But I did manage to get a spell that will keep the paparazzi off our backs for a while, so that's an improvement."

"Good." I arched a brow. "Though I'm still annoyed you didn't come to our coven."

"Next time, I promise."

"Why are you here?"

"I was hoping you would come to dinner."

"Come to dinner?" I looked around at the people who still watched us. "Surely not. We'd be a spectacle."

"Not in town." He smiled, and this time, it was more genuine. "At my house. My grandmother has been asking to properly meet you, and I don't think I can hold her off much longer."

"Right. That makes more sense."

Penelope tapped my leg, and I looked down at her. *Say yes. Dukes have good food.*

"How would you know?"

They're rich.

"That's true." I looked up at him. "My familiar is very interested in coming to dinner. She says that dukes have good food. Is this true?"

He smiled down at her. "Sometimes, it's true. I'll endeavor to do my best."

"*Your* best?" I asked, surprised.

"I'll be cooking."

I felt my brows rise. "Really?"

"Really." He gestured to the car. "Will you come?"

I found myself wanting to say yes. Not just out of obligation, but because it sounded like fun. I gave myself a hard internal pinch. *Don't fall for his games.* I'd read the news stories. I knew what kind of man he was.

But I still needed to go meet his grandmother, and Penelope was poking at my leg, clearly trying to egg me on into accepting the invitation.

"We'd be delighted, thank you."

"Excellent." He smiled and walked around the car to open my door for me.

I slipped inside, and Penelope hopped in after me, climbing onto my lap.

"Oi, watch the claws." I picked her up and sat her on the seat next to me before buckling in.

The duke climbed into his seat and turned on the car, then pulled away from his parking spot. As we drove through town, people turned to look. I felt their gazes, but hopefully, they just thought I was going over to plan the Beltane Ball. Word would have gotten out about the location by now. My coven might think we were dating, but my life would be easier if no one else knew.

"They even recognize your car," I said, horrified.

"It's not ideal."

"It's awful. How do you live with it?"

He shrugged. "I've become accustomed to it. It'd be better if I lived here permanently and came into town more. They'd get used to me and see that I'm actually quite boring."

"I find that hard to believe."

"Oh, no, I am. My hobbies are beekeeping and stamp collection."

I grimaced. "No way."

"Yeah." He laughed. "Okay, that's not entirely true. But I'm not exciting. I promise."

"I believe you."

He turned to look at me, and I shot him a cheeky grin. It was easy to forget what I'd read about him in the papers, but I shouldn't. I tried dredging up the memory of him refusing to host the party, and it helped.

We rode in silence for a few minutes before I asked, "Have you moved back for good?"

"Worried it will be awkward after we break up?" he asked.

"Yes, actually. I'm not going to love being the girl who got dumped by the local celebrity. One of my colleagues will have a field day with that."

"We'll arrange it so that you dump me."

I smiled at him. "Really?"

He nodded. "We can do it in the pub. Make it ridiculous."

"I thought you didn't like being in the papers."

He laughed. "You're planning to make it *that* ridiculous, huh?"

"*Anything* involving a duke makes it into the papers."

He sighed. "True enough."

He pulled onto the lane that led up to his estate. The guard gates opened smoothly as he approached, and he drove us toward the enormous house.

Ask him what's for dinner.

"Seriously?" I asked Penelope. "Is that all you think about?"

"What?" he asked.

"Penelope would like to know what's for dinner."

"Curry. A specialty of mine."

"I wouldn't have guessed you could cook."

"You don't know me." He smiled. "But hopefully, I'll convince you I'm not a bad one."

He was right. I didn't know him. I'd read some terrible articles about him, but they didn't match the man sitting next to me.

And I wanted to know why. Was he just a good actor?

I shouldn't care. This was just business, and I needed to keep it that way.

He shut off the car and turned to me. "Before we go in, we should probably discuss some of our history so it seems like we're actually dating."

"Good point. We don't want to be caught out by awkward questions."

Too late. Penelope scampered over my lap, claws digging into my legs, and pressed her nose against the passenger window. When I turned to see what she was looking at, I saw the dowager duchess standing in the open door, waving wildly as her dog stood at her side.

"Was she waiting at the door for us?" I asked.

"Probably. She told me not to come back without you."

"Or else?"

"Something like that." He pushed open his door. "Come on. It looks like we're going to have to wing it."

I blew out a breath. Fantastic. How wrong could this go?

This is going to go very wrong, Penelope said, as if she could read my thoughts.

"We'll be fine."

You're a terrible liar. Just try to keep your mouth shut and let me do the talking.

"No one else can understand you."

So you'll be my translator. You should be honored.

I rolled my eyes and turned to the door to push it open, but Alaric was already there, opening it for me.

"Thank you." I took his hand and stepped out, a frisson of pleasure running up my arm. I barely resisted a shiver and told myself that I was just cold. It wasn't because I found him ridiculously attractive. Definitely not.

"Hello!" his grandmother called from the step. "So glad you could come!"

I smiled and walked toward her. Alaric kept ahold of my hand, and though I knew it was all for show, I couldn't help the warmth that bloomed in my belly.

We climbed the stairs, Penelope hopping up alongside me, and I stopped in front of the dowager duchess. She put a hand on the dog's collar, just barely stopping him from leaping on me, and grinned. "I hope you like martinis."

I smiled at her and nodded. "Love them."

I'd actually never had one—I just didn't want to say no to her. She looked so happy and hopeful, and I'd always wanted a grandmother. Of course, this couldn't last, but while I had her, I would drink martinis with her.

She looked down at Penelope. "And who is this?"

"My familiar, Penelope."

Penelope looked between the dog and me. *Can I ride him?*

"Absolutely not," I whispered.

"Well, Penelope is darling," she said. "And Milo has never seen a skunk before, but I'm sure he will love her."

I looked at Milo, who was staring at Penelope with an expression of obvious doggie concern. Milo definitely did *not* love skunks, but I wasn't going to correct the duke's grandmother.

"Come along." She turned and waved for me to follow her. "We can drink in the kitchen while my grandson cooks."

I shot him a smile. "Sounds good to me."

"Her martinis will kill you," he murmured.

"I can handle it."

Ten minutes later, after I'd taken my first sip of martini, I realized that I'd probably been wrong.

"Do you like it?" the dowager duchess said, leaning forward in her seat at the kitchen table.

"Love it." I barely resisted coughing, the gin making my throat burn. "I'll have to go easy, though. These are strong."

"Of course they are." She smiled and tilted her glass toward mine. Hers gleamed a brilliant red because she'd laced it with blood. I assumed she was a vampire like her grandson, but since vampires' fangs retracted when they weren't in use, I hadn't been able to confirm it.

The kitchen table was set into a nook surrounded on all sides by windows. The setting sun turned the garden beyond into a wonderland of color. Penelope lounged in a chair by the door that led to the garden. Behind me, Alaric worked in the kitchen. I couldn't help but watch him. He'd rolled his sleeves up to reveal forearms that I couldn't look away from, and he handled his knife with chef-like skill.

After a while, I realized that his grandmother was watching me, and that we'd been sitting in silence for at least a minute.

I looked toward her. "You gave me this seat on purpose."

She grinned. "I thought you might like the view."

"The view of your grandson, you mean."

She raised her glass. "Precisely."

"Well, you're not wrong, Your Grace." And it wasn't a lie.

She waved a hand. "Enough of that 'Your Grace' malarky. Call me Vivian. It's what all my friends call me."

The words warmed me, then struck me with guilt. I didn't want it to show on my face, however, so I said the first thing that came to mind: "Did you teach your grandson to cook?"

She laughed. "Me? Heavens, no. I can't even boil an egg, and I don't plan to start now. He did a bit of cooking with his mother before her death, and then he learned on his own."

My gaze flicked to Alaric to see if he'd heard his grandmother mention his mother's death. He must have. There was music playing in the kitchen, but it wasn't loud. Still, he showed no reaction.

I knew the former duke and duchess had died in a car accident when he was young, but I didn't know the details. I certainly couldn't ask his grandmother.

"Have you had his curry before?" I asked.

She nodded. "It's wonderful. Just like him."

The genuine love in her voice made me want to swoon. They might be a small family, but they were a *family*, and thick as thieves.

It was everything I'd ever wanted.

"So, tell me about this ball." She tapped the table. "I'm dying to hear more."

This, I could do. She listened, seemingly enraptured, as I told her everything I could think of about the ball. Every now and then, I couldn't help but look at Alaric, who was working away in the kitchen with a confidence that was downright sexy.

"Well, all of this sounds lovely," she said when I finished.

"I hope so. It's a big deal for our coven, and I'm just so thrilled Alaric is letting me host it here."

"He hates crowds, so he must really love you, if he's letting them descend on this place."

No, he loves you, I thought. But I couldn't say it, so I just smiled.

"Let me help you plan it," she said. "I used to love planning parties when I was younger."

I could feel my face light up. "Really? I would love that."

After the catastrophe in the garden shed that day, I could use any help I could get. Bonus points since she wasn't in my coven.

"Oh, yes, I'm excellent at it. Would you like me to handle food and drink? We can discuss it together, of course."

"That would be amazing. Can I let you know the coven's budget? It's not bad, but it's not limitless."

She waved a hand. "Oh, don't worry about that. I want this to be amazing. It's at my family home, after all."

"I can't let you do that."

"You can't stop me." She nodded toward my glass. "Can I get you another?"

I looked down at the delicate crystal martini glass, surprised to find it empty. "Um..."

"Yes. Glad to hear it." She took the glass and went to the counter where she'd set her bottles.

"Dinner is almost ready," Alaric said. "Shall we eat in here?"

"You know I prefer the formal room," Vivian said. "But I can tolerate this. For you."

He stopped by her and pressed a kiss to her cheek. "You're a darling. Thank you, Granny."

I could only see half of her face, but it was clear that she beamed at him. I loved the two of them together.

I stood. "May I get some water?"

Alaric pointed to the cabinet to the left of the sink. "Cups are there."

Penelope hopped off her chair and took a seat at the table as I walked to the sink. I collected four cups and filled them, surreptitiously draining one before refilling it. I liked my wine as much as the next girl, but I could tell that as long as I was drinking with Vivian, I'd need to make a point to stay hydrated. She was going to put me under the table.

I carried the cups to our seats and put them next to the silverware and napkins. Alaric set down plates and naan, while his grandmother carried over two big bowls, one of rice and one of curry.

The scent of rich spices filled the air, and I inhaled deeply. "This smells divine."

"Thank you." Alaric smiled and sat across from me.

His grandmother sat at the head of the table. "Now tuck in."

They passed me the bowls first, and I filled my plates and then Penelope's. I didn't trust her with the serving spoons.

I took a bite, not even caring that it was a little too hot. Divine flavors exploded on my tongue. "This is amazing."

The corner of his mouth pulled up in an impossibly charming smile. "Thank you."

Vivian leaned close to stage whisper, "He wanted to impress you."

"Well, it worked." I took another bite.

"Now, tell me how you two met," Vivian said. "Alaric has refused to tell the story so far."

I winced. "That was out of kindness to me, I'm afraid."

"Oh?" she asked, her brows rising. "So what's the story?"

Alaric and I both spoke at the same time, our words tumbling over each other.

"We met in the men's loo," I said.

"She assaulted me with her goat," he said.

Vivian laughed. "It can't be both." She looked between us, a gleam in her eye. "Which one of you is telling the truth?"

For the briefest moment, I thought she might be on to us. Then she grinned.

"It wasn't both," he said. "I was just trying to save her the embarrassment."

"They're *both* embarrassing," I said.

He shrugged. "The goat wasn't so bad. And you improved his temperament, didn't you?"

I smiled. "I did. Mostly."

"There you have it. The loo was more embarrassing."

I laughed. Was he...teasing me?

He was.

And I liked it.

His grandmother gave a little clap. "Oh, I'm so pleased by you two. You were meant for each other."

I felt heat rise in my cheeks, but I couldn't help myself—I looked up at Alaric.

I felt the tug of guilt, yes. And I was pretty sure I could see it in his eyes, too. But there was also something else. Like a tiny fire of warm pleasure deep in my belly.

I liked him.

And I didn't like that about myself. After everything I'd read, I shouldn't like him. But I did. And I couldn't match what I knew with what I'd read.

～

ALARIC

ACROSS FROM ME, Emma blushed. How was she so damned beautiful and clever and kind? I'd never met anyone like her. And it wasn't the usual things that she was good at. Sure, she could entertain my grandmother and make conversation and do all the things a girlfriend was supposed to do.

But there was just something more—a connection between us that transcended anything I'd ever felt before. I couldn't stop thinking about it as we finished dinner and I walked her out to my car. Her skunk followed us, taking the back seat and curling up to nap.

We drove back to her flat in silence, as if the night

required some thinking. And it did. She was more than I'd expected, and I needed to get myself together. Being interested in her wasn't an option. Being interested in *any* woman wasn't an option.

But her...she could ruin me.

When we arrived, there wasn't parking close by. I found a spot about fifty meters away and I climbed out to walk her to her door. She met my gaze over the car's bonnet and said, "You don't have to walk me."

"I want to." I smiled and held out an arm for her.

She looked around, worry on her face.

"No paparazzi," I said, thinking of the London witch who had cast the spell for me. According to a recent text message from her, she was still working on the spell to silence the pap who was blackmailing me, but she would hopefully be finished soon. In the meantime, at least the ones harassing me in Charming Cove should be gone.

Her little skunk, who'd followed her out of the car, looked up at her intently. Emma looked down, appearing to listen carefully. The skunk trotted off, and Emma met my gaze. "She says she's going to do the rounds. Just to make sure they're really gone."

"That's a handy companion to have."

She smiled. "She is."

"May I?" I held out my arm for her again, knowing that any extra touch wasn't a good idea but wanting it nonetheless.

She hesitated for only the briefest moment before reaching out and slipping her arm through mine. The contact made me draw in a breath, but I tried to keep it subtle. There was no reason to let her know how she affected me.

"I think it went well," she said.

"Absolutely. My grandmother likes you. Quite a lot, in fact."

"I like her." I could hear the smile in her voice, and looked down to see a far-off look on her face.

"Are your grandmothers still around?" I asked.

"Never knew them," she said. "Or my parents. I grew up in a children's home, and then the foster system." Her voice had cooled, and I saw a crease at her brow.

"What is it?" I asked.

"Nothing."

"It's certainly not nothing, if your tone is any indication." We'd reached the door that led to her flat, and I stopped to look at her. "Tell me. I genuinely want to know."

She pulled her arm from mine and moved to stand across from me. "I looked you up before I came to ask about using the estate for the party. I saw how you pulled funding from that children's home in South London. And your father did the same." She spoke quickly, as if she needed to get the words out. "How could you?"

Ah, of course. I winced. After what she'd revealed about her childhood, she would take that information particularly poorly. "It's not like it seems."

"I have a hard time seeing how it could be any different."

"My father was a miserable man on a level that I don't want to explain right now. But one of his lesser crimes was avoiding taxes by making donations that weren't quite donations."

Her brows rose. "So the children's homes?"

I nodded, my gut churning. "He had a friend who managed the accounts for a number of homes, and they worked something out together. Because the donation was off the books, I didn't realize there was still money going to one of them. My father has been dead for years, and I've been cleaning up the estate."

"The man was pocketing it, then."

I nodded, thinking back to the miserable bastard. I'd enjoyed alerting the police, and though I hadn't kept close tabs on him since then, I knew he was embroiled in the repercussions of his actions.

"I suppose that's not as bad as I thought," she said.

I nodded, fighting the urge to tell her that I'd moved the annual donation over to an actual children's home. I kept my mouth shut, however. As much as I wanted her approval, I didn't need it. I shouldn't even want it, since relationships were off the table for me after Katrina. She'd been the one to tell the press about the children's homes, although she hadn't been fully honest with them. I'd revealed too much to her and paid the price.

She raised a brow and asked, "So you're not a bastard?"

"Oh, I'm still a bastard. Just not to orphans."

She smiled. "I suppose that's the bare minimum, but it's fine for now. Can't have people think I'm fake dating a jerk."

"Of course not."

She looked at the door. "I'd better get inside."

I nodded and reached for the door to her flat. She reached for it at the same time, and we bumped into each other.

I stilled, and so did she. We were so close that I could see her pupils dilate as she looked up at me. Her wildflower scent wrapped around me, and I drew in a deep breath, unable to help myself. It made my head go foggy.

She didn't step back. There was room to do so, but she didn't take advantage of it. Instead, she stared up at me and licked her lips.

"Emma." My voice was rough even to my own ears.

"It's a terrible idea," she whispered.

Was it, though? Despite her words, she didn't pull away. And I *couldn't* pull away. She'd bound me to herself with some kind of spell.

"I'm going to kiss you now," I said, unable to stop the words from escaping my lips. If she gave any indication that she didn't want me to, I'd back off in a heartbeat.

She didn't.

Instead, she leaned up on her tiptoes and tilted her face to mine, looking me straight in the eye. "Kiss me."

A low groan escaped me as I bent down to take her lips. She was soft and delicious and divine. She wrapped her arms around my neck and pressed herself close to me. I gripped her tighter, never wanting to let her go, and lost myself in her mouth.

The kiss went on and on, sweeping me into a maelstrom of pleasure as she moved against me.

It took every ounce of control I had to pull away. After I stepped back, she stared up at me. It took a moment for her to focus her gaze, but when she did, she gasped and stepped back.

"That's against the rules," she said. "I know I said we should do it, but I was an idiot."

"The rules?" My head was still foggy from the kiss.

"The 'how to fake date' rules. No kissing unless absolutely necessary."

"I don't recall that one." But it was a good rule.

"Well, it was." She drew in a shuddery breath. "There's too much on the line here. I know a kiss seems like a little thing, but—"

"It doesn't." I cut her off, unable to stop myself. "That kiss was not a little thing."

She blew out a breath and nodded. "You're right. That's why I'm freaking out. But I'm not looking for anything right now. *Everything* is on the line with the Beltane Ball, and I can't afford to be distracted."

I felt a smile tug at the corner of my mouth. "I'm a distraction?"

"Yes, a dangerous one. I don't want to slip up where the paparazzi can see. That's not a life I want for myself."

My smile fell. She was right. That was a real concern, and I couldn't blame her. I'd do anything to escape it.

"Of course," I said. "That makes perfect sense."

"Good." She pointed between us. "So this, whatever this is, is over. Purely professional from now on."

"Of course."

She smiled. "Good. And thanks for dinner."

Before I could say anything else, she'd turned and hurried through the door.

CHAPTER
FOURTEEN

Emma

"You kissed him?" Holly barely managed to keep her voice low, and her eyes shone with excitement. "Like, a for-real kiss?"

I nodded, my breath catching in my throat at the memory. After the kiss, I'd barely been able to sleep. It hadn't been for show.

It had been real.

"It was amazing, right?" she asked.

"Yes. Absolutely."

She let out a delighted sigh. "I'm not surprised."

"Well, I am." I stared down into my coffee cup. We'd met that morning at Margot's and snagged the most private table by the window. A soft rain pattered against the glass, but I could already see blue sky in the distance. I needed to get started on dealing with my joy battery problem, but I'd had to talk to Holly first.

"I can't believe I let it happen," I said. But he'd looked at me with those damned eyes, and I'd forgot all my plans.

"Let it happen, or participated?"

"Both. And I liked it. I think I like him."

She couldn't repress the little squeal that escaped her. "I'm so happy for you. You deserve this."

"I don't want this."

"Don't be silly."

"But the paparazzi—"

"I know. They suck. And if you break up, they'll suck even worse. But does that mean you shouldn't seize joy when you have the chance?"

I scowled at her. "It's annoying when you're brilliant."

"Does that mean you'll go for it with him?"

"No. Of course not. With the ball to plan, I can't afford to be distracted. And I really do just want a normal life. It's all I've ever wanted since I was a kid. But I appreciate your brilliance. I'm just going to be more brilliant and keep my focus on my plan."

"Well, let me know what kind of help you need."

"I'm so glad you asked." I pushed Alaric from my thoughts and leaned forward, explaining to her what we needed to do.

We spent the next two days sourcing the ingredients for the joy batteries. It involved several trips to the Garden of Enchantment to harvest mulally berries and hazelwood roots, and we'd spent long hours digging in the dirt.

Unfortunately, I didn't manage to get everything we

needed, but I was getting closer. Once I had all the ingredients that went into the glass globes to preserve the joy, we could begin assembly.

Despite the heavy workload, I couldn't stop thinking about the kiss with Alaric. I hadn't seen him in person since, but he hadn't left my thoughts. Now that I was on my way to his estate, he was front and center.

That night, we were going to make real progress with the damned ghost uprooting the garden.

The revelation stick sat on the seat beside me. Penelope was nowhere to be found, but I had my suspicions that she was at the Garden of Enchantment with Boris. She'd been very cagey about her whereabouts lately, and I'd sworn she'd been humming a love song the night before.

At least one of us was in a relationship not destined to fail.

I pulled the car to a stop in front of the grand house. It was dark out, since we needed to take advantage of the full moon, and the lights in the house gleamed golden through the windows. I could just imagine the fancy balls that had once been held there, full of people in gowns and suits.

We'd have our own ball soon enough if I could get everything sorted in time.

I climbed out of the car and walked around the side to get the revelation stick. As I opened the side door, Alaric walked out of the house. I waved.

He nodded to me, and the sight of the small smile on his face made my heart beat a little faster.

Stupid organ.

Once I had the revelation stick, I joined him. Of course he

looked divine in his thin navy sweater, like the lord of the manor on a day off. Which I supposed he was. Did he even have a job? Maybe every day was his day off.

He looked down at the bundle of herbs in my hand. "Is that the spell?"

I nodded. "It should reveal any spirits to us."

"Can we just try it on the ghost in the garden?"

I shook my head. "It works better on spirits. They're weaker and will be influenced by the spell, and maybe they can give us info that will help us force the ghost to reveal themself."

"Sounds good to me. This way."

I followed him across the grounds. Fireflies fluttered around us as we walked down the winding path that was bordered on either side by white night-blooming roses. Their scent washed over me, as did the most insane urge to reach for his hand.

No.

I was not here to be an idiot.

It was just that the fireflies lit up the night, and the full moon screamed romance. And ghosts. I wasn't sure what it said about me that I was fine with romance and ghosts being right next to each other.

Finally, we reached a little cemetery near the woods. It was a beautiful spot, with flowers blooming all around and ornate headstones marking the resting places of his family.

"It's peaceful," I said. I'd expected creepy, but that wasn't what I'd got.

He nodded. "More peaceful than the garden. Maybe you should have your ball here."

I laughed. "I'll come back to you around Halloween for that."

He smiled, and I had to turn away.

Keep your head in the game, you numpty.

"All right, here it goes." I pulled a lighter from my pocket and lit the herbs on fire. They burned slowly, their scented smoke filling the air as I said, "Reveal yourselves, spirits of Blackthorn." For good measure, I added, "Please."

Alaric raised his eyebrows at me. "Is that part of the spell?"

"No, but good manners never hurt."

"True enough."

I walked throughout the graveyard, holding the revelation stick aloft. The smoke drifted throughout the cemetery, pale gray in the moonlight. Magic shivered on the air, and an ephemeral form appeared on one of the decorative benches to the side of the graves. She was an older woman dressed in a gown that looked to be at least two hundred years out of date.

"Hello," I said, approaching her slowly. "I'm Emma. May I ask who you are?"

"Lady Fiona Hardingham." She looked me up and down, her nose wrinkling with disgust. "What *are* you wearing?"

I looked down at my jeans and sneakers, then back up at her. "Um, styles have changed a bit."

"Oh, I'm aware." She arched a brow, clearly unimpressed. "That still doesn't make *those* trousers the best choice. You'd have done better with linen. Or tweed, perhaps, depending on the season."

All right, so she was a snob. That didn't matter. "I'll keep that in mind. We were hoping you could help us."

"And that's why you bothered me?"

I grimaced. "Ah, yes. Sorry about that."

Her gaze moved from me to Alaric. "Well, hello there, handsome. Unlike this one, you certainly know how to choose appropriate attire to enhance your...assets. Who are you?"

"Alaric Ashford. Duke of Blackthorn."

Her face fell. "So my great, great-grand-something, then? A pity."

I stifled a laugh. It must be disappointing to flirt with someone and then realize they're your relative.

I stepped toward her. "We were hoping you could tell us the identity of the ghost in the garden."

"Of course you came for something boring." She adjusted her skirts. "And I'm delighted to tell you that I don't know."

"You don't know?" I frowned. "Can't you see them?"

"And hear them, yes. But I don't mix with his sort."

"So it's a man?" I asked.

"Indeed. A modern one, though not as modern as you. And quite old." She shuddered, and I resisted pointing out that she was the oldest one here. "He dresses like a damned pauper, but he's absolutely obsessed with that garden.

"Old?" I asked. That didn't match any of the names we'd found in the Bible.

"Yes. And he came far after my time, so I don't know his name."

"But you could learn it," I said.

"If I wanted to, but I don't." She looked up at the smoke

that still hung in the air around her. "It looks like your little spell is starting to fade."

Oh, bum, she was right. Once the smoke had fully dissipated, she could go. "We need to see him," I said. "What is he interested in? Or what does he hate?"

"You mean that you want to anger him into showing himself?"

I winced. "Not anger, ideally. Just entice. We're desperate, please."

"Well, he loves the garden. He doesn't like the dog who is visiting. Curses about it day and night." She pressed a hand to her face. "Drives me batty, it does."

"Anything else?" I asked.

"No." She stood, brushing off her skirts and looking at the pale smoke that was nearly gone. "And I think it's time for me to depart." She nodded at both of us, then swept off, disappearing as the smoke wafted away.

I turned to Alaric. "Not quite what I'd hoped for."

"We got a little bit of information, at least. Let's go ask my grandmother if she knew any older men who might have died on the property during her lifetime. It sounds like he was alive during it."

"Good point."

He led me back to the main house, and we found his grandmother in the cozy sitting room. Frank Sinatra played on the old record player, and she held a martini glass full of ruby-red liquid that I could only assume was gin and blood.

She smiled when she saw us enter. "Well, hello there. What have you two been up to?"

"Trying to determine the identity of a ghost in the

garden," Alaric said. Shadows fell over his grandmother's face, and he hurried to continue. "No one we know."

She relaxed a bit, and I realized there was something going on in the room that I didn't understand. Alaric hadn't wanted to ask his grandmother about ghosts before. He'd said she was sleeping, but it had obviously been a weak excuse. We could have asked her after she'd woken. But once we knew the ghost was an older man, he seemed comfortable asking her for information.

Had they lost someone?

His parents.

It was the only answer. I knew from the papers that a car crash had taken his parents, and I couldn't blame him for not wanting to dredge up old memories.

"An older man, you say?" She rose and went to the small bar set up alongside the wall that overlooked the gardens. "I'll need another drink if I'm going to think about this, and you're going to have one with me."

Oh, Hecate. More martinis? They'd definitely done a number on me the other night. Before I could ask for wine, she pressed a martini into my hand. Vampires were faster and more graceful than most other types of supernaturals, and she'd whipped up that martini more quickly than my eye could follow.

"Thank you." I held out my glass to toast her, then took a sip.

"You can mix your own," she said to Alaric, then took her seat on the couch. "When do you think this ghost lived?"

"During your lifetime."

"I don't remember an older man dying while I was here. A young woman, yes. But not an older man."

I blinked at her. That was it?

"Is there anything else you want to ask me?" She sipped her martini.

"Yes," I said.

She smiled between the two of us. "Good, then. We can enjoy our drinks."

I didn't really have time to sit around drinking martinis, but then I realized what she meant. She wanted the company.

And I wanted to be there. With her *and* with the duke. Even though this was supposed to be fake, it didn't feel like it. Sure, there was tension between the duke and me, since we were keeping a pretty big secret and trying to avoid any thought of the kiss we'd shared. But there was still something immensely comfortable about being together.

"I do know someone who might be able to help, though." She looked at Alaric. "Your Aunt Madeline knows everything about the estate. And her boyfriend Harold is a medium. She could bring him along."

A medium could help, especially if they were strong. Perhaps we could combine our powers—whatever mine were—and try to force the ghost to show themself.

"That could work," Alaric said. "Could you call her?"

"Absolutely." She raised her glass in a toast, meeting my gaze. "Madeline is my daughter. I'm sure she could be here first thing tomorrow."

"More help would be amazing," I said, so happy that I

risked another sip of my martini. It burned its way down my throat, but I was developing a taste for it.

"Excellent. Why don't we play a game of pool to celebrate?" She stood and gestured to a door on the far side of the room.

I'd never played pool before, but I was willing to try. I'd seen enough lads play it at the pub to know the basics.

Alaric looked at me, his gaze questioning. I was pretty sure it said something along the lines of *You don't have to.*

But I wanted to. Just like I wanted to be there with him and his grandmother. Being in that room with them felt like being wrapped up in a warm blanket, and I wanted more of it.

"I'm terrible, but I'm a quick study," I said.

Vivian pointed at me. "Just don't use your witchy powers to cheat, all right?"

I gasped, laying it on thick. "I would *never.*"

I also didn't have any spells for it. With time, I could develop one, perhaps. But I didn't care if I lost. I just wanted to be there.

We went into the room next door, which looked like an old-fashioned gentleman's study or game room. It was all dark wood and gleaming leather, with golden sconces glowing on the walls. There was a large oval table that I assumed was for poker, along with a pool table in front of the windows on the far side of the room. There was even a skittles lane on the far left side of the room, with the wooden pins lined up at the end, waiting for the ball.

Vivian set her drink on a little table by the hearth and went to the rack of cues. She selected one with a confidence that I could only admire, and I followed suit. Alaric joined us, and I looked up at him. "Any tips for choosing a cue?"

He examined the cues, then picked one from the left side and handed it to me. "This one is good luck."

"She's going to need more than luck to beat me, darling," Vivian said.

I turned to Vivian and grinned. "You're on."

She smiled. "I like your attitude."

Alaric's gaze burned into me, and I turned to look at him. "What?"

"Nothing." He looked away, as if embarrassed to have been caught staring at me, then looked toward his grandmother. "I just like seeing her happy, is all."

Was he implying that I made his grandmother happy? I liked the idea of it.

"I'll break." Vivian set up the table and scattered the balls with her cue. She sank three of them before missing, then turned to me. "Your turn, darling."

I went to the table and leaned over it, trying to position my cue.

"Oh, no, that's terrible," she said. "Your form is atrocious. Alaric, help her."

I looked between Alaric and his grandmother. She had a cunning gleam in her eye, and I was pretty sure it had nothing to do with winning the game.

Alaric walked over to me and stopped by my side. "May I?"

May he what?

He held his hand out by my hip.

Oh, boy. I nodded. "Sure."

He pressed his hands to my hips and adjusted them. Heat raced through me, and I realized that Vivian had set us up.

She was incorrigible. I'd have looked over to see what I was sure would be delight on her face, but I was too distracted by Alaric's hands on me. He kept his touches brief and professional, but it didn't matter. Every one of them burned through my clothes and made my heart race.

The kiss had not been a fluke.

No one had ever made me feel this way.

That had to mean something, right?

Yeah—that he was handsome and nice. That was all it meant, and there were plenty of handsome, nice men out there. And most of them didn't come with the baggage of a dukedom.

When he was finished showing me how to properly strike the balls, I felt like I was vibrating. Maybe it was the martini I'd drunk, but I knew deep down that it was all from him.

We played three games, each more fun than the last. With Alaric's help and the relaxation caused by another martini, I actually improved. His grandmother still wiped the floor with me, but I didn't care. I was buzzing from the alcohol and fun and Alaric's touch.

But eventually, it became too much. Too much fun, too much of Alaric. I liked my life, but I wanted *this*.

Family.

A man like Alaric.

And that scared me.

"I'm going to go get some air," I said. "You two play a match."

"Are you all right?" Alaric asked, his voice low.

"Yeah, fine." Not really, but he nodded, so I figured I sold it pretty well. "Now kick your grandmother's butt for me."

"I heard that!" she called, a laugh in her voice.

It broke my heart the tiniest bit. Not because I didn't like her, but because I did. She reminded me of the family I'd never had and the one that I wanted so desperately.

And this was all fake.

I was *tricking* her.

The guilt was too much.

I hurried from the room, finding a door that led out to the gardens. The fresh air helped, but not entirely. So I walked as quickly as I could, with no destination in mind. When I found myself at the maze, I stopped dead.

That damned ghost.

"Show yourself!" I screamed, wanting control of something. Penelope appeared at my side, and I frowned down at her. "How did you get here?"

I sensed that you were having a mini-crisis.

"Just a mini one?"

So far. She looked around. *Has the ghost shown up?*

"No." Frustration surged through me. "I hate that I'm tricking Vivian, and I hate that the damned ghost could ruin the ball and make my lying worth nothing."

To my left, several gardenia bushes uprooted themselves. Golden magic sparked around them, and my anger surged.

Penelope laid a paw on my leg, and a little comfort ran through me. Power, too, as if she were a conduit for magic. She was, in a sense. A familiar was meant to enhance a witch's power.

"Come here." I bent down and swooped her up. She made a little squawk of surprise, but it was cut off by my shout. "Show yourself, old man! Quit messing about with the garden and show yourself, or I'll bring that huge dog out here and let him have a go."

"That damned dog?" The ghost appeared, offense written all over this face. "You had better not."

"Then talk to me."

He harrumphed. "Why are you disturbing me?"

"Why are you destroying the garden?"

"Because I don't want you to host a party here, you halfwit."

"Halfwit?" I felt my brows rise, and I wanted to turn Penelope around and tell her to do her worst. It would be pointless, though, since I doubted a smell could stick to a ghost. "Well, I'm a powerful halfwit, then, because I forced you to show yourself."

"That's all you can do." He bent down and pulled a tuft of white flowers from the ground, then chucked them over his shoulder and gave me a challenging glare. "Couldn't stop me from doing that, could you?"

I growled—actually growled—and said, "What the heck is your problem?"

"I told you, I—"

"Don't want me to host the ball here, I heard you. But why?"

"They'll trample the garden."

I laughed. "But *you're* destroying the garden yourself. I think you're the halfwit here."

"It's my garden to destroy." He crossed his arms over his

chest and glared. "Anyway, I can put it back. And I can't do nearly the damage that five hundred people can do."

"No one is going to ruin the garden," I said.

"You can't know that."

"Yes, I can." I softened, trying to remember that this was an elderly man with unfinished business and I should try to be sensitive. "What's your name?"

"None of your business."

"I'm Emma." I held up Penelope. "This is my familiar, Penelope."

His eyes softened when he looked at her. "I've always liked skunks. I'm Barnaby."

"Barnaby." I smiled, hoping I was making progress. "Well, Penelope and I would love it if you would stop destroying the garden."

Thunderclouds passed over his face, and he turned and strode toward a huge old rosebush. With a grunt, he pulled the thing out of the ground and chucked it aside. He moved to the next one with surprising speed and uprooted it as well.

In my arms, Penelope looked up at me. *He's mad.*

"I know." I turned, frustration boiling within me. "Let's get out of here before we piss him off any more."

She nodded. *Good plan.*

It wasn't, really—we still needed to come up with one of those. But at least I now knew his name and could maybe figure out what his unfinished business was. There were people who could banish malicious ghosts, but that wasn't Barnaby, despite his destructive nature. I needed to solve this by helping him pass on, not by destroying him.

CHAPTER
FIFTEEN

ALARIC

WHEN EMMA DIDN'T RETURN to the house within twenty minutes, I went to look for her. My grandmother was delighted to shove me out the door in search of my lady, as she called Emma, and I was happy to see *her* so happy. Her health seemed to be improving with Emma there, though she still slept far later than I was comfortable with.

Perhaps she was just enjoying her retirement.

I found Emma stomping up the path toward the house, her skunk clutched in her arms. She was so damned adorable that it took my breath away, though I was certain I shouldn't tell her that. Grown women rarely liked hearing that they were adorable.

"Everything all right?" I asked.

"Fine," she shouted, then blushed. I could just barely see the darkening at her cheekbones as she passed under the lights that bordered the patio and climbed the stairs. "I met our ghost."

"Oh?"

"A grumpy old bastard named Barnaby who won't see reason." She stumbled on the last step, and I caught her. Gasping, she looked up at me. "Thanks, I almost took a header down the stairs."

"We certainly wouldn't want that." Up close, I could see that her gaze was a bit fuzzy. "How many martinis did my grandmother give you?"

"Two? Three?"

"I think it was at least three."

She winced. "I really need to tell her I'm not used to liquor."

Penelope squirmed out of her arms, and Emma laughed as the skunk jumped to the ground.

"What did your skunk say?" I asked.

"Penelope likes me better this way. Says I'm more fun."

"You're always fun." I looked toward her car, which I could just barely see behind a tree. "But I don't think you can drive yourself home. I'll take you."

"No, I'll be fine. I can walk."

"It's at least an hour's walk, and it's too late."

"Good point."

"Why don't I get you a room upstairs?"

"Are you sure?"

Sure? I was one thousand percent sure that I wanted her in *my* room, but a guest suite would have to do. "Of course, come on."

She hiccupped before she followed me, and I made a

point to stop by the kitchen to get her water. She drank the entire thing, and I refilled the glass for her, then handed it to her before sweeping her into my arms.

She gasped. "I feel like I'm in a romance novel."

I chuckled. "Hold on tight to that water cup."

She drew in a breath. "My head is spinning. I think that third martini is hitting me."

"I think so." I tried to hide the smile in my voice and made a note to tell my grandmother to stop pushing drinks on her. "You could tell her you don't want one."

She gasped. "And disappoint her?"

I knew that feeling. "I promise she won't mind."

"Hmmm. Maybe."

Penelope disappeared at some point as I helped Emma to a room near mine. It was a few doors down because there was no way I'd be able to sleep if she were right next to me, but I had a feeling this wouldn't make much difference.

She looked up at me as I carried her through the door. "You're taking care of me. I like it."

I like it, too.

I managed to bite back the words, at least. Though it might not have mattered, since there was every chance she wouldn't remember this in the morning.

Careful not to jostle her, I flicked on the light switch to reveal the large bedroom, which was dominated by an enormous wooden bed covered in blue silk. I carried her to it and sat her gently on the side.

"I'm just down the hall," I said. "Have you got it from here?"

"Definitely." She set her water on the coaster on the

table, then flopped onto her back, throwing her arms over her head. Within seconds, she was asleep. I removed her shoes and draped the duvet over her, then turned off the light and left the room.

Emma

THE NEXT MORNING, I woke with a pounding headache and the memory of Alaric taking care of me.

I rolled over and buried my face in my pillow. I had *not* handled that well.

But I had made progress with the ghost.

That made me smile.

The movement made my head ache, and I drew in a deep breath.

Regrets.

It didn't matter that I felt like a fish that had done a round in the spin cycle of a washing machine, I had to start my day. There was just too much to do.

A yawn escaped me as I climbed from the bed and looked around. The room was pretty, as if it had been decorated by a duchess at some point when women wore big dresses. The furniture was a gleaming golden wood and the duvet a gorgeous soft blue silk. Across the room, a door beckoned.

I found a bathroom on the other side, and it was magnificent. There was no way this was original to the house—they'd probably turned another bedroom into this oasis of marble and glass. The toilet was hidden in one of those tiny rooms, and double vanities occupied the space on either side of the entrance. A massive tub sat in front of an expanse of windows, providing a glorious view of the back gardens. As much as I wanted to sink into it, I didn't have the time.

Instead, I stripped down and headed to the shower, which had six shower heads—five more than I'd ever experienced at once.

It was difficult, but I forced myself to hurry through the shower. The pounding spray went a long way toward clearing my head and waking me up, and by the time I put on my old clothes, I was ready to figure out exactly what Barnaby wanted and give it to him.

I found Alaric in the kitchen, leaning one trim hip against the counter as he poured a cup of coffee. He smiled when he saw me and held up the cup. "Can I get you one?"

"Sure." I wished I'd looked closer at my reflection in the mirror that morning to make sure I didn't look a mess. I'd showered solely to wake myself up, not for looks. Now that I was standing in front of Alaric, who looked perfect with his windblown hair and dark, thin sweater that fit him gloriously, I felt like a troll.

I didn't hear him as he approached, but I did sense when he neared me, as if I were some kind of animal who could feel minute changes in the air. I turned and smiled, trying to look like a normal person instead of the idiot I felt like, and took the cup. "Thank you."

"Sure. Can I get you breakfast?"

"Oh, you don't have to go to the trouble. Maybe just a piece of toast?"

"I can do better than that." He nodded toward the table, where a plate of muffins was laid out next to butter and jam. "Start with that, and I'll make up something more substantial. Anything you don't eat?"

"No." I shook my head, watching as he walked back to the big old iron stove. It was a proper Aga, with all the little doors on the front and burners on the top.

I took a seat at the table and looked at the muffins. There had to be half a dozen varieties. "Please tell me you didn't make these. It would give me a serious inferiority complex."

He laughed. "No, I picked them up in town."

"This early?" I looked up at the clock and realized it was half past ten. "No way. I slept that long?"

"You were in a bit of a state when I took you up to bed last night."

"Oh, I know." I blew out a breath. "Not doing that again any time soon."

"Help yourself to a muffin. It'll make you feel better."

I selected a blueberry one with a crumble topping and bit in, barely resisting a groan. It was divine.

Alaric turned back to the Aga and began breakfast, his movements once again as practiced and precise as a professional chef's.

"Where did you learn to cook?" I asked.

"My mother, a bit. Then on my own."

Oh, right. His grandmother had mentioned he'd learned from his mother before her early death. It made my heart hurt to think of a young Alaric continuing to cook as a way to be close to his mother.

Fortunately, Vivian arrived at just that moment, calling

out in a cheerful voice as she swept into the room in her lined silk dressing gown. "Good morning, my darlings!"

I smiled at her. She looked no worse for wear, considering our indulgences the previous night.

"I'm a bit tied up at the moment, so you'll have to pour your own coffee," Alaric said. "Sorry, Granny."

She waved a hand at him. "Oh, I can do that. Don't apologize, you goose."

With the grace of a dancer, she glided over to the coffee machine and poured herself a cup, then came to join me at the table.

"Now, what have we here?" she asked as she sat. Her eyes lit, and she picked up a chocolate muffin. "Alaric, you devil. You'll be the death of my waistline."

"Worth it," I said. "The blueberry was amazing."

"Oh, no, I'm a chocolate girl myself." Vivian bit into the muffin.

"Fried eggs all right?" Alaric called over to me.

"Perfect, thanks." I looked between Alaric and his grandmother. The late morning sun lit them with a golden glow, and the whole setting felt so homey that it made my heart twist. This was the second meal that I'd shared with them, and it just made me feel like I wanted to share more.

This was the life I wanted. A home, a family. I loved my little flat, but this was better.

A few moments later, Alaric appeared with two plates and laid them in front of his grandmother and me.

"You must be joking." I stared down at the eggs, toast, mushrooms, tomatoes, bacon, blood sausage, and baked beans. "A full English?"

"We've got a lot of work ahead of us if we're going to get rid of that ghost," he said, carrying over his own plate.

My stomach grumbled, and I dug in. I could never resist a proper breakfast.

"So, Emma, I'm pleased to find you here this morning." Delight sounded in Vivian's words.

"Your martinis got the better of me," I said, almost telling her that I'd slept in the lovely blue bedroom. It would be better if she thought I'd slept with Alaric.

But I needed to get her off this topic of conversation. "Did you ever know a man named Barnaby?"

Her brow furrowed, but recognition lit in her eyes. "Why, yes. He was a gardener here a long time ago."

Bingo. I shared a smiled with Alaric.

"He's the ghost in the garden," I said. "When did he die?"

"Oh, darling, I have no idea. I haven't seen him in decades. He left the estate when he was about thirty."

"So he didn't die here?"

"No, certainly not."

"And you probably don't know what his unfinished business is, then?"

"Sadly, no." There was some hesitation in her voice, though. Before I could press further, she shoved a big bite of eggs in her mouth and looked away.

Well, that was that. If I wanted more information out of her, I'd probably have to give her a martini. That would need to wait for later. I couldn't even face the smell of one right now.

"Granny," Alaric said, his voice gentle. "Are you sure you don't know anything more about Barnaby?"

"I've told you what I know." Her voice was so short and her expression so fierce that Alaric just nodded and smiled.

"All right then, thank you."

Oh, there was a story there, all right. But I wasn't in the business of harassing grandmothers, so getting the answers would have to wait.

From somewhere else in the house, a door slammed. Footsteps echoed quickly down the halls, followed by a voice. "My loves! Where are you?"

It was a woman, though I didn't recognize who. Vivian must have, because she smiled broadly and stood. "Your aunt is here!"

I looked at Alaric, who looked both happy and tired at the same time. When the whirlwind of a woman arrived in the doorway, I had an idea why. She looked fun but exhausting.

For one, she was dressed in every color of the rainbow. And yet, somehow, it looked chic instead of clown-like. The floor-length sundress flowed around her like a dream, and a massive hat made of delicate woven straw sat on her head. A mass of red curls tumbled down her back. She could have been anywhere from thirty-five to sixty-five, and I liked the look of her immediately.

"I've brought Harold." She turned and gestured to a man standing behind her.

He was tall and slight, with sandy blond hair and brilliant green eyes. He was probably in his fifties, and a summer linen suit draped perfectly over his slim form. He was the polar opposite of Alaric's aunt.

"He's the medium." She grinned widely. "I hear you have a bit of a ghost problem?"

"We do, and you've arrived in time to save the day," Alaric said.

She preened, and it was obvious he knew her well. Her gaze moved to me, and a wide smile split her face. Excitement echoed in her voice. "And who is this, my darling?"

"This is Emma." There was an unexpected amount of warmth in Alaric's voice as he walked over to me. "Emma, this is Madeline."

I stood to join him, and his aunt swept toward us. As she reached out her hand for mine, I wished I weren't lying to her. Not just because I hated to hurt any of these lovely people, but because I wanted this to be real.

"Lovely to meet you, Lady Madeline." I shook her hand.

Alaric put his arm around my waist, and a shiver ran over my skin. It drove the last of the hangover from my head, and I leaned into him, unable to help myself. With every minute that passed, I was forgetting this was a ruse.

Harold approached and held out a hand. We shook, and he stilled as soon as his skin touched mine.

"You have the gift," he said, not releasing my hand.

"The gift?"

"Of seeing and speaking to the dead." He smiled. "Quite a powerful one, too, from the feel of it. I'm not sure if I'm needed here."

"Oh, you are," I rushed to say. "If I have the gift, then I just got it last night. I'd never seen a ghost before that."

"Ah." His brows rose. "It came late in life, then?"

"Very."

"Hardly." Vivian waved a hand. "You're a spring chicken. This isn't even close to late in life."

For a witch developing her specialty, it was very late indeed. But there was no point in trying to correct her.

"So, tell me all about our ghost." Madeline walked to the table and sat down in a cloud of billowing fabric. "I love mysteries like this."

"That's not all we have to do, dear," Vivian said. "We've got to plan all the catering for the witches' Beltane Ball."

She didn't have to, of course, but she sounded so excited about it that I didn't correct her. Instead, I would count myself grateful for their help.

CHAPTER
SIXTEEN

EMMA

LATER THAT DAY, after updating Alaric's family on everything I could about the ball and Barnaby, I returned to the coven shopfront on Foxglove Lane. We planned to visit Barnaby again at night, and until then, there was a lot left to do for the party.

My job that afternoon would be to make plans for the spectacular events that would awe and delight the crowd. Presuming Barnaby let us host the ball, I'd need to have plenty of things to entertain people.

I'd been present at the last two balls, but the ones before were a mystery. I'd need to consult the book again to see what had been done so that I didn't repeat anything.

Fortunately, Cleo was working the front desk. I'd have preferred Holly, of course, but I was grateful that it wasn't

Lily. I waved at her as I passed, heading upstairs to where the book was kept.

Within minutes, I was so engrossed in the text that I didn't hear someone come in.

"Emma! Just the person I was looking for." Hazel's voice caught me unawares.

I looked up at the official witch and smiled. "Hi, Hazel. What can I do for you?"

"You can bring your young man to quiz night, that's what."

Oh, Hecate. I barely kept myself from grimacing.

I'd forgot that that night was quiz night down at The Sea Shanty, our local pub. The coven always put up a team, generally comprised of official witches and whichever apprentices they invited that week.

It was my week, apparently.

And she wanted me to bring Alaric.

"Um, he's really trying to avoid the paparazzi." For good measure, I held up the book. "And I'm pretty busy with planning the ball."

"Nonsense, you've got it under control. And I'll talk to the coven—we'll enchant the pub to repel cameras and other electronic devices. No one will know he's there except for the other patrons." Her tone suggested she wouldn't take no for an answer. "You know quiz nights are important to us, and we want to meet the duke and make sure he's good enough for you."

Her words warmed me because I believed them.

"Thanks." I smiled. "I'll ask him."

"You'll be there."

"We'll be there."

"Good." She turned and swept from the room.

I looked down at the book.

Oh, bum.

A few moments later, Holly swept through the door, calling out, "Hello! Party planning committee here to help!" She carried two takeaway coffees, and the paper cups bore Margot's signature logo.

I grinned up at her. "You are a lifesaver. I could really use some brainstorming help."

"I'd be delighted to storm your brain."

I laughed. "You're ridiculous, but truly the best." I reached for a coffee, and she handed it to me. The scent curled around me, lovely and rich. "Thank you."

"There's more where that came from." She threw herself into the chair opposite me and dug into her bag, withdrawing a paper sack. "Shortbread. The good kind."

My mouth started watering. Margot's buttery, sweet shortbread was the absolute best, and I was pretty sure that the secret was a sprinkle of sea salt on the top.

Did someone say shortbread? Penelope's voice sounded from the window.

I turned to see her perched on the sill. I'd opened it to the breeze, not skunks, but there she was.

"How the heck do you do that?" I asked.

She shrugged a furry little shoulder, jostling her bow. *I have a gift.*

Holly pulled a slice of shortbread out of the bag and handed it to Penelope, who took it with a delicate paw and began to nibble at it.

I frowned. "I hope you didn't just give her mine."

"Oh, no. I'm far too clever. I bought her her own."

I love her.

"Penelope says she loves you."

"Well, I love you back, you little stink queen."

Penelope preened. *Stink queen. I like that.*

"Thought you might." I looked at Holly. "She likes the nickname. But enough of that. We need to get started with some serious planning. The ball is only three weeks away."

Holly nodded. "How are you coming with finding supplies for more joy batteries?"

"Pretty well. I've got most, but there are still two more that Aria is trying to find for me."

Holly raised her hand, showing me her crossed fingers. "Here's hoping she finds them. And how is the catering coming along?"

"Great, as far as I know. It's being entirely taken care of by the dowager duchess and her daughter."

Holly's brows shot up. "Wow. You've made quite the connections lately."

"She's lovely." My heart warmed just to think of her. "Honestly, she's just the best."

"I think you're falling in love. With the dowager duchess, that is."

"Oh, totally. I want her to be my own grandmother." I winced. "I just hope she never figures out that I'm lying to her. I couldn't bear to hurt her."

"It'll be fine." Holly reached over and squeezed by hand. "It'll all work out. I'm here to help. The ball will be so grand

and she'll have such a fun time, she won't even mind when you and the duke stage your breakup."

The words caused the strangest little twinge in my heart. I frowned. It was silly to feel sad over something I knew was going to happen. Anyway, it was for the best.

"Okay, we need to move on before you get too caught up in those thoughts, whatever they are." Holly reached for the book and pulled it into her lap. "Have you found any good ideas from the really old balls? I'm sure we can do some repeats if they're old enough."

I dragged my thoughts away from Alaric and turned them toward the ball. "Well, there was one ball about fifty years ago where they enchanted fireflies to spell out predictions about people's futures. It was powered by a divination witch, and a guest could go to a special spot where the fireflies would give them a hint about their future."

"Hmm. That's quite cool." She frowned. "What if they gave bad news? Seeing it lit up in lights would be pretty terrible."

"Good point. Let's forget that."

"Well, you'll need plenty of fun activities and events, so we'll put it on the list. And what about that maze? I'm sure we can do something with that."

If Barnaby will leave it alone.

I shot Penelope a nod of agreement, then looked at Holly. "Perhaps a game inside the maze."

We spent the next two hours planning the events and what kind of magic would be required to make them happen. When we were done, I put the book back on the shelf and gave her a hug. "I've got to head over to the estate and invite the duke to quiz night," I said.

"No!" She grinned. "Really?"

"Really. Hazel cornered me here and insisted."

Holly blew out a breath. "Good luck, friend. It'll be fun, but those witches are observant."

"Yeah. I'll have to be on my game."

She gave me one more hug for good luck, and we parted ways. Penelope disappeared through the window without a word, so I was on my own as I drove to the estate. For a moment, I thought a paparazzi car was following me, but it turned off before I got to the lane leading to the main house.

When I reached the house, I parked in the driveway. Madeline answered the door, a big smile on her face and another colorful sundress billowing around her legs. "Emma! Lovely to see you again."

"Hi, Madeline. I'm looking for the—" I barely stopped myself from calling him *the duke*. It would be weird as hell for his girlfriend to call him that. "Alaric. I'm looking for Alaric."

She grinned and tilted her head to the right. "He's around the side of the house in the bee garden."

"Thank you."

"No, thank *you*." She reached out and squeezed my arm. "We all think you're just perfect for Alaric. We're so glad he's finally seeing a nice girl."

"Thanks. I, ah...like him a lot."

"We can tell. And he likes you. I haven't seen him look at someone like this in years. Maybe ever."

"Really?" My heart fluttered. Madeline seemed sincere.

"Really. Now go get him. He's in his happy place, and it will only get better once you're there."

His happy place? I wouldn't have expected the bee garden to be his happy place. I didn't say it, though. That was something a girlfriend should know.

We said our goodbyes, and I went around the house to the bee garden. The rain had departed in favor of a beautiful sunny day, and the garden was alive with colorful blooms. Round, industrious bees buzzed from one flower to the next, and the sight of them made me smile.

There was no sign of Alaric, however.

I followed the path deeper into the garden, inhaling the sweet scent of the flowers as my feet crunched the pea gravel. Finally, I reached the back of the garden where the beehives were kept. There were three of them, and one had the doors swung wide open, revealing the honey comb inside.

Alaric stood in front of it, bees buzzing around him as he harvested some of the honey. He wasn't even wearing one of those silly suits to protect him from the bees.

"Aren't you worried you'll get stung?" I asked from behind him.

I could hear the smile in his voice when he spoke. "No. They're used to me. And bees have an affinity for vampires, though I've no idea why. Unless I'm aggressive with them, they won't bother me."

"I didn't realize that." I walked around to the side so that I could see his face as he worked. "I didn't realize you were serious about bees being your hobby."

"I was only joking about *one* of those hobbies."

"Oh, I'm aware. But I assumed you collected stamps."

A grin tugged at the side of his mouth. "As thrilling as stamps sound, I inherited this garden and a love for the bees from my mother. I enjoy taking care of it when I'm home."

I smiled. It was a lovely thought, though also a bit sad. "I'm sorry you lost her so young."

"Me, too." His face turned more sober. "It was terrible."

"I'm here to talk about it, if you ever want." I hurried to add, "Not that you have to, of course. Just wanted to...you know, let you know I'm there for you."

He turned to me, his gaze intent. "You're really something, you know that, Emma?"

"Something good or something bad?"

"Good. Very good." The intensity in his voice made me feel funny inside, but in a good way.

"Thanks. You're something else, too." I pointed to the beehives, needing to move the conversation away from anything remotely intense, which was the direction in which we seemed to be headed. "Honestly, though, I never pegged you for a bee guy. How much of this do you do? Do you sell it?"

"No, there's not enough of it to make it worth my while. I give some of it to Elena at the Starlight Café. She was close with my mother, who would always give her some every year to use in her baking there. I continued the tradition."

The Starlight Café.

I closed my eyes and winced. "That's what was in the box when Clive headbutted you in the arse."

"No matter. I'll be giving her some of this."

"What do you do with the rest? Do you eat it?"

"Fates, no." He grimaced. "Can't stand the stuff, myself. Too sweet."

I laughed. "You do all this work, and you don't even eat it?"

"It's not about that." He smiled at me. "Bees are vital to the health of the earth. This is just a tiny group of them, but they're the ones—along with my mother—who ignited my passion for it. They give me purpose."

I looked at the hives. I'd never expected him to be such a passionate gardener and beehive expert, if that's even what they were called.

"Not just this hive," he said, no doubt seeing the surprise on my face. "It's a good bit of work but not enough to keep me busy. I work with several NGOs dedicated to protecting bees and the environment. But it was these specific hives that got me started."

"Oh, wow, so like—a job?"

He smiled. "Does that surprise you?"

"Maybe. I didn't know if you had one."

"Well, they don't pay me because it would be a bit ridiculous for me to take a salary from a nonprofit." He inclined his head back toward the massive house to indicate the absurdity. "But I need to do something with my time, and that seemed like a good way to honor my mother and do something decent for the world."

Well, now I just wanted to swoon. How amazing was that? The prickly, reclusive duke spent his time taking care of prickly little creatures who were good for the world. They had a lot in common, actually.

"You're more than I expected," I said. "I like it."

He smiled. "Careful. That must be against your fake dating rules."

"Good point. We've got to keep it professional." I drew in a bracing breath. "Speaking of, my boss insists that you attend the pub quiz night with us. She's not really the type that I want to tell no."

He glanced over at me, brows raised. "Quiz night?"

"At The Sea Shanty. Tonight. You'll be on our team." I winced. "I know it's a pretty big ask. She promised that the coven would enchant the pub so that no one could take pictures."

"I'd love to come."

"Really?"

I nodded. "Honestly, I would. I don't get to do things like that often. It'll be fun."

"Oh, my gosh, thank you." Relief rushed through me.

"It's no problem. You're faking it for my grandmother, I can fake it for your coven."

"Excellent. See you there at seven?"

"I'll be there."

Alaric

I approached the pub, feeling like a teenager with his parents coming along for his big date. As I'd been leaving the house, Madeline and Harold had stopped me to say how much they liked Emma. Things had snowballed from there.

"Oh, I'm so excited for this," my grandmother said. "I haven't been to a pub in ages."

"It'll be a blast," Madeline said. "I love a good quiz."

"I'm quite handy with the etymology questions," Harold said. "And anything about beetles."

Fantastic. I was bringing my grandmother, my aunt, and her beetle-obsessed boyfriend to quiz night with my fake girlfriend. At least the paparazzi wouldn't be there.

"You'll have to be on your own team," I said. "Emma never mentioned me bringing along three interlopers."

My grandmother laughed. "Oh, we'll wipe the floor with you, my lad."

"I wouldn't be surprised if you did." I leaned over to press a quick kiss to the top of her head.

It was a beautiful night in Charming Cove, with the soft breeze carrying the salty scent of the sea mixed with flowers.

"I do love it here," my grandmother said as we stopped at the door of the pub. "I don't know why I ever moved."

"You wanted the night life in London." I pulled open the door so she could sail through.

"Of course. That's right. But perhaps I'll come back."

"I'd like that. The house is certainly big enough."

Inside the pub, the tables were already mostly full. Excited chatter sounded from people holding glasses full of golden beer. The sound died as they all noticed us.

Not ideal.

To my left, a formidable woman with short dark hair stood abruptly and glared at the crowd. They immediately looked away from us and resumed talking. Emma stood next to the woman, and I had to assume she was Hazel, the leader of the coven.

"Well, she's quite impressive," my grandmother said. "I like her already."

I smiled. "Let's go meet her."

As much as I wanted to shuffle my family off to the corner like an embarrassed teenager, I was, in fact, an adult.

The coven table was one of the bigger ones in the pub, located right in front of the fire that cracked merrily despite the warm weather outside. It wasn't too warm, at least. Six witches sat around it, and Emma made the introductions.

"You must join us," Hazel said to my grandmother, aunt, and Harold. "We'll make room."

"Oh, but there aren't enough seats," Madeline said.

"Nonsense." Hazel grinned, then waved her hand and murmured something under her breath. Magic sparked on the air, and three more chairs appeared at a table that was suddenly larger. The oddest thing was, we didn't even bump into the tables that surrounded us. It was still a tight fit, but somehow, she'd created more space in the pub.

"Told you she was powerful," Emma murmured at my side.

"She's quite something."

Emma peered around me to see my companions, who were settling themselves into the seats that had been created for them. "I'm glad you brought them along."

"They insisted."

"Well, the more, the merrier." She took a seat, and I lowered myself into the one next to her.

The table might have become bigger, but our chairs in

particular were still very close together. Mine was so close to Emma's that my shoulder pressed against hers. Heat raced through me, and I drew in a low breath. Every time she moved, her body brushed against mine. I did my best to ignore it, but it was impossible.

I stood. "Why don't I get a round of beers?"

Most people at the table already had them, but I needed a reason to get up and pull myself together. She was having an embarrassingly strong effect on me.

"All right, but hurry," Emma said. "The quiz starts soon."

I made my way to the bar and placed an order for enough pints of the local ale that everyone at the table would have one. As I waited for the bartender to fill the order, one of the witches appeared at my side. Lily, she'd been called during the introductions.

She smiled at me, and there was something cunning in it that put me on my guard. When she spoke, her voice was friendly, "I thought you could use some help carrying."

"Thank you."

"So, you and Emma, huh? When did that start?"

"Oh, not long ago."

"Hmm. Interesting." She smiled at me again. "How did you meet, exactly?"

"It depends on who you ask," I said, thinking about the night with my grandmother.

"Well, I'm asking you." She poked me in the shoulder, and there was something distinctly flirtatious about it.

This was one to be wary of. "We met in the loo at the new pub down the road."

She laughed. "Those aren't gender-neutral."

"Exactly."

"So, who was in the wrong restroom?" She arched a brow. "I'm sure it was Emma."

Irritation pricked. Lily was no friend of Emma's. "Actually, it was me." I smiled and shrugged. "Wasn't paying attention to where I was going and ended up in the ladies."

"Well, lucky Emma." She sighed. "Though I must say your relationship is a surprise."

"Really?"

"You just don't seem like a match."

"I know what you mean. She's far too good for me."

"Hmm." She smiled. "You're a good boyfriend, Your Grace."

"Hmm." Fortunately, the bartender finished the last of the beers. I handed over a hundred-pound note and told her to keep the change just to get away from Lily as quickly as possible. "Why don't we get these back to the table? I think the quiz is starting soon."

"Sure thing, Your Grace."

I felt her gaze on me as I led the way back to the table. She was definitely one to be wary of.

CHAPTER
SEVENTEEN

EMMA

THE QUIZ TURNED out to be pretty fun, actually. Alaric was better at the music questions than I'd have expected him to be, and his grandmother was killer with pop culture. His aunt spent most of the time drinking gin and tonics and flirting with Harold, who waited at the edge of his seat for an etymology question.

The witches were the same as they always were, fiercely competitive and full of ridiculous jokes. The beers were flowing, with the bartender making unusual stops at the table to offer refills. I had to assume that Alaric tipped well, from the way she kept smiling at him, although it could just be that he was handsome and charming. When I'd seen Lily follow him to the bar, I'd wanted to tackle her like a rugby player. Fortunately, I'd decided against it.

There had been questions about my relationship with

Alaric, but we'd managed them. Still, there had been a few stressful moments.

Hazel leaned close to me and whispered, "I like him."

"Me, too." It was the truth, though I wished it weren't. When this was all over, it would make it even harder to break up.

"Even more than that, I think he's good enough for you."

I shot her a surprised look. "What?"

"You deserve only the best, Emma." She wrapped an arm around my shoulder and gave me a hug.

Happy warmth exploded within me, and I hugged her back. Hazel spent most of her time being the businesslike leader of the coven, but she did have a soft side. I rarely saw it, but when I did, it made me feel like I finally had the family I was searching for. True, it was a work family, but beggars couldn't be choosers, and I truly loved the coven.

"Thank you." I pulled back, my shoulder brushing against Alaric. It happened every thirty seconds, and it was really doing a number on my equilibrium. "I'm going to head to the loo."

Hazel nodded. "Hurry back. The next round is starting soon."

"Will do." I stood and wove my way between the tables, slipping inside the quiet bathroom. I didn't really need to use the loo—I had barely touched the beer Alaric had got me since tonight was so important—but I did need the break.

As I was washing my hands in the sink and staring at my reflection in the mirror, the bathroom door opened. For the briefest moment, déjà vu had me expecting Alaric to walk in.

Instead, it was Lily.

It took everything I had to plaster a smile on my face. I hadn't expected her to be there that night, but hadn't been terribly surprised when I'd seen her. She had a habit of turning up when it was least convenient for me.

"Well, he's quite something, isn't he?" she asked as she walked to the other sink and checked her lipstick,.

"Alaric?"

"No, Harold." She shot me a deadpan look. "Of course, Alaric. I must say I'm surprised you managed to bag yourself a man like him."

I felt my jaw slacken slightly. That was boldly rude even for her. "I guess I just got lucky."

"I'll say. I wish I'd been in the ladies' loo when he got confused and walked in."

"Oh?" I frowned. That wasn't quite what had happened.

"He told me how you met," she said. "That he walked in on you in the ladies' loo at the new pub."

Oh, Alaric. I smiled. How impossibly kind of him.

"Like I said, I'm just lucky."

"Hmmm." Her gaze caught mine in the mirror, and for the briefest moment, I thought I saw suspicion there.

Yep, it was definitely suspicion. I swallowed hard.

Lily was clever. Like, really clever. If anyone could figure out that this was a ruse, it was her.

I needed to get the heck out of here. "I'd better head back out there, I think the next round is about to start."

"Sure." She smiled.

I hurried out, feeling like a mouse who had just escaped the claws of a cat.

When I reached the table, they were cheering. Vivian

grinned up at me and said, "There was finally an etymology question, and Harold delivered."

I looked over at Harold, who was grinning from ear to ear. "Well done, Harold."

He smiled at me. "I knew my time would come."

The next round went quickly, and I was surprised by how well Alaric and his family got along with my coven. It was like they'd always been there, and it made me hope for more.

Silly.

During a break between rounds, after Alaric had returned with more beer for the group, Lily leaned forward and said, "Well, I think it's time for a kiss."

I blinked at her. "What?"

"Kiss your man, silly." She pointed to Alaric, a clever smile on her face.

What a witch. She was totally putting me on the spot, and it was because she suspected we were up to something.

Right?

Honestly, I couldn't tell with her.

Fortunately, Alaric had no problem playing along. "An excellent suggestion." He turned to me and cupped the back of my head.

His gaze burned into mine before he moved his lips to my ear. His breath brushed across the sensitive curve, and I shivered. "May I kiss you?"

The request, and how it was delivered, was so sexy that I almost swooned backward. My breath came short as I said, "You'd better."

He moved his lips to mine and gave me a kiss that made my mind go blank as pleasure swept through me. The pub disappeared as his lips parted mine. From the outside, the kiss probably looked chaste.

It didn't feel chaste.

It felt like I was burning up inside.

"All right, I think that's as much as I can handle," Madeline's voice broke in. "At the risk of sounding like I'm in an American movie, you two will have to get a room if you want to keep going."

Alaric drew back, his gaze meeting mine briefly. The heat in his gaze made me blush, and I looked away.

Fortunately, the next round pulled everyone's attention away from the kiss. Not mine, though. My body was at the table, but my mind wasn't present for a single question.

I didn't even notice when the game ended, but suddenly, everyone was standing up, and it was time to go. Alaric stood next to me and took my arm like any good boyfriend would do, but I wanted to shove him away. Or pull him closer, I wasn't sure. If he wasn't going to carry me to bed right now, I wasn't sure I could handle any more touching. Tonight, I would be going to bed lit up like a firework.

"Thank you for inviting me," he said to Hazel. "It was lovely to meet you all."

She smiled. "Likewise. Just be sure you take care of our girl, here."

Her words distracted me a bit, for which I was grateful. I could at least get my mind out of the gutter long enough to say my goodbyes.

Alaric told his family that he would meet them at the car after walking me to my flat, and I didn't object. We left the pub, and by the time we were out of earshot of the others, my head cleared a bit, and I laughed.

"I can't believe that worked," I whispered to him.

"We put on a good show, I think."

I looked up at him, drawn in by the camaraderie of maintaining a ruse in front of everyone. It was like we were in our own little world, and I loved it.

When we reached the door to my flat, I stopped and turned to him. "Thank you, Alaric. I appreciate it."

"Of course. It's no more than you've done for me."

"You told Lily that you were the idiot who went into the wrong loo."

He smiled, but then his gaze darkened slightly. "She's one to be careful around. If anyone suspects anything, it's her."

"Yeah." I nodded, worry tugging at me. "We'll need to be careful. She'll go digging if she thinks something is up, and she won't hesitate to rat me out."

"That's a shame."

"I know." Across the street, something caught my eye.

Three of the senior witches were walking down the street, headed back to their flats and houses. Alaric followed my gaze, spotting them.

When he turned back to me, heat had entered his eyes. "I suppose we'd better keep up the ruse with a good night kiss?"

Desire flushed through me. We could just stand here talking until the witches passed and then say goodbye like the business partners we were.

Or we could kiss.

Sure, we were using the witches' presence as a weak excuse. But I was okay with it.

From the way he devoured me with his eyes, he was okay with it, too.

"We'd better do it," I said, leaning up to wrap my arms around his neck. I kissed him for the second time that night, but that time, I was in control. I pulled him down to me and parted his lips with my own, slipping my tongue between. He groaned, a low sound that sent desire shooting through me. I wanted to climb him like a tree, but I settled for pulling him back into the corner of the nook where my door sat.

He wrapped his big hands around my waist and lifted me up to him, pressing me against the firm expanse of his chest. I clung to him as I ran my mouth down his neck, tasting the salty skin there.

When he pulled away, my head was spinning.

"My family," he said, his voice a low rasp. "They're waiting."

"Right." I gasped, trying to catch my breath. "Of course. You should go."

"I really should." The look he gave me made it clear that he didn't want to leave. But there wasn't any other option.

I gave him a little shove and a smile. The grin that he shot me was so charming, I felt compelled to press my hands to my chest and laugh like some ridiculous schoolgirl.

Embarrassed, I turned and let myself into my house. I was being ridiculous. Totally ridiculous.

But it was so damned fun.

CHAPTER
EIGHTEEN

Emma

THE NEXT MORNING, I went directly to the Enchanted Garden to talk to Aria about the remaining ingredients for the joy batteries. I'd wanted to head over to Alaric's place first, but that was out of the question.

I needed some space to get my head together. The night before, I'd tossed and turned for hours, memories of the kiss haunting me in the best—and most frustrating—way. When I'd finally fallen asleep, I'd been hounded by dreams that made me wake up sweating.

I was starting to fall for him.

The racing heart and distracted thoughts made that clear enough. But he didn't want that, and I couldn't afford it. The paparazzi might be leaving us alone just then, but they wouldn't always.

I arrived at the gates of the Enchanted Garden before I could answer that question and threw myself into the distraction. When I reached the little cottage that acted as the main office building, I caught sight of Aria kissing a tall, dark-haired man: Callan Hawthorne, her husband and the wealthiest and most powerful man in town until Alaric had arrived. He was also a nice guy, despite all that.

I stepped on a twig, and the cracking sound made them pull apart.

"Sorry!" I called out. "The gate was open, so I thought..."

"No worries!" Aria grinned at me, then nudged Callan with her elbow. "He's got to get to work, anyway."

"True enough." He smiled at me, then leaned down to press a kiss to Aria's cheek.

They were the loveliest couple and had been married about a year. He gave me a little wave as he headed down the path toward the exit.

"You're here for the rest of the supplies?" Aria asked, patting down her hair to make sure it was neat.

"Yes. Did they come in?"

"The sunspark berries did, yes." She frowned. "But I'm afraid the moon thistle didn't make it. They're entirely out. In fact, there's only one place that has it, and they're unwilling to part with it."

"What?" Horrified, I stared at her. We needed that ingredient *desperately*.

"Yeah." She grimaced. "It's on the estate of the Marquis of Dale. He's a retired botanist, along with his wife, and they don't like to sell their stock."

"Oh, bum." I was going to have to find a way to convince them.

"There is one possibility, though," she said. "He's a vampire like the duke. If you can get your guy to call him up... then maybe he can sort something?"

I blew out a breath. "I'm going to have to try it. Thank you for tracking it down."

"Anytime. How many of these things have you got to make, though? You've been placing some pretty big orders."

"I know. It's going to be a lot. At least a hundred."

Aria winced. "They take a lot of magic to put together. If you need help, let me know. I can rope Tabitha and my gran in as well."

"Oh, my gosh, thank you so much." It was an amazing offer. "I think I might have to take you up on that."

"Do it. We'll make it a party."

I grinned, liking the sound of that. The more I hung around with Aria, the more I liked her.

"Let me get what you came for." She turned and hurried into the cottage, then came back out with a cardboard box. Boris and Penelope followed her, looking sheepish. "Look who I found snuggled in the chair by the fire."

"Oh!" I grinned at Penelope.

She glared at me. *I won't ask you about your love life if you won't ask me about mine.*

"I wouldn't dare," I said to her.

"Is she telling you off?" Aria asked. "Because Boris already had a word with me."

"She did indeed."

"I find that bacon sandwiches can often get the info or help I need."

Penelope's brows rose. *Bacon sandwiches are an option?*

I took a page out of Aria's book, but I didn't actually want to know about her love life. I would need help, though. "Maybe. If you'll help me set up for the ball later."

I can be persuaded.

I grinned. "Excellent." Bacon sandwiches were much easier than promising her open favors, but I didn't tell her that.

LATER THAT AFTERNOON, I drove up to Blackthorn Hall to meet Harold. He'd agreed to visit Barnaby with me and give me some tips, and I was grateful.

As I climbed out of my car, he appeared on the front steps of the house, right on time. He wore another pale suit, this one also in a summery fabric. He was the picture of titled leisure. Madeline appeared behind him, along with Alaric and his grandmother.

I smiled and waved. "You're quite the welcome party."

"What can we say? We like you." Vivian swept down the stairs, dressed in a perfect wool skirt and silk blouse. She gave me a peck on either cheek, her hands gripping my upper arms. "We're hoping you'll stay for dinner."

I looked at Alaric, who nodded.

"I'd love to," I said.

Harold clapped his hands together. "Now that that's

settled, we should get to work! If you're new to this, there will be a bit of a learning curve."

"You can count on it," I said. "Can you give me a moment with Alaric?"

Before he could say anything, Madeline grabbed his arm and pulled him away. "Come show me the roses, darling."

"But I don't know anything about roses," he said.

"I know." She winked at me.

"I'll see you for drinks at eight," Vivian said before she turned and swept up the stairs.

"You're going to have to tell her, you know." Alaric grinned at me.

"I need to learn a spell to weaken the strength of gin." I laughed. "Although it will probably just be easier to request wine."

His gaze dropped to my lips, then rose to my eyes. "What did you need to talk to me about?"

"Do you know the Marquis of Dale?"

"A bit. Stuffy old man, lives up north in the Lakes District."

"Well, I need a favor."

"Anything." He said it with such quick agreement that I had to smile before telling him what Aria had shared with me.

When I was finished, he nodded and said, "I'll call him today and see what I can do."

"Thank you."

He smiled. "Now go meet Harold. He keeps staring at you over the rose bushes. Once he sets his mind to something, he wants to get it done. It's how he became the foremost beetle expert in the United Kingdom, you know."

I smiled, loving the adorable ridiculousness of it. "See you later."

I found Harold by the roses, shooting me glances as Madeline tried to distract him.

"Oh, thank fates you're here," Madeline said. "Once this one gets his mind on something, it's impossible to slow him down."

"It's true, I'm rather one-track." He tapped the side of his head. "But I'm serious about getting you up to speed with your skills. This ball is coming up, and we need to deal with this ghost."

"Thank you, Harold. I truly appreciate it." And I meant it. He was like a gift dropped from the sky, because I needed all the help I could get.

"Come, now, show me where the ghost usually stays."

Madeline waved her fingers at us. "Bye-bye. Have fun. Don't anger the spirits."

"We'll try, my dear." He pressed a kiss to her cheek, then followed me toward Barnaby, talking as we went. "Tell me what you know about this ghost. I think it's important to know everything we can if we want to be successful."

"For one, I don't think he's a violent ghost. Unless you're a rosebush." I frowned. "He's ornery, though. I can't get him to see reason, or to even talk to me."

"That's what I'm here to help with. Tell me the rest."

I went through everything I knew about Barnaby, which wasn't much. Harold didn't seem disappointed, though, and by the time we reached the garden maze, I'd finished talking.

"Vivian informs me you have a familiar?" he asked.

"I do. A skunk named Penelope."

"Can you call her to you? A familiar can enhance a witch's powers, correct?"

"Yes." I should have thought of that and asked her to come. "I can try. She usually shows up when I need her."

"Go on, then."

"Penelope?" I called, my voice hesitant. I cleared my throat. "Penelope, I need your help. Come, please."

I'm here. Her voice sounded from behind me, and I turned to see her. I still didn't know how she got to me so quickly. Did she run? Did she appear out of thin air?

She looked around me toward the maze. *We're trying with the ghost again?*

"We are."

All right, then. She raised her arms like a toddler wanting to be picked up, and I lifted her up against my chest. She snuggled close, and I'd have been lying if I said I didn't like it.

"Right, you look like you're in position," Harold said. He turned toward the maze. "Ask that he show himself."

Last time I'd screamed and threatened until he'd shown himself, but I had a feeling that wasn't what Harold was asking for.

Good instinct, Penelope said.

I looked down at her. "Can you read my mind?"

No, but you don't hide things on your face very well. And I remember the last time just as well as you do.

"Fair enough." I looked back at the maze and called out in my nicest voice, "Barnaby? Will you please come out to speak to us?"

Nothing happened. I shot Harold a doubtful look.

"Honestly, that was a bit weak, my dear. Also, I could hear the frustration in your voice."

"You could?"

"And see it on your face."

I frowned. "Oh, bum."

"It's all right. This is about making a connection, and you're better suited than most people. I know he's frustrating you, but you need to control that. Spirits are more emotional than people. They are driven by their last desires and a strong need to fulfill them. You need to control your own desires and emotions so that you can use your power to understand theirs."

"How, though? What are the actual mechanics of that?"

He drew in a deep breath and raised his hands, palms out. "Feel the magic in the air—that special signature, the one that isn't the ether. That's the spirit world You need to feel it and open yourself up to it."

"Is that what the golden sparkles were when he would appear and damage the garden?"

"Yes, exactly. It was a visible manifestation of that otherworldly magic in the air. You just need to feel it even if the sparkles aren't there."

"All right." I hugged Penelope close and closed my eyes, then reached out with all of my senses. Immediately, I felt the magic that was in the ether. It filled the air, something that nearly all witches could feel easily. To me, it felt like bubbles against my skin. I could draw them to me and use them to manifest my will through spells and potions.

Being a witch was awesome.

I forced my mind back on the task, looking for the other type of magic in the air. I was pretty sure I'd never felt it before, so I wasn't totally clear on what I was looking for.

Eventually, though, I thought I felt something a little different. It was like a fine mist, cool and damp. I opened my eyes to make sure that it hadn't just got misty, but the day was still bright and clear.

"I think I've got it," I said.

"All right, excellent." Harold grinned. "Spells, like the one that Alaric told me you used in the graveyard, can force spirits to appear. But the true skill is in making the ghost or spirit comfortable enough to communicate. You can make a connection with them that others cannot make, and you can convince them to talk to you."

"I presume that doesn't involve yelling?"

He stared at me, aghast. "Certainly not. Is that how you got him to show himself before?"

I blushed. "Maybe."

"Well, none of that today. Feel for the magic and make a connection with it. See if you can convince him to show himself."

"Okay." I closed my eyes again and hugged Penelope, who seemed to have fallen asleep in my arms. She snored softly against my neck.

I drew in a deep breath and focused on the misty magic that I could feel all around me. If I reached out to it, I could direct it through the air, like my will had become a breeze. I worked on instinct, gathering the magic close to me.

More and more, it coalesced in front of me. Once it felt like there was a lot of it, I spoke. "Barnaby? I want to apologize for yelling the other day." I hesitated, hating what I had to admit to next. "And for threatening to bring the dog. I hate that you are destroying the garden, but that was wrong of me. I was hoping you could come out and we could chat."

I could actually *feel* his presence begin to appear in front of me.

When I opened my eyes, he stood in front of me, only partially visible.

"Hi, Barnaby," I said.

His gaze moved to Penelope, still snoring, and he smiled.

"I was hoping we could talk," I said.

He glared at me and said nothing. Tentatively, I reached out my hand toward his. My heart thundered wildly, but I followed my gut. He looked down and saw me coming so he had an opportunity to move, but he stood still.

As soon as my fingertips made contact with his pale hand, a zap of magic ran up my arm. I could immediately feel what he felt. Regret and love and longing. Excitement flashed through me.

"You regret something and feel longing for it," I said. "And love."

He glared at me and disappeared.

"Oh, bum." I scowled.

"You went too fast," Harold said. "Couldn't you feel his hesitation?"

"No, I got too excited that I was succeeding."

"True, you did. It's important to remove yourself from the equation and just be there to listen. To make connections. Take time before you speak or move—twice as much time as you think you need."

"All right. Can we try again?"

"Tomorrow at the earliest. He's not a blank slate. He's upset now, just like a living person would be. Give him time."

Guilt pricked me. "Good idea."

As we walked away, I vowed that I would get better at this.

CHAPTER
NINETEEN

EMMA

ALARIC SENT a car for me the next morning. I'd expected him
to pick me up as he usually did when we went to his
house, but the driver had said that Alaric had to meet the
boat.

"A boat?" I asked as I climbed into the back of the big
dark car.

"You'll be traveling by boat today, ma'am." He smiled
and shut the door.

He hadn't introduced himself when he'd picked me up
and I'd been so surprised by the mention of a boat that I'd
forgot to ask. Now that he'd climbed into the front of the car
and turned on the music just a bit too loud, I figured that I
shouldn't.

Instead, I settled down on the cloud-like seat and looked
out the window. We left the charm of Foxglove Lane behind

and headed out into the countryside, which was beautiful on that late spring morning.

We arrived at the coast forty minutes later, having driven farther west into Cornwall. The driver pulled to a stop at a small quay in a village I'd never visited. It was a pretty place, with pennants strung over the streets to celebrate a festival of some sort. I peered out the window to catch sight of the scrolled writing on one of the signs hung in a shop window. This weekend was the Seagull Serenade, a festival dedicated to all things seagull.

I grinned, then turned my attention to the harbor. It was one of the small, stone-walled harbors so common on the coast of England, with little boats bobbing on the water. Most appeared to be fishing and tourist boats, but then my gaze was drawn to the beautiful wooden cruiser moored just outside the harbor, on the other side of the jetty. It was huge, but not overly ostentatious, probably because it was one of those classic ones that was so pretty, it was impossible to think it was too much.

The driver opened the door for me, and I climbed out. The boat was even more impressive from this side of the car window.

I blew out a breath and whispered, "Penelope, you're going to want to see this."

She hadn't come with me, but at my words, she appeared at my side. I'd missed if she'd scampered up from somewhere, but it had to be impossible since we were so far from home. She'd either stowed away in the car or she'd used magic to appear.

Whoa. She sat back on her hind legs. *That's something.*

"Isn't it?" I grinned down at her. "I bet the kitchen is good."

I bet you're right. I'm going to go find out. She waddled toward the water, where a small wooden boat was approaching, piloted by Alaric. He smiled and waved.

"Sorry I couldn't pick you up," he called over. "You would have had to wake up far earlier to meet the boat with me." He nodded back to the huge yacht, and I wasn't surprised to find that this was his boat. It had *billionaire duke* written all over it.

"I wouldn't have minded." I ran my gaze from bow to stern. "It's beautiful."

"Thank you. It was my mother's." The smile on his face was genuine, if a little sad.

As the boat neared the side of the dock, the chauffeur approached and held out his hands for the line. Alaric slowed the boat, pulling up alongside with expert precision before tossing a line to driver. Once they'd secured the boat to the side of the wharf, which was quite a bit higher than the water level, Alaric reached up to pick up Penelope, who'd stuck out her little arms like a child waiting to be helped down into the boat. He lowered her into the vessel, and she scampered onto a seat and looked out to sea, the wind in her whiskers.

Because the tide was so low, I had to sit on the wharf and let Alaric grip my waist in two hands to lower me into the boat. My body ran along his as he lowered me, and his touch sent a rush of heat through me. Once I stood in front of him, I looked up and met his gaze.

"Hello." His voice was rough and soft, and he leaned down to press a kiss to my cheek.

It warmed me from the inside, and I leaned into him just briefly. There was no one here to put on a show for, unless he expected the driver to report back to his grandmother. Since that was highly doubtful, he was kissing me just to kiss me.

And I liked it.

He pulled back and smiled down at me, his hair windswept and his green eyes flecked with bits of gold that I'd never seen before. The chauffeur passed my bag down to Alaric, then handed the rope to me. I wrapped it into a neat pile and set it on the seat while Alaric headed back to the steering wheel. A moment later, the engine was rumbling, and we were off.

"It'll only take a couple of minutes to get to the *Anne Marie*," he said from his spot at the helm.

"That's the boat's name?" I looked out at the vessel bobbing peacefully on the small waves.

"My mother named her for her mother, who died before I was born."

"Oh, I'm sorry. If she was anywhere near as cool as Vivian, it's a shame not to have known her."

He nodded. "I'm lucky to have one grandmother, at least."

I nodded, a bit sad. "True."

"I'm sorry, that was insensitive." He looked truly apologetic, and I tried to give him a reassuring shrug.

"Oh, don't worry. It's fine. I'm used to it."

"That doesn't make it easier, I imagine."

How was he so kind?

Since I didn't want to explore how much I was growing to like him, I turned my attention to the *Anne Marie*.

"Where does the marquis live if we need to take a boat to him?"

"America."

"No!" I looked at him, aghast.

"Just joking." He smiled. "He lives with his wife on a private island about three hours from shore. We can get underway as soon as we're on board."

As we neared the *Anne Marie*, I realized that it was quite a bit bigger than I'd thought. "That thing has a real captain, right?" I asked.

Alaric laughed. "Worried about my driving?"

"Maybe."

"It does. And a crew of five."

"Crew?" I blew out a breath. "Quite a boat. Or is it a ship?"

"A boat? I don't know what the difference is."

Our small vessel pulled up alongside the yacht, and we were met by two crewmen in matching navy uniforms. They caught the rope that Alaric passed them, and we stepped onto a low wooden platform on the back. I thought it might be called the fantail, but I didn't know enough about boats to be sure.

"Do you ever take this thing down to the Mediterranean?" I asked as I climbed up onto the back sitting area. It had a huge table for meals and a large U-shaped couch with cushions upholstered in navy with white trim. I could just imagine the holidays down there, hanging out on the beautiful deck and swimming in the crystal blue water.

"We could, if you like." He smiled.

The words caught my breath. They sounded so natural, and like he meant it. "I'm not sure if that's within the fake dating rules."

"My grandmother could come."

"All right." I grinned. I didn't mind keeping up the ruse, and not just for the free holiday. I *wanted* to keep seeing him.

This train of thought was dangerous. There wasn't a future here.

"Show me around?" I asked, wanting a distraction.

"Sure. Follow me."

As the *Anne Marie*'s engine rumbled to a start and the boat headed out to sea, Alaric showed me around the interior of the vessel. There were eight full bedrooms that looked nothing like I expected of boat bedrooms. They could have been straight out of a posh home decorating magazine. There were also multiple sitting rooms and bathrooms and an impressive kitchen, where Penelope was already eyeing the cook.

But it was the deck that was my favorite part of the tour. There were various sitting areas with chairs and sun loungers, each covered in a navy cushion. The sea breeze was delightfully cool and fresh as the brilliant green hills of Cornwall shrunk into the distance and gulls circled overhead. I wanted to tell them to head toward land and the festival in their honor, but I hadn't figured out if the festival celebrated the birds themselves or different ways to eat them. Could you eat a seagull? I didn't want to try.

I turned my face up to the clouds, enjoying the warmth of the sun on my skin.

"You like the sea," he said.

"It's hard not to on a day like today. On a boat like this."

"I mean it when I say we can take a holiday."

"I'm tempted to take you up on it." But I wouldn't. "So, tell me about the marquis and marchioness. What's our angle here? We've got to convince them to give us the moon thistle, I assume."

"Yes. It was my grandmother who convinced the marquis to see us. Or rather, she probably convinced the marchioness, who convinced the marquis. He's always been a grumpy old bastard, but he loves his wife, who has been good friends with my grandmother for a long time."

"So you know them, too? And like them?"

"How'd you know?"

"Your voice. There's fondness there despite the fact that the marquis is grumpy."

He nodded. "We would visit when I was young. I still remember her sneaking me sweets."

"So this shouldn't be too hard."

"Unfortunately, she's not the one we have to convince to give us the moon thistle. But her husband loves her dearly, so she'll be good to have in our corner."

"All right, 'Operation Charm the Marchioness' commences." I grinned at him. "Maybe you focus on that, and I'll focus on the marquis."

"Careful, or you'll make me jealous." He smiled, and there was something distinctly flirtatious in his tone that I loved.

"Oh, really?"

"Indeed. The marquis is a bit older than me, but there's a distinct air of sophistication about him."

"Hmmm. You'd better watch out, then."

He smiled and turned toward the water, looking out over the glittering waves. We chatted as the hours passed, and there was something so easy and natural about it. At one point, one of the staff members delivered a beautiful lunch to the deck, and we ate it as the breeze blew my hair back from my face and Penelope lay on a sun lounger with her white belly to the sky.

Eventually, an island rose up in the distance, crowned with a small green hill. Trees covered the left side, and a house sat near the top. It was a beautiful old estate, though I couldn't see much from that distance.

The boat dropped anchor about a football pitch's distance from the small dock on the shore, and one of the crew members prepared the smaller boat to take us to land. They loaded our luggage, and then we boarded for the short ride.

As we neared, I spotted two figures standing at the dock, waiting for us.

"They've come to greet us," Alaric said.

"*That's* the Marquis and Marchioness of Dale?"

"The very same."

I laughed at the idea of either of us flirting with them.

They were the epitome of an adorable elderly couple who were deeply in love. Both were tiny, with pale white hair and lined faces. They wore matching wax jackets to keep out the wind, and even their Le Chameau boots were identical, coming up to the knees of baggy trousers that looked like they'd donned them for gardening or walking.

But it was the way that they held hands that caught my eye, and the way the marchioness leaned into the marquis. He leaned toward her as well, and it made my heart go warm.

I shot Alaric a look and murmured, "I think I'm going to have a hard time making you jealous by flirting with the marquis."

"I suppose you're right," he said. "He does only have eyes for his wife."

I'd been nervous about this dinner, but maybe it wouldn't be too bad.

As the boat pulled up to the dock, Alaric waved at the couple. The marchioness waved back, but the marquis just stared.

Hmm. Maybe this wouldn't be as easy as I'd thought.

Alaric climbed onto the dock first, then turned around and held out his hand to help me. I gripped his strong palm and stepped off. Penelope scampered after me, probably already thinking about the kitchens in the big house on the hill.

He led me toward the couple, and I put on my best friendly smile.

"Alaric!" The marchioness grinned widely and let go of her husband's hand, holding out her arms for a hug. "It's so lovely to see you, my boy."

"Eileen." The warmth in his voice was genuine as he stooped low to wrap his arms around her. They hugged, and when they pulled back, both had enormous smiles on their faces.

It was downright adorable.

Alaric held his hand out to the marquis, who shook it heartily and gave him a small smile. It looked genuine, at least, but this was a man whose admiration you had to earn.

"Please let me introduce you to Emma Willowby, my girlfriend."

I smiled, liking the sound of that, even though I knew it was fake. "Lovely to meet you, My Lord, My Lady."

The marchioness clapped. "Oh, it's so wonderful to meet *you*, my dear. Vivian has told me all about you, and I'm just so thrilled that our dear Alaric has found someone worthy of him." She reached for the marquis's hand and squeezed it as she looked at him. "Aren't we, dear?"

"We are, indeed." His voice was gruff, but like his small smile, the words sounded genuine. "Please, call me Rupert."

"And call me Eileen." She smiled broadly.

The guilt hit me then, of course. This was another group of people I'd disappoint with my lies, and I'd need to make sure that I ended this as well as I could.

Eileen looked down at Penelope, who sat patiently at my side, her pink bow fluttering in the wind. "And who is this little one?"

"My familiar, Penelope."

"Oh, of course. Vivian mentioned that you were a witch." Eileen smiled at me. "And you must be quite a strong one if you have a familiar."

"I am a witch, though whether I'm a strong one I have yet to see. I'm working on it."

"You'll do fine, my dear," she said.

"Vivian says you're here about the moon thistle?" Rupert said, a scowl on his face. "You know we don't sell any of our garden."

"I'm aware." Alaric's voice was so perfectly diplomatic, with a tone and volume that he'd clearly developed for just this sort of situation. "But we're hoping to convince you that this is a special occasion."

"Ha." Rupert grunted. "Unlikely."

Eileen gave him a little nudge with her shoulder. "Oh, Rupert. Don't be such a grouch. Let the children try."

The children? I had to resist a laugh.

"Fine. You can try." He glared at us. "But don't expect success."

TWENTY

ALARIC

RUPERT AND EILEEN escorted us to a sitting room at the back of the house. A fire cracked merrily on one side of the room, and wide windows provided a view of the garden and sea on the other side. It reminded me of my childhood, and it was easy to see my mother in this room. She'd often come on our visits, but my father had not. They had been some of our happiest times.

"Tea?" Eileen asked, shaking me away from my thoughts.

"Please," I said, taking a seat on the brocade couch and leaving a spot for Emma.

She sat so close that she could reach out and hold my hand, which she did. When she leaned her shoulder into mine, I realized that she was mimicking the body language of Rupert and Eileen from when we'd seen them on the dock.

Clever.

"This room is beautiful," she said as Eileen poured the tea that had been delivered by one of the household staff.

"Oh, thank you." Eileen looked around and smiled, her gaze lingering on the windows that overlooked the garden and sea. A brilliant profusion of purple flowers bloomed right in the middle. They were more than a hundred meters away from where we sat, but they were so profuse that they were impossible not to notice. They were also incredibly tall.

"Those flowers are beautiful," Emma said. "What are they?"

"They're what you came here for," Rupert grumbled.

"Those are the moon thistle?" I asked, surprised. "I would have thought they'd bloom at night."

"They do. This is their dormant state." Rupert looked out the window. "They are the prize of our garden."

Bloody hell. No wonder they didn't want to part with them. If they became more beautiful at night, they'd be a sight to behold.

"They're truly glorious at night when the moon is large," Eileen said, her voice full of wonder. "They glow."

This task was growing more impossible by the minute.

Eileen handed teacups to us, then put a plate of biscuits on the table. She sat next to Rupert and sipped her own tea. "When we're done here, we can walk amongst them. After dinner, you really should visit them again when the moon is out."

"We'll be sure to," I said, wondering how I was going to convince them to part with their beloved moon thistle.

As we finished our tea, Eileen asked about our relationship. We put on a pretty good show, adding as much charm as possible, though it only seemed to work on Eileen. Rupert was as inscrutable as ever, though he did mow through at least half the biscuits. He'd always done that, and the reminder helped humanize him. Penelope worked on the other half, much to Eileen's delight.

"Shall we walk in the garden?" Eileen asked after our tea. "Then we can dress for dinner."

We followed them out to the garden, which was beautiful. It was clear they adored the moon thistle, which grew up a little higher than my head. Both Rupert and Eileen seemed to light up when they talked about it. After about an hour, we finished the walk and retreated to our bedroom to change for dinner.

I shut the bedroom door behind us, noting the fact that there was only one bed. Of course there was, and I couldn't request another room since we were supposed to be dating.

Emma didn't seem as concerned with the bed situation, though. She groaned and threw herself onto it, arm draped over her forehead. "They are never going to part with those flowers."

"I'm getting the same impression." I walked to the window and realized that we could see the flowers from there, their tall stalks leaning in the wind.

"I'd say we should lay on the charm more thickly, but I don't know how to."

"You're doing an excellent job."

"Well, don't get too excited, because I'm distinctly sure I heard Eileen say *dress for dinner*. That means formal dinner, right? Because I didn't bring anything appropriate."

"Madeline packed you a bag," I said. "She would visit

with us when I was young, and she's familiar with how they do things."

She sat upright. "She did? Really?"

I nodded and went to the side wall, where the staff had delivered our bags. "She put a few things in there, she said." I set the bag on the bench at the foot of the bed and unzipped it.

"That's so thoughtful." She grinned widely and crawled across the mattress to look down at the bag I'd opened.

The sight of her on the bed made something tighten inside me.

I needed to get myself together.

"I'm going to shower."

"All right." She was already sorting through the clothing that Madeline had packed for her, and I left her to it.

The bathroom was huge and modern, no doubt a product of the same sort of renovation that Blackthorn Hall had undergone decades ago. As I showered, I couldn't get Emma out of my mind.

That day had been...wonderful.

It was a ridiculous, soft word, but it was the only one that suited. I hadn't spent this much time with Emma since we'd met, and I'd liked it. A lot. Especially since she'd been doing her best to be a doting girlfriend.

I want it to be real.

The thought was loud in my head, and impossible to banish. I tilted my head back and let the shower pound down over me.

Emma

I TRIED on every dress that Madeline had packed for me, unable to believe how gorgeous they were. And comfortable. Was this what you got when you paid thousands of pounds for clothing?

It must be. But I shouldn't get used to it.

You look nice.

Penelope's voice drew my attention from the mirror, and I looked down to see her staring up at me. "When did you get here?"

A few minutes ago. I felt like something fun was happening.

"You can sense that?"

She shrugged. *I can sense whenever something I might like is happening. That's usually food, but I also like sparkles.*

"Then you like this one?" I asked, looking back in the mirror. It was a pale gold sheath dress that glimmered with the faintest flicks of gold throughout the fabric. It glided over my skin like water, and I could have worn it forever.

I do. But I also think you should try the pink.

I looked back at the bag, spotting another dress that I hadn't seen. There were shoes and jewelry as well, everything in brands I'd only read about and some I didn't even recognize. Beautiful clothing had never been in my budget, so I'd thought I wasn't interested in it.

I'd been wrong.

It was glorious.

I tried on the pink dress, much to Penelope's delight. She still preferred the pale gold, and so did I. I changed back into it and neatly folded the dresses that I hadn't chosen. Next, I pulled out a pair of heels that fit like a dream. I felt the faintest fizz of magic and smiled. They'd been enchanted to fit anyone. I finished the look with a gold waterfall necklace of thin, smooth chains.

"Look what I found." I held up a pretty gold bracelet dotted with blue gems. "I think this would make a very fine replacement for your bow tonight."

Ooooh! Penelope hopped up and ran toward me, making grabby hands.

"I'll put it on you."

Of course. She turned around and let me take off her bow and put on the makeshift collar, then she ran to the mirror to admire herself. I grinned, watching her turn left and right to better see the necklace in the mirror.

The door behind me opened, and Alaric appeared. He wore a dark blue suit and a shirt the color of snow. The top button was open at the throat, giving him an air of casual elegance. The whole effect made him so handsome that I couldn't help a small gasp from escaping.

He stopped dead still as he looked at me, his eyes darkening. "You look..."

I waited for him to think of what he wanted to say. Penelope turned, too, clearly interested.

"Amazing," he finished. "I was searching for a better word, but that's all I could come up with." He chuckled faintly, and I loved the sound of it.

"Thank you." I smiled. "You look pretty good yourself." I nodded at Penelope so that he would notice her.

He looked down, seemingly surprised to see her. "I'm

sorry, Penelope. I had eyes only for your witch. But you look lovely in that collar."

She preened. *I hope they've set a place at the table for me.*

"I'm sure they have. You got your own cup at tea."

Good point. This house doesn't have the anti-skunk bias of so many places. I'm impressed.

I smiled, then translated for Alaric, who laughed.

He held out his arm for me. "May I?"

"Absolutely." I took his arm, shivering at the contact, and let him lead me downstairs.

Rupert and Eileen were already waiting for us in the drawing room, each holding a glass of bright red liquid. Matilda's was a champagne flute, while Rupert held a lowball. Whether they'd spiked it with something else was hard to tell, and I just hoped I wasn't offered a martini.

"Emma, you look lovely, dear," Eileen said.

"Thank you. So do you." She really did. She'd put on a pale blue dress embellished with a silvery lace that looked so delicate, I'd be too scared to wear it. She wore it with confidence, though, and looked incredible. Rupert wore a suit in an older style, but one that was impeccably fitted.

He raised his glass to Alaric. "May I get you one?"

"Thank you."

"Champagne, dear?" Eileen asked me. "Plain, of course."

I smiled. "Thank you."

"And one for your lovely companion?" Eileen smiled down at Penelope, who stood at my side.

"I think she'd love that," I said.

Congratulations, you think correctly. Your prize is one happy skunk.

That was far better than an angry skunk, so I would take it.

Rupert and Alaric went to a bar cart that sat near the door. Rupert poured me a glass of champagne, then poured a smaller one for Penelope. He brought them to us, bending low to give the little cup to Penelope, who had taken a seat on one of the upholstered footstools by the fire. He returned to join Alaric near the bar cart and began to mix his drink.

Eileen raised her glass toward mine. "To a long and happy life for you both, together as we have been."

I quite liked the sound of the together part, actually. It would be better if I didn't, but I did.

"Thank you." I gently tapped my glass to hers. It glittered gold in the warm light of the chandeliers. We drank, and the golden bubbles exploded on my tongue, delicious and cold. "This is wonderful."

"It's my favorite vintage." She gave me a cheeky smile. "I'd suggest you try it the way I drink it, but I imagine it's not to your taste."

"Perhaps after I've had a couple."

She laughed. "Oh, I like you."

I grinned at her as she sipped her blood cocktail. I hadn't met many vampires in my life, but it didn't bother me to watch them drink. It was like watching a person eat a hamburger. Or, more accurately, eat a blood sausage.

Most vampires didn't drink directly from humans anyway, since it wasn't a particularly comfortable process for the human. Instead, they preferred to source their blood from magical suppliers, who in turn purchased it from willing sellers.

It was all very civilized, for which I was grateful.

Once they had their drinks, Alaric and Rupert joined us. The duke wrapped his arm around my waist, shifting me closer to him. I leaned against him, smiling up at him in an attempt to look like an adoring girlfriend. He looked down at me, and from the way his eyes heated, I thought I might have managed it.

"Oh, I just love the way you two look at each other," Eileen said. "Reminds me of us, Rupert. Don't you agree?"

"Hmm." He grunted, but when I looked at him, there was the faintest twinkle in his eye.

Maybe this was working?

"I've never met anyone like her," Alaric said. Though I knew the words were for the benefit of Rupert and Eileen, his tone was entirely believable. "She's kind, smart, strong, beautiful. She's perfect."

"Oh, you charmer." I gave him a playful nudge. "You're all right, too."

Rupert laughed, the first genuine sound of pleasure I'd heard from him all day.

Alaric and I spent the rest of drinks and dinner trying to charm them, until Rupert finally asked us what we wanted the moon thistle for. I explained about the joy batteries and the ball, but his stern expression never shifted. Eileen seemed intrigued, though.

"You really ought to come," I said. "It will be a beautiful party. I think you'd enjoy it."

"Oh, that sounds lovely, dear." Eileen looked at Rupert. "We should go."

"It would be rude to go if we didn't give them the moon thistle," Rupert said. "Which we aren't going to do."

"We would still love to have you," I said, though I wasn't sure if there even *would* be a ball if I couldn't get the moon thistle. Without it, we'd have no joy batteries. And without a way to collect the joy at the ball, there wouldn't be much reason to throw one. We wouldn't be able to afford the cost without the promise of work for the future year.

"Hmm." Rupert took a sip of his whiskey.

"You really ought to go out and see the flowers after dinner," Eileen said.

"You should join us," I said.

"Oh, no, we'll be turning in early. Tonight is the final episode *of Murder in the West Country.*"

I hadn't heard of it, but assumed it was one of the murder mystery shows that were so popular.

We finished dinner without speaking of the moon thistle again, and I had a nice time despite the stress hanging over my head. This wasn't going as well as I'd hoped, and we were running out of time. After dessert, Eileen and Rupert departed for their bedroom. We made plans to meet for breakfast, and it would be my last shot at convincing them.

"Well, that didn't go as well as I hoped," I said.

"No." Alaric frowned. "He's very determined to hold on to those flowers."

"I'm going to need to think of some way to convince him." But I had no idea how.

"Shall we go for a walk?" he asked. "See the flowers like they suggested?"

"Sure." I looked over at Penelope, who had curled up on

her chair halfway through dinner and fallen asleep. "Let's leave her. She looks so peaceful."

Alaric stood and held out his arm for me. I took it, liking how naturally we fell into this rhythm, and let him escort me out to the garden. I could hear the sound of the sea crashing in the distance and smell the fresh grass and flowers that bloomed all around.

The moon hid behind clouds, but there was enough light from the house that we were able to make our way toward the moon thistle. The sweet scent wrapped around me, and I inhaled deeply.

The flowers had been planted in rows, and between each row was a soft strip of grass. The flower stems grew about two or three meters tall, with soft purple blooms all the way up. The stems themselves looked a bit prickly, so perhaps that's where the name had come from. Alaric led me down one of the rows in the center of the garden, until we disappeared amongst the blooms. I ran my hand gently along the flowers at my side. Magic sparkled against my fingertips wherever I touched them, and it sent a little jolt of happiness through me.

"These flowers really are amazing," I said.

Alaric stopped in the middle of the row. We were fully hidden from the house, with the flowers towering all around us. He turned to me. "*You're* amazing."

I smiled at him. "There's no one around. You don't have to put on a show."

"I'm not. And I mean it. You're incredible." His green gaze bore into mine, and the intensity on his face made a shiver rush through me. "As soon as I saw you in that dress tonight, I couldn't keep my eyes off you."

Above us, the moon came out from behind the clouds. Its light illuminated the purple blooms around us, making them glow a pale, iridescent lavender. It was otherworldly, and the light that lit Alaric's face made him so impossibly handsome that it took my breath away.

It felt as if we were in our own world there amongst the flowers, with the moonlight and the blooms creating a paradise just for us. It was intoxicating, and I felt my gaze drop to his lips.

CHAPTER
TWENTY-ONE

ALARIC

EMMA LOOKED like a goddess amongst the moon thistle. Her hair glowed as golden as her dress, and her enormous brown eyes had gone liquid with desire.

"Alaric," she murmured. "You're looking at me like you want to kiss me."

"I want to do more than that."

"So do it." The low challenge in her voice was the sexiest thing I'd ever heard.

I drew in a shuddery breath, my body tightening with desire. "Isn't it against your rules?"

"I don't care." She pressed a hand to my chest, and her palm burned through the fabric of my shirt. "Just once? What's the harm?"

I'll lose myself to you.

I would be a changed man if we did this. If I gave into what I'd been fantasizing about...

There would be no going back.

But still, I found that I couldn't stop myself.

I raised a hand and cupped the back of her head, tilting her face upward. She licked her lips, and a soft noise tore from my throat. "Emma, are you sure?"

She threw her arms around my neck and pressed her lips to mine, fitting the length of her body against my own. The pure pleasure of it was maddening, and I devoured her mouth, wanting to taste every inch of her.

She was sweet and soft and sexy as hell, and I wanted to live inside that moment forever. My heart raced, desire flushing through me. She clung to me as she returned this kiss with equal passion.

Wanting more of her, I ran my hands down her sides, relishing the smooth curves of her body underneath the silk.

The flowers waved around us in the faint breeze as I dragged my lips down her neck, tasting the sweet salt of her skin. I pressed kisses right above the neckline of her dress, holding her waist to keep her close.

"Alaric." Her voice was dreamy with desire, and I drew back just enough to see her. She had her head tilted back, her golden hair a waterfall behind her in the moonlight. A blissful smile curved her lips.

I'd never seen anything so beautiful in my life.

"Do you want me to stop?" I asked.

"You'd better not."

With a groan, I went to my knees in front of her. I wanted to worship her, and this was the best way I knew how. I ran my hands up her legs, looking up to meet her eyes as I pushed her skirt up her thighs. She released a shuddery breath.

"May I?" I asked.

She nodded, licking her lips as her gaze clung to mine.

I turned my attention back to the treasure before me, revealing the scrap of silk that covered the soft center of her.

I pressed a kiss to that silk, the heat and fragrance of her making my entire body go hard with want. She sank her hands into my hair, holding tight. Desire gripped me, and I was ravenous to taste her fully. With a trembling hand, I moved her underwear aside and ran my tongue over her folds. She cried out, and a groan tore from my throat.

I kissed her deeper, disappearing into the moment and into her.

"More, Alaric, I want more." She pulled away and went to her knees in front of me, pushing the coat off my shoulders and moving to the buttons of my shirt. She fumbled, then laughed, her eyes bright and beautiful. "Take this off. Now."

I tore the shirt off, not caring about the expensive fabric. Her eyes fell to my chest, and she blew out a breath. "Someone spends some time in the gym."

I chuckled, unable to help smiling at the appreciation in her eyes.

She drew her dress over her head, revealing pale ivory undergarments that gleamed in the moonlight. All around her, the blue moon thistle glowed with an otherworldly light.

"Take off your trousers and lie down," she said, a wicked gleam in her eye.

The air rushed from my lungs, and I hurried to comply. She removed her undergarments, and her beauty took my breath. I did as she commanded, and she climbed on top of me, rising up in the moonlight, her golden hair blowing in the breeze.

"You look like goddess," I said.

"I feel like one when you look at me like that."

Regret tugged at me. "I don't have protection."

She smiled. "I'd be a sorry witch indeed if I didn't have that taken care of."

Oh, thank fates.

I reached up to run my hands down her curves, and she lowered herself until her warmth hovered over me. Desperation gripped me, making my heart pound and my hips arch just slightly. She sank onto me with a moan, her hands on my chest.

The pleasure nearly blinded me, and I began to move beneath her, finding a rhythm that made her cry out. We rode the waves of pleasure as the flowers rose all around us, the moonlight streaming down. She tightened around me, her pleasure sweeping me up in a maelstrom and taking me with her.

Emma

THE NEXT MORNING, I woke with my head on Alaric's chest, the sunlight streaming golden into the room. For the briefest moment, I didn't know where I was, but I did know that I'd never felt happier.

"Good morning," he rumbled from above me.

I looked up, smiling at the sight of him. He looked sleep tousled and happy, and it made *me* happy. I knew I shouldn't get wrapped up in this—it was a one-time thing, we'd said—but it was hard not to enjoy waking up with him.

"Last night was amazing," I said.

"Agreed." He looked over at the clock above the door, then frowned. "Bloody hell, we're going to be late for breakfast."

"Oh, bum."

"Bum?" He smiled. "*That's* how you curse?"

I grinned as I climbed off of him. "Yep. It's all about how you say it. Now get up and get dressed. This is our last chance to convince Rupert to let us have the moon thistle."

"Maybe if we told him what we did in it last night, he won't want it anymore."

I laughed and threw a pillow at him. "Don't even think about it."

"I suppose you're right."

I went to my bag to find something to wear, and he climbed out of bed to do the same.

Once we were dressed and packed, we joined Rupert and Eileen for breakfast before departing. Even though I knew they couldn't have seen us amongst the moon thistle, I couldn't help the blush that formed on my cheeks.

"Was it wonderful?" Eileen asked as soon as she saw us.

I felt my jaw slacken. How did she know?

The blush got even hotter.

"The moon thistle, dear," Eileen prodded. "Was it wonderful in the moonlight?"

"Oh, yes! It was just amazing. Best flowers of my life. Thank you so much for letting us experience that." The words tumbled out of my mouth, and I shot a look at Alaric. He grinned at me, and his eyes sparkled, and I realized how my words must have sounded.

I stuck by them, though. It really had been the best of my life.

We made small talk over breakfast, which was a delicious full English cooked by the kitchen staff and delivered by a young man who couldn't have been more than twenty. I wondered what he did there when he wasn't working. There was nothing on this island but the estate.

Once we'd finished and were lingering over coffee, Alaric leaned toward Rupert and asked, "Are you sure there isn't anything we could do to convince you to part with your moon thistle?"

He shook his head. "Your grandmother told us the quantities you'd need, and frankly, my lad, it would be all of it. We just can't part with it."

My heart thudded. *No.* This wasn't how it was supposed to go.

"Perhaps a large donation to the charity of your choice?" Alaric asked.

"We make plenty of donations, lad."

"Of course you do, I didn't meant to offend."

Well, bum. This was just getting worse. I looked at Eileen, and she looked disappointed but understanding. Her husband must really love those flowers.

Rupert pulled a beautiful old timepiece out of his pocket and looked at it. "Your boat will be here any minute."

Double bum.

Something about the watch distracted me from my disappointment, though. It had a strange energy emitting from it, and I frowned. It was familiar, but in a way that didn't make any sense.

"Are you all right, dear?" Rupert asked me.

"Um, yes. Fine."

"Are you sure?"

"Yes, why?"

"You're looking at my pocket watch like it stole your ice cream."

A little laugh escaped me, but he was right. I could feel the scowl on my face. "Is it a very old watch?"

"Indeed. It was my grandfather's." He held it out to me, and I took it.

As soon as my skin made contact with the metal, I gasped. Magic vibrated though it, feeling distinctly like the magic that hovered around graveyards and the maze when Barnaby was present.

"Were you close to your grandfather?" I asked.

"Very." His gaze grew a bit distant. "He was a wonderful man, though it's been nearly sixty years now since I've seen him."

Oh, how unbearably sad to have not seen someone you love for that long. And yet he carried that watch around with him as a reminder of his grandfather.

"Careful you don't crush it, now," he said, nodding to the watch.

I looked down and realized I was holding it quite tightly. Not tightly enough to crush metal, of course. I didn't have that power. But my knuckles were white.

"You do look a bit peaky," Eileen said. "Are you sure you're all right, Emma?"

I nodded. "This watch has magic. Did you know that?"

Rupert frowned. "What do you mean?"

"I can feel the magic in it. It feels like a spirit."

"A spirit?" He frowned. "How so?"

"I'm not sure. I'm new at this, but I have a gift for connecting with spirits and ghosts. Usually, I can only do it when I'm in a cemetery or a place that they are haunting, but I feel something similar in this watch."

Rupert chuckled. "Well, I can assure you my grandfather isn't haunting the watch."

"No, of course not." Objects weren't usually haunted, though it wasn't unheard of. If that watch were *actually* haunted, however, it would be a lot more obvious. And likely destructive. "But this is one of your most cherished possessions, correct? Because it reminds you of your grandfather?"

"Yes. Although I don't see what you're getting at."

I wasn't sure what I was getting at, either, but I was pretty sure that something about Rupert's feeling for his grandfather, and the fact that the watch had once belonged to the man, meant that part of the grandfather's spirit might linger with the watch. Or perhaps it was a conduit with the spirit realm. I would need to do more research.

But right then, I wanted to try something.

"I won't hurt the watch, but do you mind if I try to understand the magic a little better?" I asked.

"What would it involve?"

"Just sitting here, really. I need some time with it."

"All right, then. I'll have another cup of coffee."

The others got coffee while I held the watch, feeling the magic within it. Penelope, as if sensing I needed her help, abandoned her plate and climbed onto my lap. Her magic flowed into me.

"Rupert?" I said. "Will you think of your grandfather, please? Thoughts that evoke emotion, ideally."

"Happy to."

I felt the magic in the watch flare, pulsing against my hand, and looked up at Rupert. His eyes were closed, his brow slightly furrowed.

It was working.

I reached for the magic in the watch, trying to draw it out. It resisted at first, but as Rupert continued to think of his grandfather, I had better luck.

The air in front of me began to shimmer, and an older man in a tweed suit suddenly stood before me. He wore wire-framed glasses that looked like something from a different century, which they certainly were, and he had a smile that was very similar to Rupert's.

"Sir? Can you see me?" I asked him.

"I can indeed, young lady." He looked at Rupert. "And is that my grandson, now an old man?"

I nodded. "It is."

"What do you see?" Rupert asked.

I moved closer to Rupert and touched the back of his hand, sharing some of my magic with him. He blinked, suddenly able to see his grandfather. His eyes widened.

"Granddad! Is it really you?"

"It is, dear lad." His grandfather smiled widely. "This young lady has made a connection with the spirit world."

Rupert looked at me, shocked. Then he looked back at my grandfather. "How are you? Are you happy?"

"I am, my lad. Though I can't give you details about the beyond, I can say that it is lovely. And that I'm very proud of the man you've become."

Rupert smiled, a sheen of tears in his eyes.

"I love you, Rupert." His grandfather reached out and gripped his shoulder. "Be good, now."

With that, he faded away.

I released a shuddery breath, tired from the effort of keeping him on this plane. The magic in the stopwatch shimmered more powerfully than ever. Probably because Rupert was thinking about his grandfather, and with quite a lot of emotion.

I handed the watch back to him.

He took it, eyes still damp. "That was incredible. Thank you."

I smiled. "You're welcome."

"You have a special gift," he said. "To be able to bring distant spirits like that forward...I've never heard of it."

Neither had I. I'd only ever heard of people seeing spirits and ghosts that had chosen to stay on this plane. But Rupert's grandfather had been in the spirit world. The fact that I'd drawn him forward using the watch as a conduit was...unexpected, to say the least.

"Darling." Eileen reached for Rupert's hand and squeezed it. Her voice was heavy with meaning.

"I know, dear. You don't need to say it." Rupert turned to me. "You've given me quite a gift. And I must return the favor. For this year only, you may have our entire crop of moon thistle."

I gasped. "Really?"

"One good turn deserves another," he said. "And what you did for me, Emma...it was incredible."

"I'm glad I could."

"Thank you, dear. You really are something special."

TWENTY-TWO

Emma

THE NEXT DAY, I woke early to get started on assembling the joy batteries. The day before had been wonderful. Alaric and I had spent the day helping his crew harvest and pack the moon thistle.

It had been a bit sad to see it all cut down, but it would grow again next spring, and the blooms we'd taken would go to excellent use. I'd used my magic to dry the flowers and shrink them down so that they were highly concentrated for use in the joy batteries, and the effort had left me sapped.

Once the blooms were packed onto the boat, we'd left Rupert and Eileen's island and taken the boat back to Cornwall, where we'd had dinner with Alaric's family. The entire thing had been like a dream.

It certainly hadn't felt fake.

But I had no idea if he felt the same way, and even

wondering about it made me nervous. I'd gone home after dinner, needing some space, but I hadn't been able to drive him from my thoughts. I needed to, though, because the work ahead would require every bit of my focus.

I wasn't the only one going into the shop that day, though. The previous night at dinner, Vivian and Madeline had requested to visit, so I was waiting for them outside the shop that morning. They were getting more and more excited about the party. It should have made me feel better, like Vivian would want to host the ball whether or not I was dating her grandson.

But it just meant I would hurt her more if she found out I was lying to her. It would taint the ball as well as myself. And the more I got to know her, the more terrible I felt about the lies.

But were they lies anymore?

Yes, though everything I had with Alaric was begging to feel more and more real.

I shook the thoughts away and waved to Vivian and Madeline, who had just got out of their car across the street from the shop. They were dressed in their finest, which meant nothing like normal people. Vivian was always dressed to the nines in a fantastic suit of wool or silk or linen. Sometimes a skirt, sometimes trousers—always fabulous. And *always* decorated with jewels that blew my mind. As ever, her white hair was swept into a sophisticated wave back from her forehead.

Madeline was dressed like Madeline—as if another billionaire had invited her on his yacht off the French Riviera and she needed to be prepared in her best sundress and giant hat. That day's outfit was brilliant pink with yellow flowers, and it somehow looked magnificent against her red hair instead of terrible like it would on a normal human. She held onto her sun hat as they hurried across the road.

"We're so pleased you invited us," Vivian said. "I've always wanted to understand more about covens. I love the idea of a business full of women."

"Me, too." I grinned at her. It was one of the other things I loved about being a witch: all of the support and camaraderie from my coven. "Come on. We'll go up to the workshop, and I'll show you the space and how we're making the joy batteries. You can consult the planning book to see what kind of food and drink was served at previous parties to get an idea for what you can do."

Madeline clapped. "I do so love planning a party, and it's been far too long since we've had one at the estate."

Vivien gripped her hand, almost a comforting gesture despite Madeline's excitement. When she spoke, there was something a bit sad in her voice. "Too long indeed, my dear."

There was a story there, and one that I desperately wanted to know. Not my place, though.

"This way." I turned and entered the shop, holding open the door for them.

Of course Lily was at the desk. She gave me a catlike smile as I entered, and it was impossible not to imagine the cunning in her eyes.

I was totally losing it. She couldn't be that bad.

"Hi, Lily."

"Hello." She looked past me toward Vivian and Madeline.

"Bringing your friends for show and tell today? Shame the rest of the class isn't here."

Okay, scratch what I'd previously said. She really could be that bad.

Madeline and Vivian both gave her lovely smiles, as if to prove their breeding couldn't be brought low by a snide comment.

"We're just so excited to see the place," Madeline said.

"Indeed. We've been fascinated by covens," Vivian said. "Vampires are such solitary creatures, and it gets a bit tiresome, to be honest."

Lily softened. "I agree. That is one nice thing about a coven."

"This way." I headed toward the stairs, not wanting to dawdle and give Lily time to remember that she was out to destroy me.

"Emma?" Lily called after me.

"Yes?" I gestured for Vivian and Madeline to go up the stairs as I turned back to Lily.

"There was a journalist here earlier, asking about you."

Ice skated down my spine. "A journalist?"

She laughed, and it wasn't entirely nice. "Well, I'd say they were more a low-budget paparazzo. But they were definitely interested in you and the duke."

Oh, bum. I'd hoped to keep this out of the press. They would destroy me if they found I was dating the duke and then we broke up. "Did you tell him anything?"

She glared at me. "I'm not that bad."

"No, I'm sorry. Of course. Thank you for not saying anything."

"You'd better be careful, though. He seemed very keen to catch more photos of you."

"More?"

She nodded. "That's what he said. Didn't show me the ones he had, but he certainly implied they existed."

Double bum. "Thanks, Lily."

I joined the women in the workshop. The space was bright and sunny in the morning light, and the scent of herbs welcomed me in. Holly was already there, and she was making introductions with Vivian and Madeline.

Vivian turned to me. "Well, this is just lovely!"

"Thank you." I pointed to the chairs by the windows. "Those chairs are comfortable. And the big book on the bookshelf next to them is the record of all the parties. You can get an idea of past catering."

"Excellent." Vivian rubbed her hands together and strode toward the book.

They squeezed into one of the big chairs together and began to flip through the pages.

I joined Holly, who leaned close and whispered, "They're lovely."

"Right? I can't believe they want to help. And so enthusiastically."

"It'll be right posh, too, with those two in control."

"Much better than I could have done." I looked at the boxes of ingredients that she'd started to unpack. "How are we looking?"

"Well, we've got everything we need to recreate the batteries, but it's going to be a job."

"I know. I'm hoping we don't have to ask for help."

"We'll see."

"Emma?" Vivian called out.

"Yes?"

"It looks like there are a lot of incredible activities planned for each party. What have you got in mind?"

"A few things so far." I rattled them off, and finished with, "But we haven't thought of the big thing yet. I need something really spectacular to wow people."

"I can see what you mean," Madeline said. "Everything you have planned is excellent and will be delightful, but you need something on par with the big events at the last balls."

"What about a fountain of gold?" Vivian asked. "People love money. They could take it with them."

And here I'd thought she was down to earth.

"That's true, people do love money. But I don't have enough gold." Or any, in fact.

"I do." She smiled at me.

"I couldn't." I stared back at her, shocked. "That's so kind of you, but it's too much."

"Oh, darling, anything for you. After the way you've made my grandson look, I'd give you rivers of gold."

Rivers of gold. I closed my eyes, at once bemused and guilt stricken. Even if we managed to keep up the ruse and have a civil breakup when this was all over, she would be hurt.

I hated these lies.

Slowly, I drew in a breath and opened my eyes. "That's truly thoughtful, it is. But it's just too much. And anyway, I'm supposed to do something that proves my magic."

"Ah, of course." She nodded. "That makes sense. I'll give it another thought."

"Thank you." I turned back to the ingredients for the joy batteries.

Holly and I got to work while Madeline and Vivian spoke quietly by the windows, planning the food and drink. They were going all out, and I couldn't have been more grateful. I also wouldn't be surprised if someone chipped a tooth on a gold coin hidden in a cupcake, since that seemed to be Vivian's vibe.

After a while, Hazel appeared in the doorway. "I heard that you had helpers."

I smiled at her while inwardly cursing Lily. It was obvious who had ratted me out. "I'm so lucky they insisted on taking care of the catering."

It seemed like the subtlest way I could say that I hadn't gone searching for their help. I was grateful for it, but I was still wary of Willow's warning about seeking too much help and not proving my skills.

"It's excellent that you can get so much help from outside the coven," Hazel said, sounding truly impressed. "It's an excellent skill and is quite a boon to our little group."

Whew. It sounded like she genuinely approved.

Vivian stood and approached. "It's so lovely to see you again, Hazel. Why don't Madeline and I take you to lunch?"

"I would enjoy that." Hazel gave them a genuine smile.

The three of them left, and I turned to Holly. "Well, that wasn't so bad."

She grinned. "I think you came out on top."

"Now I just need to keep doing that."

"Let's see how we make out with the joy batteries. We can each make one."

"All right. Race you?"

Her smile widened. "You're on."

We had the instructions laid out in front of us, and all the ingredients sorted. Now it had just come time to assemble and feed some magic into the batteries to get them going.

I scanned the directions once more, even though I'd memorized them. There weren't enough ingredients that I could afford to make mistakes, though.

As quickly as I could, I tied the unicorn hair around the bundle of faerie willow reeds. There were quite a few bits and pieces that needed to go into the glass globes that formed the shell of the battery, and they had to be tied or linked together in some way that always turned out to be time consuming and difficult. An hour had passed by the time I'd got it just right. Holly was right behind me.

The completed battery sat in front of me, just a shell until I jumpstarted it with magic from the ether. I placed a hand on the battery and called into the ether around me, drawing the magic into myself and feeding it into the battery.

Obnoxiously, the battery resisted.

Just my luck.

I tried harder, clearing my mind so that I could be an open conduit for the power. Gradually, I could feel the power trickle into the battery. It wasn't that different than electricity. When a device charged slowly, it lasted longer.

I wasn't even filling it with the joy it would eventually store, either. I was just priming it to receive the joy. The better the job I did, the more joy it would hold.

Unfortunately, it took a long time—at least an hour, though I lost track of the clock.

Once it was done, I was damp with sweat. I looked over at Holly, and she didn't look much better. Her gaze met mine. "We're in trouble."

I nodded. "There's no way we'll finish them all before the ball. There just aren't enough hours in the day, especially with all the other planning to do."

"Even if there were enough hours, I don't have the strength. It took a lot out of me just to do one. I'm sure I'll get better at it, but not that much better."

I squeezed her hand. "Thank you so much for the help. And don't worry. I have an idea for where we can get more help. We'll only ask the coven if we really need to."

"Good, because I've got a lot riding on you making it to official witch." She grinned. "Not only do I not want to lose you if this thing is a bust, but I'd love to have someone on the other side, padding my chances at being promoted in the next couple years."

"Don't worry, I'm your girl." I heaved a sigh and looked toward the window, where the sky was darkening as afternoon became evening. "I've got a date with a ghost."

"Of course. I'll take care of all this stuff. You go find your guy."

My guy. As soon as she said it, I thought of Alaric. She meant Barnaby, of course, but I couldn't help but see the duke's face in my head.

"Thanks, you're a hero."

"Of course I am."

CHAPTER
TWENTY-THREE

EMMA

HAROLD WAS WAITING for me when I arrived at the estate, his usual linen suit replaced with trousers, a perfectly cut sweater, and Le Chameau boots. His hair was neatly combed, of course.

Penelope and I hopped out of the car and approached. He grinned as we neared and stuck out his foot, which was clad in one of the brand-new wellies favored by the residents of Buckingham Palace. "Since we're going into the garden, I thought I'd dress for the occasion."

"You look smashing," I said. "And I can see why you and Madeline suit. You both have quite the eye for fashion."

He pressed a hand to his heart. "Ah, Madeline. Never was there a woman like her."

He was freaking adorable, but I refrained from saying so. "Shall we?"

"Indeed."

Together, we set off for the maze. I went over my plan in my head—keep calm, listen, speak last.

When we reached the maze, I immediately felt the magic of a ghost in the air. I gasped. "I feel it already."

Harold grinned. "You're getting better. Soon, you'll feel it without even trying."

"Does this mean he's here?"

He nodded. "Yes. Interested in what you have to say, no doubt."

"Then I'd better not screw it up."

"Better not. You're running out of time before the ball."

"Thanks, Harold," I said dryly. "I needed the reminder."

He patted my shoulder in a fatherly gesture, and I didn't hate it. "You'll be just fine, dear. Give it your best."

I loved that even more, but I hated how much I was growing to care for the people I was lying to.

I shoved the thoughts away and picked up Penelope, then turned to the maze.

You've got this, she said, then immediately fell asleep.

"Lazy skunk," I murmured. I could still feel her power, though, and it enhanced mine. This was probably easier without her squirming, anyway.

Calling out to Barnaby came more easily than I expected, and within minutes, he was standing in front of me. I looked at him, trying to project a sense of calm and understanding.

He looked back at me, appearing tired and a bit sad.

"It's not easy being a ghost, is it?" I asked.

He harrumphed.

I waited for him to speak again, but he didn't. So I

thought carefully before my next words. "I know we got off to a bad start. It's my fault, and I apologize. But I really would like to help you with whatever you're seeking."

"Hmmm." He stared at me, looking between me and Penelope. "You must not be all bad if that skunk trusts you."

A small laugh escaped me. "She is quite a picky judge of character."

"Skunks often are."

Excitement flashed within me. We were getting somewhere! This was definitely a rapport if there ever was one.

"What is it you've stayed behind for?" I asked. "Why did you come to this garden?"

He glared at me. "That's my business, lass."

"Of course. Of course." I reached out a comforting hand, wanting to lay it on his shoulder to show that I understood.

As soon as I laid my fingertips on his ephemeral shoulder, he disappeared. But not before I got a glimpse of Vivian's face. She was younger in the image by at least fifty years, but it was definitely her.

"Not ideal," Harold said.

"No, but I think I know why he's here."

"Really?" Harold smiled. "You saw something?"

"I did. Vivian. About fifty years ago."

He frowned, clearly searching his memories. "She would have been about twenty or so and still living here with her father and mother, I believe."

"He could have been the gardener."

"There's only one thing for it," he said. "Martinis and mysteries!"

"Martinis and mysteries?" I asked.

He nodded. "We give her a martini, and then we solve this mystery."

I grinned. "That sounds like it should work. Let's go."

Harold and I left the garden and made our way to the main house. The lights glowed golden in the windows, welcoming us up the stairs. I didn't want to feel like I was going home, but I did.

When we reached the family kitchen, we found Madeline laying out packages of fish and chips from Codswollop's, the chippy in town.

"We fancied something a bit easier tonight," Vivian said from where she was gathering plates from the cupboard.

"Come on, Mama, we don't need plates," Madeline said. "We'll just eat out of the packaging."

Vivian gasped. "I didn't raise you to be a heathen."

Madeline laughed and held out her hand. "Fine, give me the plates."

"We got you some," Vivian said to me. "In case you decided to stay for dinner."

"I'd love to." I said the words before I even thought about them. But of course I would love to. I wanted as much of this family time as I could get. I loved Vivian, Madeline, and Harold.

But mostly, I just wanted to see Alaric.

He appeared in the doorway, stopping as soon as he saw me. A slow smile spread across his face, and heat warmed my belly.

"Hello," he said, his voice soft.

"Hi." I grinned at him.

He approached and gave me a kiss on the cheek. It was

chaste, but it carried with it all the memories from our trip, and I could feel my blush.

Madeline gave a low wolf whistle.

"Oh, get ahold of yourself, Madeline," Vivian said. "I swear, sometimes you're no better than a schoolboy."

Madeline smiled widely and shrugged. "If the shoe fits."

"Did you have any luck with the ghost?" Vivian asked as she sat.

"We did." I joined them, taking a seat next to her and reaching for one of the takeaways. As I unwrapped the fish, I asked. "You knew Barnaby, didn't you?"

She looked over at me, sharp as a hawk. "How do you know that?"

"Well, you seemed to know him when we asked you last, but you didn't want to talk about it."

"So you're asking now?"

I nodded. "Only because he wants to see you. I thought that might change things."

Her hands, which had been unwrapping the fish, stilled, and her face softened. "He does?"

I nodded. "What was he to you?"

She sighed. "A schoolgirl crush. I thought it could be more, of course. But he left."

"Why? The war?"

She glared. "I'm not that old."

"Right, sorry!" I shrugged. "I thought maybe there was another war. Which, I realize, was stupid of me. It's just that there's such romance in your voice when you speak of him. And then you said he left, and my mind immediately went to lovers being torn apart by tragedy."

"Not tragedy." She glared down at her fish. "Just him being an idiot." She looked up at her daughter. "It worked out, though, dear. I don't want you thinking otherwise. Because Barnaby left, I was free to meet your father and have the loveliest life. I truly adored that man."

I could hear it in her voice. She'd loved him to pieces.

"I know that, Mama." Madeline reached across the table and gripped her hand. "But tell us about this Barnaby."

She sighed. "Fine. We met when I was eighteen and visiting Blackthorn Hall for the summer." She looked at me as she went on to clarify. "My mother was friends with the Duchess of Blackthorn before I married into the title. We visited one summer for two months, though Alaric's grandfather was away when we arrived. Barnaby, however, was here. He was twenty-six, and the gardener. I was in love immediately, of course. He ignored me. Then he didn't. Probably because I insisted on wearing a bikini in the garden. Far too obvious of me, not subtle at all. But it worked. It got his attention."

Madeline whistled. "Bold, Mama."

"Well, he wouldn't speak to me until I put on clothes. But we grew close. I loved him. He insisted he wasn't right for me, though, and eventually, he left. Said that the gardener couldn't be with one of my class and disappeared one day."

Madeline sighed. "How noble. And misguided."

"Misguided is right." Vivian nodded. "But as I said, it wasn't meant to be. I met your father later that summer when he came back from his trip abroad."

"Well, I'm quite happy to be here," Madeline said. "So I agree, it was for the best."

"Same," Alaric said, his laughing gaze meeting mine.

"I'll throw my hat into that ring." Harold squeezed Madeline's shoulder in a loving gesture. "I'm quite glad you're here, too."

Vivian turned to me. "But you say he's here at the estate? And he wants to see me?"

"Yes. Well, he's a ghost. But he is here, and he wants to see you. Would you like to see him?"

"Indeed, I would." She smiled widely. "That would be wonderful."

"Excellent. Maybe tomorrow?"

"I'll be ready." She turned to Madeline. "But don't think I'm going to let you help me pick my outfit. You'd put me in some ridiculous rainbow dress."

Madeline grinned. "True enough. But I can do your makeup."

"I'll concede you're quite good at that, so yes, you may."

Inwardly, I sighed, just so happy to be around them all. When Alaric's gaze met mine, things were perfect.

CHAPTER
TWENTY-FOUR

EMMA

I DIDN'T SPEND the night at Alaric's house. We'd agreed that our romp would be a one-time thing, and spending the night was explicitly against those rules. I'd felt him looking at me more than normal, though, and I'd tossed and turned with dreams of him.

Holly had met me at the shop in the morning, and we'd spent the day assembling joy batteries while brainstorming special events for the party. We were running out of time, and I needed to think of my big surprise. What would *I* plan that would wow everyone and get me promoted to official member of the coven?

I still had no idea by the time work was over and it was time to go create a reunion between a ghost and a dowager duchess.

Vivian was ready precisely at seven, when we'd agreed to

go see Barnaby. I'd already discussed the plan with Harold. We'd be ambushing Barnaby, in a way, just by bringing Vivian without asking him. But he wouldn't have to show himself if he didn't want to.

And since he was so reticent to share with me, it seemed best to avoid asking him any more questions and just try to give him what he wanted.

Alaric waited with his grandmother in the front sitting room. He rose when Penelope and I entered, and I approached him for my usual kiss on the cheek. My heart raced as I neared, and he lingered for a moment, his lips pressed to the sensitive skin of my cheek.

When he pulled back, he said, "I thought we could take a walk while my grandmother speaks to Barnaby."

"I think I have to be there," I said, disappointment streaking through me. "Or Harold. Barnaby is a ghost, and not a particularly strong one since he didn't die here. He needs a medium to make contact."

Vivian laughed. "Don't let Barnaby hear you say he isn't strong."

I smiled. "I would never." I turned my attention to Alaric. "A walk afterward?"

"Perfect."

"Where is Harold?" Vivian asked. "We should get going."

"We need only one medium for this," I said. "And we thought it best to give you some privacy with Barnaby. As much as we could manage with me being there."

"All right." She stood and clapped her hands together. "Lead the way, then."

I waved goodbye to Alaric and headed out the door, Penelope and Vivian at my side.

Tell her she looks fabulous, Penelope said.

I passed the message to Vivian, who did indeed look fabulous. She'd chosen a powder blue suit made of the finest wool, with a cream silk blouse and a brooch of flowers crafted from jewels of all colors. I had a feeling that was a nod to Barnaby being a gardener, and I loved the thoughtfulness.

As we walked toward the garden, she chattered away about Barnaby, sharing everything she could remember.

"You're not nervous at all, are you?" I asked.

"Oh, I stopped being nervous about things years ago," she said. "Absolute waste of time."

"I like how you think."

"Stick around for more helpful tips."

I smiled.

When we reached the maze, I put a hand on her arm to stop her. "Here will be good."

"All right. Do your thing." She searched the space in front of her as if looking for Barnaby.

"It would be best if you held my hand," I said. "Might make it easier for you to see him."

She gripped my hand in hers, and I smiled. Penelope pressed herself against my leg, and I felt her power seep into me. That familiar magic was in the air again, feeling like a cool mist. I let it flow around me, using my power to call it to me.

"Barnaby?" I said. "We've come to see you. I think you might know who this is."

There was no response.

"Oh, come now, Barnaby. I dressed up and came all this way to see you," Vivian said. "Please show yourself."

A few moments later, he appeared, his gaze on Vivian. "You always were demanding."

She smiled. "That's one of the things you liked about me."

"Indeed, it was."

"Lovely to see you again, after all this time."

"Very nice to see you as well." There was emotion in his eyes, but not in his voice. That was stiff and formal.

Well, shite.

This wasn't going well, and it was all because I was here.

"What have you been doing lately?" Vivian asked, reaching for conversation.

"Besides dying?"

She gave a horrified laugh. "Well, yes. I'm sorry about that, by the way. I'd have loved to have seen you on this side."

He nodded, the gesture as stiff as his voice. But there was still that longing in his voice, and if I reached out to touch him, I was sure I would feel it.

I was the problem here, that was clear enough.

"This was lovely, Vivian. Thank you for coming. But I must go." He disappeared, and I barely resisted cursing.

Vivian turned to me. "Well, that was anticlimactic."

"You're telling me." And Barnaby was definitely still there. I could feel that he hadn't passed on peacefully. I could stay and try to ask him why, but I was pretty sure I knew.

"Let's go back," I said. "I think I need to work on

something."

"Oh?"

"Yes. I've got an idea."

"Excellent."

We turned to leave, but before we'd got very far, Barnaby appeared in front of me. Vivian kept walking, indicating that she couldn't see him without touching me.

"You brought her here just to get me to leave, didn't you?"

"Um, no. I mean, that was part of it. But I knew you wanted to see her, so I brought her."

Vivian turned to look at me. "Has he returned?'

Barnaby ignored her. "It won't work. You might want to banish me, but I won't let you. And I certainly won't let you host your confounded party here."

The anger in his voice echoed in the air as he disappeared. To my right, a bed of lilies began to uproot.

"You're making a poor impression, Barnaby," Vivian said. "I thought you were better than this."

The lilies stopped uprooting themselves, but Barnaby didn't reappear.

"Come on, dear. We need a drink." Vivian turned and left.

"Can we make it wine?" I called after her.

"*You* can. But after that, I want something stronger."

I laughed. She had a point—maybe I needed something stronger as well.

~

ALARIC

. . .

EMMA and my grandmother returned to the house shortly after they left, which couldn't be good. A successful meeting should have taken longer, shouldn't it?

My grandmother sailed into the drawing room, discarding her blue wool suit coat on the chair near the door. "I need a drink. Anyone else?"

"Me, obviously," Emma said. "Though I'll stick to wine." She grinned at me, clearly proud of herself for having told my grandmother no to the martinis.

"It wasn't a success?" I asked.

"He was a grumpy bastard." My grandmother poured gin into a shaker, then topped it with blood before giving it a good, hard shake. As she poured, she looked at me, "I don't know what his problem is."

"I do," Emma said. "I think he wants to be alone with you. He can't talk about his feelings if I'm there."

My grandmother paused with her glass partway to her mouth. "Really?"

Emma shrugged. "It's my best guess."

"Can you make that happen?"

"I'm not sure. I can ask Harold."

"Well, where is he?" my grandmother asked me.

"He's gone down to the pub with Madeline. There's live music tonight, and they wanted a date."

"Hmmm." She shot Emma a stern look. "Well, get on with it when you see him, dear. I want to hear what Barnaby has to say."

"I'll do my best." Emma tried for a confident smile, but I

255

could see the hesitation in her eyes. I tried to shoot her a reassuring smile. She would come up with something, I was sure of it.

"Good." My grandmother tilted her glass toward us in a toast. "Now, I'm heading off to bed. I will see you both in the morning."

"It's early," I said.

"I'm a bit tired, is all." She smiled. "I'll see you tomorrow." With that, she swept from the room.

I looked after her, worry twisting in my chest. Emma approached. "Are you all right? You look concerned."

I drew in a breath, hating to voice my concerns aloud because then they would feel more true. Emma made me want to share, though. It was a first. Even Katrina had had to pull my secrets from me.

"I'm worried about her," I confess. "She sleeps later, goes to bed earlier. Then in the daytime, she seems tired."

Emma laughed.

I stared at her, horrified. "What?"

"Oh, Alaric." She cupped my cheek and looked into my eyes, a small smile on her face. "Your grandmother isn't sick. She's addicted to riveting long-form storytelling as provided by internet streaming services."

"Wait...what?"

She nodded. "She didn't want you to know because she thought you wouldn't approve. She's been devouring *Breaking Bad* and *The Walking Dead*."

"I thought she was dying. Or at least very ill. It's one of the reasons I wanted her to stay here with me."

"I can see that now. And if she knew, she would tell you

the truth, I'm sure of it."

"So you're telling me that my grandmother has been burning the midnight oil over Netflix?"

"Or HBO, or whatever." She nodded. "But yes, that's basically what is happening."

I tilted my head back and looked at the ceiling, a relieved laugh escaping me. "That's unexpected, but the best news I could hope for."

"Maybe you could watch them with her?"

"Television?" I scowled at her. "No. I'm not a fan."

"What?" She stared at me, shocked.

"Really."

"Snob." She laughed. "There's so much good television these days. So many incredible stories! I can't believe you don't like it. You're probably the only one."

I winced. "I can see why my grandmother didn't share."

"Well, you don't want to know what *my* favorite program is."

"Oh, don't tell me."

"*Love Island.*" She grinned broadly, clearly wanting to horrify me.

I couldn't let her. "Oh, that's fine. That's like a documentary."

She laughed. "A documentary?"

"Yes, of the human condition in the twenty-first century. People will study it millennia from now."

"All right." She nodded. "I'll go with that."

"Shall I get you a glass of wine?" I asked, recalling her request when my grandmother had asked who had wanted to join her in a drink.

"Sure." She went toward the couch and curled up in the corner, looking right at home. I liked seeing her there, I realized.

"What kind?" I asked.

"There are options?"

"Um, yes?"

"Have you got a wine cellar?"

"Of course."

She laughed. "It's not *of course* for most people."

"Fair enough."

"Any kind of white will do." She smiled.

I retrieved a bottle and two glasses, then sat with her and poured us each a drink. She didn't snuggle up to me the way I'd hoped she might, but why would she?

This wasn't meant to be real.

I banished the thought, wanting to enjoy the night. "My grandmother did seem happy when she came back from the maze. Thank you."

"You think so?"

He nodded. "She was acting annoyed, but there was a twinkle in her eye. I like seeing it."

"You're close, aren't you?"

"Yes. After my parents' deaths, it was just her and me. Madeline would visit occasionally, and then Harold appeared on the scene. But for the most part, it was just the two of us."

"It must have been hard on you to lose your father," she said, her voice low with concern. "And hard on your grandmother to lose a son."

"Not really," I said. "It was my mother's loss that wrecked us both."

"What?" she asked, her voice slightly horrified. "You weren't sad to lose your father?"

"Good riddance. Though my grandmother might not agree. She cares for him still. Of course." And I still wanted to protect her from ever knowing the truth.

"Oh, no." She squeezed my hand. "I'm so sorry. He must have been difficult."

"*Difficult* doesn't even begin to describe it. Laundering money through false donations to orphanages was nothing compared to some of his other crimes." I looked down into my wine glass, pinching my lips closed.

"We don't have to talk about it if you don't want." She squeezed my hand again. "We can just listen to music or something. Or I can tell you about coven drama, and I'll embellish it to make it hilarious and ridiculous."

I smiled, liking the idea. But something compelled me to share. Maybe it was the way she didn't prod. Maybe it was just her.

I also wanted her to know the truth behind this ridiculous fake dating plan. To know what I was protecting my grandmother from so that she didn't think it was a stupid reason on my part.

"He was an alcoholic, but that wasn't actually the bad part."

"It sounds pretty bad," she said.

I nodded. "It's an illness, so I can understand, to an extent. But he was a mean-spirited bastard before the drink.

It just made it worse. My grandmother never knew the extent of it, though."

She waited in silence, and I played over my next words in my head before speaking. "The night my parents died, he was drunk or high on something. I don't know what. But he dragged my mother out of the house for a drive, and they never came back. The police found their car at the bottom of the River Tamar."

She gasped. "Oh, Alaric. I'm so sorry."

"We'll never know if he did it on purpose or if it was an accident, but we do know that she didn't want to go with him." My grandmother hadn't been there that night, which I was thankful for. Though I hadn't seen what had happened, I'd overheard the upstairs maid telling the police what she'd witnessed as my father had dragged my mother from the house. "My father had a friend in the police. He covered up the nature of the accident, making it look innocent. It wasn't."

Emma wrapped an arm around me and snuggled up to my side, offering what comfort she could. I leaned into her, appreciating the connection.

"I've never told anyone except you and Katrina, my previous girlfriend."

"You haven't mentioned her."

"She...wasn't a good person." It was the politest way I could put it. "She badgered the information out of me. That, and other family secrets. I didn't realize it at the time, but in hindsight, I can see what she was doing. I was about to propose when the first journalist came to me."

"Journalist?"

"She sold the secrets. Apparently, she was tired of waiting for me to propose. She said she deserved the life of her dreams, and she thought that she'd get it by becoming a duchess. But then I took too long to propose, and she thought it wouldn't happen. So she sold the secrets for a mint."

"That's despicable," she said, her voice vibrating with anger.

"I agree. The journalist—although that's a generous term for him—published most of them, but not the one about the accident. The other stories devastated my grandmother, though seeing that dirty laundry about her son in the press… she didn't know half the stories."

Understanding echoed in her voice as she spoke. "The story about the orphanages was one of those, wasn't it? I'm so sorry I brought it up."

"No, it's fine. And it's fair. He did do that. And I don't give a damn if people know the truth. It's for her that I worry. And when I thought her health was poor…I didn't want her to have to deal with more trauma. I still don't want her to know the truth about the accident."

"I haven't seen the story about your parents' deaths in the news, though."

"It's one of the reasons I wanted to pretend we were dating. I knew my grandmother would stay longer if you were around. I want her here if the news breaks before I can bury it."

"Can't you silence the journalist with a spell?" she asked. "They're difficult, but I would be happy to help you. My coven, too."

I nodded. "Thank you, but I've already got a witch in London working on one."

"Ah, of course. You wouldn't want the locals knowing anything about this."

"Ideally not. My grandmother loves this place, and I wouldn't want her to feel strange when she goes into the village."

"Does she think I'm Katrina?"

"Not Katrina specifically, but she thinks you're the person I talked about liking on the phone. They'd never met, and I don't think I mentioned her name specifically. I played it close to the vest and promised to introduce them in good time."

She nodded, then tightened her arm around me. "I can see why you did it. I wouldn't want her to know, either."

"Thank you."

"When will this London witch be finished with the spell? Do you want me to help?"

"She updated me yesterday. Should be done by the end of the week."

"I don't think I'd be able to speed her up..."

"I'll just hope the journalist doesn't get bored of black-mailing me before then."

She chuckled dryly. "What a thing to hope for."

"It's better than the alternative."

"True enough."

"Thank you for letting her and Madeline help with the ball, by the way. They used to love hosting parties here before my parents died."

"Why did they stop?"

"Without my mother, it was too sad. But with you here, the place is brighter, somehow."

She looked up at me, a brilliant smile on her face. The sight hit me like a punch to the chest.

I'm falling for her.

There was no denying it. What I was beginning to feel for Emma was nothing like what I'd felt for Katrina.

For one, I knew it was real. She cared for my family, and they cared for her. And she was strong, smart, and so beautiful, she shone like the sun. She had no interest in the dukedom. It was a negative, as far as she was concerned.

And I could trust her.

Somehow, I knew that I could trust her. And that meant everything.

"Why are you looking at me like that?" she asked.

"Like what?"

"I don't know. All...intense and stuff."

A smile tugged at the corner of my mouth. "I could blame you for that."

"Blame me for you being intense?" She laughed.

"You bring it out in me." My gaze dropped to her lips, and I knew I needed to give her an opportunity to leave if she wanted to. "I'll take you home, if you like."

"What if I don't like?"

"Then you want to stay?" I smiled. "I might not be able to abide by the rules of our fake dating."

"I might not want you to." She set her glass on the table and leaned forward, her lips hovering over mine. "In fact, I want to tear those rules up."

CHAPTER
TWENTY-FIVE

EMMA

WHEN I WOKE, Alaric was nowhere to be found. There was a single rose on the pillow next to my head, though. I smiled and held it up to my nose, giving it a sniff. The rich fragrance smelled divine.

The night itself had been divine, actually. We fit so well together.

Yawning, I climbed from the bed. The scent of roses filled the room, and I realized that one of the windows had been thrown open to let in the cool spring breeze. I leaned out to get a better view and realized that the rose vines that climbed the house made it all the way up to the window. Alaric must have cut one off for me. The image made my smile again.

It was a gorgeous day, and I was ready to get started with my plan. I still didn't know if it was possible to get Barnaby and Vivian together without my presence, but I was going to find out. And I was going to assemble a whole bunch of joy batteries, Hecate permitting.

After a quick shower in Alaric's amazing bathroom, I went down to the kitchen and found him making a full breakfast at the stove.

"It smells amazing in here," I said, inhaling the scent of bacon and coffee.

Penelope already sat at the table, a cup of coffee in front of her and her eager eyes glued to Alaric. No one else was in the kitchen, so I walked up to him and pressed a kiss to his lips. He smiled against me and kissed me back.

"Now go," he said. "You're distracting a master from his craft."

"I don't mind burned bacon."

I do. Save it for your own time.

I laughed at Penelope, but she didn't laugh back. She looked deadly serious.

As I poured myself a cup of coffee, Harold and Madeline entered.

Madeline smiled widely at me. "Glad to see you here this morning."

I just smiled and asked, "How are you?"

"Good," she said. "Going to see a caterer in Plymouth about doing the canapés for the ball."

"Thank you so much. I can't tell you how helpful you and Vivian have been."

She waved the comment away as she poured herself a coffee. "We enjoy it."

Harold, who eschewed coffee for the carafe of orange

juice on the table, joined Penelope and me. I leaned toward him. "Harold, do you think it's possible for Vivian and Barnaby to spend time alone together?"

"Without you or me there?" He frowned. "I think not. He's not a proper ghost haunting this place—he's visiting for another purpose. On the positive side, that means he's not angry or violent. On the downside, his form is weak enough that he needs a medium to help him make contact."

"Hmm." That wasn't ideal.

"It's never been done before," he said.

"Not yet." I smiled.

"That's what I like to hear. Let me know if you need help."

"Thank you."

Alaric brought plates over, but my mind was already spinning with ideas for how to get Vivian and Barnaby alone.

It took two days for the idea to come to me, during which I was entirely preoccupied with doing research about the Vivian/Barnaby situation or assembling the joy batteries. Holly and Penelope spent every spare second helping me, but the task was seemingly insurmountable. I didn't see Alaric, to say the least. There was just no time to go over to Blackthorn Hall.

I thought about Alaric, though. And he thought about me, if the text he'd sent me was any indication. It had been almost painfully short, but he'd wanted to make sure I was doing okay.

There was no time to dwell on thoughts of him, though. The day of the ball was barreling toward us, and there was a mountain of work to do.

I turned back to the book in front of me. I'd been flipping through for the perfect spell to help me get Barnaby and Vivian together alone, and I was pretty sure I'd just found it.

"What's that smile on your face for?" Holly asked. She stood at the table, assembling more of the joy batteries.

I looked up. "I think I've found it."

"Oh, yeah?" She grinned at me. "Think you can do it?"

"Yes. It'll take all day, though."

"Better than taking all week. We're running out of time."

I blew out a breath, all too aware.

Emma? Penelope called from the front window. *You might want to come see this.*

"What is it?"

There's a bloke lingering across the street, looking at the shop.

For the briefest moment, hope flared. Alaric had come to see me. Then Penelope spoke again. *He's got a big camera around his neck.*

"Oh, bum." I put some extra emphasis on the word to really convey my frustration. "Paparazzi?"

Sure looks like it. Rumpled, unwashed, a stalker gleam to the eye.

I joined her, and she was right. The man was definitely paparazzi, and he had his eye on the shop. Did he know about Alaric and me? Did he know we were faking?

Of course he didn't know. How could he?

But did he suspect? Was I doing such a poor job of pretending that someone had noticed? The idea sent a chill down my spine.

"Do you think someone mentioned your relationship?" Holly asked.

"No idea. I didn't think so." I frowned, looking at the guy. "But his presence makes me think otherwise."

I'll take care of him. Penelope climbed out the open window and scrambled down the side of the house, using the eaves and shutters to get to the ground below. Once there, she scampered across the road, running full tilt toward the man.

He spotted her and paled, then turned and ran for it.

I grinned, shouting, "Thank you, Penelope!"

She ignored me and kept chasing him, clearly determined to teach him a lesson. I left her to it, turning back to Holly and joining her by the joy batteries. "I'm going to do a bit of research, then I'll work on getting us more help with these." I reached for her hand and squeezed it, meeting her eyes. "Thank you so much for the help with this. I couldn't ask for a better friend."

She grinned. "Oh, don't you worry. I'll call in the favor one day."

"You'd better."

Her smile turned a bit evil. "It'll be something horrific. Like, I'll start a hot dog stand, and you'll have to dress as the hot dog and dance on the street to get me some customers."

I laughed. "You know I love hot dogs *and* theatre. I'll be the best hot dog you've ever seen. You'll have to think of something worse than that."

"Hmmm." She frowned, her expression thoughtful. "I'll think of something. Now get to work on your solution for Vivian and Barnaby."

I did as she instructed, burying myself in the work. My plan was to make a revelation stick like the kind I'd used before, when Alaric and I had compelled the spirit in the cemetery to show herself. This one would have a special twist, though. Revelation sticks really only worked well when used by someone with my kind of power, and Vivian needed a good bit of time with Barnaby. For this stick to work, I had to put some of my power and skill into it.

That was the tricky part, though. This was different than jumpstarting a joy battery. When I did that, I was just a conduit, moving magic from the ether into a receptacle. I wasn't putting any of myself or my particular gift into the receptacle. To do something like that, I'd needed to find a special spell.

Fortunately, I just had. It took time to craft the elements of the spell and the revelation stick itself, but I managed it.

By the time I finished, it was nearly dinner, and I was tapped out. Holly had already left, and my stomach was grumbling.

I needed to deliver the special revelation stick to Vivian, and I wanted to see Alaric.

I pulled my phone from my pocket and texted Madeline, asking if they wanted me to bring a takeaway over for everyone for dinner. She immediately responded with a yes, and I grinned.

An hour later, I was driving up to the estate. Penelope had found me as I'd been picking up the takeaway and invited herself along. I wasn't surprised, though. I knew as soon as I placed an order that she would sense it, so I'd got her favorite.

I don't know why you won't let me eat in the car. She glared at me from the passenger seat. *The smell is killing me.*

"It isn't a Happy Meal," I said. "And you're not a child. Anyway, the last thing I need is greasy skunk footprints all over the upholstery of my fine vehicle."

She eyed the dash of my old car, an invisible eyebrow raised. *Fine vehicle?*

"One more word, and I won't give you the sweet I bought you."

She mimed twisting a key near her mouth and throwing it away. I grinned and turned onto the lane that led up to the estate. The lights glowed golden in the windows, and the near-dark made the roses blooming on the sides of the house look almost black. Fireflies glittered in the air. It was gorgeous, and the night of the ball would be something truly spectacular.

Vivian opened the door almost immediately after I knocked, grinning widely at me. "I'm so glad you came."

I held up the bag, which smelled invitingly of fish and chips from Codswollop's. "I come bearing gifts."

"My favorite." She turned and gestured for Penelope and me to enter. "Come in, come in."

She led us toward the kitchen, but Alaric was nowhere to be seen. Disappointment tugged at me. If he'd really been my boyfriend, he would have met me at the door.

I really needed to remember that this wasn't real. Despite what we'd shared, we were still bound by the rules of our ruse.

As I was putting the takeaway on the kitchen table, Alaric appeared in the doorway. He smiled at me as he approached, and I turned to him.

"Hey, stranger," I said, unable to keep the flirtation out of my voice. It was good for the charade, of course, but I wasn't acting. Even though I knew I was supposed to hold part of myself back, I couldn't.

He smiled and leaned down to kiss me. I pressed myself against him, savoring the short moment. I didn't know if I should lean into this experience and enjoy it while it lasted or try to protect myself from the inevitable hurt when we broke up.

"How has work been?" he asked.

"Good." I gestured to the food. "I had a breakthrough today, so I wanted to celebrate."

"Smells amazing."

Vivian brought plates to the table, where Penelope had already taken her seat.

I looked at Vivian. "I've found the spell that will allow you and Barnaby to see each other without me there."

She arched a white brow. "Oh, really?"

I nodded, smiling. "That is, if you still want to try."

"I do." She looked down at the fish and chips she'd put on her plate, as if debating whether she should eat first. Then she picked up a chip. "I'm not delaying my food for a man, that's for sure."

"Amen, Mama." Madeline raised her ruby-red cocktail. I grinned at them, then looked at Alaric.

He smiled back at me, and it was so easy to believe this all was real.

Harold was the last to join us, and we ate as we discussed the ball and Vivian's upcoming meeting with Barnaby. It was all so lovely that it made me even more afraid to lose it.

When the meal was over, Vivian stood. "I'm going to go freshen up, and then I believe I have a date."

"I'll come with you." Madeline stood. "Your brows could use some work."

Vivian glared at her daughter, then rolled her eyes, which was pretty funny to witness on a duchess. "Fine, I'll let you have a try at my face again."

"Oh, come off it." Madeline's voice was fond. "You loved how you looked last time. And I really think you ought to give some serious consideration to wearing the dress I suggested."

"Over my dead body." Vivian scowled.

"You want to be buried in it?" Madeline's voice was rich with put-on excitement. "Why, Mother, I'm honored."

Vivian laughed, and the two departed.

"I'll take care of the dishes," Harold said. "Why don't you two go have a drink in the drawing room?"

"Thank you, Harold." Alaric smiled and stood, offering me his arm.

I took it, and we went to the drawing room, where Alaric poured me a glass of white wine and lit the fire. There was still the faintest chill in the evening air, but I was pretty sure he was lighting it mostly for the ambiance. It sent a golden glow over the cozy room, and I settled onto the couch.

CHAPTER
TWENTY-SIX

ALARIC

I POURED myself a glass of whisky and walked toward Emma. She'd curled up in the corner of the couch with her glass of wine, and she looked beautiful in the firelight. She also looked cozy, and I could imagine her there in all seasons—in the autumn, with a sweater on, or in the winter with a glass of mulled wine.

The thought was so impossible that I shoved it aside. I was falling for her, but it seemed too good to be true. *She* seemed too good to be true.

Katrina had been the same. With her, I'd thought I'd met the woman I would spend my life with. What I'd learned was that I couldn't trust my own judgement, and the resulting fallout threatened my grandmother and the rest of my family.

I couldn't risk that again.

And yet I couldn't seem to help myself around Emma. She drew me to her like the sun, and I was a helpless planet in her orbit. I would need to be careful to keep as much of myself reserved as I could. This was just too dangerous.

I took a seat next to her, and she turned to face me, curling her legs up under her. She frowned before she spoke. "There was a paparazzo standing outside my shop today."

"What?" The word snapped out of me, and I pulled back. "Sorry, I'm just surprised. How did they find out about us?"

"I don't know. And maybe they haven't figure it out for sure? Maybe it's just speculation."

I dragged my hand down my face. This wasn't good.

"I'll be careful," she said. "But I'm glad this isn't real. I couldn't handle that kind of life."

I'm glad this isn't real.

Her words were a thin dagger between the ribs, and I needed to remember them. What she shared with me was part of her job, not part of her real life, and she wanted to keep it that way.

"Some people don't mind this life," I said, searching for something to say. "Considering all the benefits it offers."

She looked around at the drawing room, her brow arched. "You mean the big house and all that?"

I shrugged. It was what Katrina had wanted, though she'd been too impatient to wait for me to propose. Thank fates. Even though it had blown up in the end, it would have been far more harmful to marry her.

"No, thanks," Emma said. "The house is lovely but too big. I want a real life."

"This is real," I said, offended.

"You know what I mean."

"Do I?"

She shrugged, her face a bit sad. "Maybe not. Your childhood wasn't much more normal than mine. But you had Vivian, which I envy."

I nodded. She had a point. Between the boarding schools and the cruel father, my life hadn't been normal. But it had had its good parts.

She turned and looked into the fire. "Don't you wonder what it would be like? A normal life with a home and a family?" She gestured to the estate. "Not this kind of home, I mean. But a regular one."

"Not really. This is all I've ever known. It has its downsides, but overall, it's a good life."

"I know, I'm sorry. I don't mean to sound dismissive of it. I think I just grew up addicted to those movies and TV shows about wholesome nuclear families."

An ache for her settled deep in my chest, and I couldn't stop myself from reaching out and wrapping an arm around her to pull her close. She curled into me, laying her head on my shoulder, and it felt like the most natural thing in the world, even though I knew it couldn't last.

"It makes sense," I murmured against your hair. "You didn't have that, and most children want it."

"All children want it," she said. "A desire for stability and love and family are hardwired into our DNA. Some of us may grow out of it, but we all start out with it."

"I suppose you're right." I pressed a kiss to the top of her head. There were tragedies in my past and things I mourned, but I'd had love. First from my mother, then from my grandmother.

Emma hadn't had that, so of course she wanted it.

"How is the London witch coming with the spell to silence your blackmailing journalist?" she asked.

"It'll be delivered by the end of the week."

"So we'll no longer need to pretend."

I looked down at her, trying to see if she was relieved about that. She probably was, given how much she disliked the paparazzo who'd shown up on her doorstep. She wasn't falling for me the same way I was falling for her, and I needed to remember that. I couldn't trust my own judgment, especially when something seemed too good to be true.

I settled on saying, "We can't break up yet. We'll have to wait until after the ball, at least."

"Of course." She grinned at me. "Should we stage something public where I throw a drink in your face and then storm out?"

I laughed. "Maybe not so dramatic."

"What if it was your favorite beer?"

"I'd call it a waste."

"Fair enough." She looked toward the window, then leaned forward. "I think I see your grandmother returning."

A few minutes later, my grandmother swept into the room, her cheeks rosy and her eyes bright with happiness. Madeline and Harold hurried in behind her, both with expectant looks on their faces.

"Well?" Emma asked, excitement in her voice. "How did it go?"

"It worked a treat, darling." My grandmother glided

toward the bar cart and poured herself a healthy measure of gin, which she topped off with blood. She added ice to the shaker and shook it, then poured it into her usual martini glass and held the cup up to the light. "To renewing old flames."

Madeline gave a little wolf whistle, and I grinned at my aunt.

"Renewing old flames, Mother?" she asked.

"Yes." My grandmother shot her a saucy look. "Just because he's incorporeal doesn't mean we can't have fun." She turned to Emma. "Presuming you can make me another revelation stick?"

"I can." Emma gave a little clap of excitement. "I'm just so pleased it worked! I wasn't sure it would."

"You're incredibly talented, my dear," Harold said. "We're lucky to have you."

The rest of my family nodded, and worry shot through me. They weren't going to take it well when we broke up. I hadn't expected them to like her so much, and this was a serious downside of my plan.

"So, tell us the details, Mama!" Madeline demanded, joining her on the other sofa, her own drink in hand.

"Well, he was much more charming this time. I don't think he's particularly fond of our Emma here. His mistake, of course. He'll see the light as to how wonderful she is."

"Oh, thank you," Emma said. "I'm not sure he will, but I appreciate the kind words."

"Well, either way, I've convinced him to let you host the ball here. I told him how important it was, and he agreed."

"Thank you!" Emma pressed her hands to her chest, her

eyes gleaming with excitement. "I can't tell you how much that means to me."

"Well, he wants to see me more, of course. That will convince him to let us host the ball, he said." She winked at us. "And I'd like to see him, too, if I'm being honest."

"He could attend the ball!" Madeline said. "Wouldn't that be lovely? You'd have a date."

"Oh, that would be divine." My grandmother looked at Emma. "That's possible, right? I'd just need to use a revelation stick that night?"

"Um, yes." Emma stared into the middle distance, looking like her mind had gone somewhere else. It was like I could see the thoughts going a mile a minute in her head. Slowly, she set her nearly untouched glass of wine on the table in front of her and stood. When she spoke, there was a hint of excitement in her voice. "Excuse me, but I need to go."

"What?" I leaned forward, surprised by her abruptness.

"Oh, stay!" Madeline said. "We can play a game."

"Thank you, but I have some work to do." From the look in her eyes, her thoughts were already a million miles away. "I've just figured out something really important, but I need to see if it will work."

"All right, then." Madeline looked at her glass. "You can drive?"

"I only had a sip," Emma said. "I'm fine." She turned to me. "I'll see you later."

Without another word, she hurried from the room.

Emma

FINALLY, I knew what my big surprise would be for the party. Vivian's happiness after seeing Barnaby had planted the seed in my mind, and Madeline's comment about Barnaby attending the ball had watered it. The last part of the puzzle was Rupert's watch, which had connected him to the spirit of his grandfather.

I just didn't know if my idea was possible, so I had to get into the shop and get to work. I would *make* it possible. Ideas ran through my mind as I drove back toward Charming Cove. It was approaching my bedtime, but I didn't care. I needed to find a way to implement my vision.

It wasn't until I arrived at the shop that I realized I'd left Penelope at Blackthorn Hall. She probably preferred it, though. Their cupboard was far better stocked than mine.

The shop was quiet as I let myself in and went upstairs, going immediately to the bookshelves to see if I could find a way to implement my plan. Hours passed as I scanned the books, my eyelids growing heavier and heavier.

It wasn't until Holly's voice woke me that I realized I'd fallen asleep over the books.

"What are you doing here so early?" she demanded. "You look awful."

I rubbed my face. "Thanks, mate."

"I mean it, you need to get yourself cleaned up before the big meeting."

"Big meeting?" I blinked at her.

"Yes, we have a coven meeting, remember? It's why I'm

here early, to get a little work done on these joy batteries beforehand." She went to the table and began to sort through the ingredients, setting up to assemble a few.

"Oh, you're the best."

"Which is why I'm telling you that you need to go take a shower and get yourself together. You don't want the official witches to think you're out of your depth."

"Good point." I groaned and looked at the ceiling, feeling like a truck had hit me. Body aching, I rose to my feet. "I know what my big surprise will be at the ball."

"Really?" She looked up from where she was fiddling with a particularly difficult ribbon wrapped around a bundle of herbs. "Go on."

I told her my idea, leaving out no details.

"You're insane," she said. "I don't think that's possible."

"Not yet, it's not. But I have an idea for how to do it on a mass scale. That's all I was missing, and I think I found out how last night."

"I mean, if you can manage it, people will love it. But if you can't..."

"I'll have no surprise for everyone." And then there was no way I'd be made an official member of the coven. "But now that I have my mind set on it, I have to try. People would love it. And it would truly prove my magic."

"That's true." She sighed, looking down at the joy batteries. "That's going to take all your time, which means we'll need help assembling these."

"I've got an idea for that, too." I didn't want to jinx us by making it seem like I had everything in hand, but I was feeling pretty good. All the other elements of the party were shaping up as well. "Now I just need to report this to the official witches, and they'll know I've got it all under control."

Holly waved me away. "Well, go get cleaned up. You look like you crawled out of a hole in the forest."

I laughed as I saluted her, then turned and left.

When I returned for the big meeting, freshly showered and dressed, I found Lily manning the desk in the main shop. She looked up when I entered, a frown on her face. "There was a paparazzo at my desk ten minutes ago," she said.

"What?" My stomach pitched. "*Inside?*"

"He wanted to speak to you."

I blew out a breath, nerves prickling. "Did he say why?"

"No, but he seemed excited." She arched a brow. "What have you been up to?"

"Dating the duke. That's got to be why the paparazzo wants to talk to me." I hesitated before speaking, but I couldn't help myself. "Did you tell him anything about me?"

"Of course not. I might not like you, but you're still coven. I'm not going to sell you out to the paparazzi."

"Well, someone did." My anxiety made me speak without thinking, and that was really the last thing I should do around Lily.

"Maybe it's just that you've been around town together? They could have spotted you."

"Maybe." I pinched the bridge of my nose. I really needed to keep my head in the game. The official witches would want a status report at the meeting, and I couldn't let that rattle me.

Willow appeared at the door that led to the meeting

room. "Come on, ladies. Put the sign up and get back here. Meeting is about to start."

Lily rose and put the *Closed* sign at the door.

I filed into the meeting room with everyone else, my heart pounding. It shouldn't be—I had this all in hand, and my idea would make the ball a success.

But it was all just so important to me. I couldn't help but be nervous. And anyway, I hadn't actually implemented my idea yet.

Fortunately, the meeting went off without a hitch. I told them what I'd planned, and everyone was more than impressed. I could see doubt in a few eyes about my ability to scale up the operation, but I would manage it. We agreed to change the invitations so that people knew to bring something that connected them to a loved one they'd lost, so there was no going back now.

I got started immediately, losing myself in my work. There were a couple missing pieces of the puzzle that was my idea, and I needed to sort them out.

When Alaric appeared at the door of the workshop, my muscles ached from sitting in the same place for so long.

"Holly says you haven't left this room all day." He looked at his watch. "And it's dinnertime. Have you eaten?"

I smiled, touched. "Are you here to make sure I've eaten?"

"Maybe." He returned my smile. "And to make sure everything is all right. You ran out last night like your tail was on fire."

"It was. With my fabulous idea."

He smiled. "Then come on and tell me about it while I get you something to eat."

"I don't have time."

"You have to eat, or you won't be able to keep going. We'll get something quick."

He had a point, and I liked that the was taking care of me. I rose, stretching out the kinks from sitting all day. "All right. I'm coming. But let's just do sandwiches."

"Perfect."

He escorted me out onto Foxglove Lane, where twilight had already settled. The street lamps glowed golden against the sky, and people sat at outside cafés and pub tables, laughing over pints and plates. The ubiquitous flowers that characterized Charming Cove blossomed wildly in pots and beds, and seagulls circled out over the sea.

"It's Friday already, isn't it?" I asked, having lost track of the days.

"It is, indeed." He looked around. "We wouldn't find a table even if we wanted one."

"It's no trouble." I led him to the little shop a few doors down, and we bought premade sandwiches and soft drinks. Then we found a seat at one of the benches overlooking the sea. It was hidden behind a particularly wild honeysuckle bush, so no one would see us. Foxglove and lavender bloomed around us, scenting the air with a delicate fragrance as the sea breeze blew gently off the water.

We chatted as we ate, and it was quite simply lovely.

Then we repeated the ritual for the next three nights. During the day, I would work until I almost dropped, and then Alaric would come and take me for sandwiches. We'd eat on the hidden bench, and not once did we mention that this was a fake relationship.

CHAPTER
TWENTY-SEVEN

EMMA

AS I WAS LETTING myself into work the next morning, it was one of the rare cloudy days in Charming Cove. A raincloud hovered out over the sea, threatening to drift over us later.

My key stuck as I fiddled with it in the lock, and I felt a presence behind me. I turned away from the shop door to face the person standing behind me.

It was a man with a scruffy beard and large camera hanging around his neck. I swallowed hard and put on my iciest expression. "Yes?"

"Emma Willowby? I'm Clark Smith. Any comment for the *Magic Mirror* about your relationship with the Duke of Blackthorn?"

Oh, bum. "I've got no idea what you're talking about."

"Yes, you have."

"I really don't, and I need to be getting into work." I

turned from him to jiggle the key once more. *Come on, work, you bastard.*

"You might want to look at this, then."

His words sent a chill down my spine, and I looked back at him. He held his camera out toward me, the little screen lit up with an image that was clearly two people kissing.

My stomach dropped, and I leaned closer. It was definitely me, kissing a man whose face was mostly obscured but not entirely. The embrace was passionate—so much so that Alaric would be horrified. *I* was horrified. I didn't want my life in the paper like this.

I looked up at him, ready to do whatever he wanted. "You can't print that."

"I can't, but my paper can."

I scowled. "That's what I meant. And you can't. I don't want to be in the papers like that."

"So, no comment? Because if you don't have one, the *Mirror* will speculate, and I promise, it won't be pretty."

I didn't want that, but I couldn't give a comment, either. There was literally nothing I could say that could protect me from the attention I was about to receive. And Alaric...he would hate this.

"There's speculation this isn't a real relationship," he said, eyes glinting with interest. "Care to comment on that?"

"From where?"

"Can't reveal my sources."

Was he making this up? Did it matter? Vivian would be devastated if she found out through the papers. I couldn't let that happen.

"What do you want? I'll give you anything I can if you'll delete that photo."

"You don't have what I want."

"Try me." I pointed to the sign above the door that advertised the Aurora Coven. "I'm a witch. A powerful one. I can make you spells. Lots of them. Whatever you want."

He sighed. "I'd really just rather have a comment."

"Well, I can't give you one. I don't want my life in the *Magic Mirror*. People will be hurt."

"That's your problem."

"Ugh!" I wanted to grab his camera and break it, but that wouldn't do any good. Those photos were probably already in the cloud.

"If that's all, I'll be going." He jerked his head toward the beat-up car on the other side of the road.

"Go, then."

"I'll give you a few days to decide if you want to give a comment. Then I'm going to the *Mirror*, and they'll say what they want." He shrugged. "You'd be better off giving me a comment when I come back."

"It's not going to happen."

He just grunted and turned, ambling across the road.

I ground my teeth as I watched him go, wishing I could shoot a hex at his back. Something like boils on his butt or making him quack like a duck whenever he tried to drink a beer.

What a jerk.

A few days wasn't long enough for my coven to create a spell that would silence him, but maybe Alaric's London witch had made a double batch of hers. I would tell Alaric, and he could ask her.

My head was pounding as I turned back to the door and let myself into the shop. I had work to do, and there were still a few days left before the paparazzo returned for a comment. I'd see Alaric that night and ask him.

Fortunately, no one was at the desk that early. The workshop was a reprieve from the worries outside. The herbs hanging from the ceiling scented the air with the calming aroma of lavender and rosemary, and I inhaled deeply. As I flicked on the lights, I vowed I would focus on batching my surprise spells for the ball. That way, I'd get something done and escape from the worry for a little while.

I set about my task, losing myself in the work. By late afternoon, I was starving and still needed to meet with Vivian about where to put the buffet tables at the party. She'd invited the caterer over, and we needed to speak to him.

Holly stopped me on my way out of the shop, where she was closing up the desk for the day. "Where are you off to?"

"Blackthorn Hall. Want to come?"

"Love to." She grinned. "I've always wanted to see the place. And maybe we can get an idea for how big the party will be, geographically speaking."

"That's what I was thinking. We need to determine how many joy batteries we need to cover the whole area."

"Perfect. Lead the way."

We locked up the shop and headed to my car, then drove over to the estate. Vivian and Madeline were already outside with the caterer, walking around to the back garden and patio. The threat of rain had passed, though there were still plenty of clouds in the sky. We hurried to catch up to them, and I introduced myself and Holly to the caterer. He was a young man in his late twenties, with a shock of purple hair and a T-shirt with a cartoon rat cooking on it.

"I am *so* excited to be catering this event," he said, speaking quickly. "I cannot tell you how excited."

"Fantastic." I smiled. "I'm here to answer any questions."

We spent thirty minutes going through the menu and where things could be set up outside, then Holly and I headed off to get to work on plotting out the rest of the party and what events would happen at each part of the grounds. Besides the joy batteries and my big surprise, we'd done a lot of work to enchant different elements of the party, and they'd all need the perfect setting.

Alaric

Emma wasn't at her shop when I stopped by late that afternoon, but there was a man on the bench across the street. He had a scruffy beard and the ubiquitous big camera carried by paparazzi, and I turned away from him quickly.

The spell that had been cast to protect my family and me from the paparazzi should have worked to keep him from taking a direct photo of my face, but everything was fallible.

Before I could climb back into my car, he approached. "Your Grace?"

I turned to him. "You really don't need to bother with the honorific if you're also planning on invading my privacy."

He shrugged. "Thought it might soften the blow."

"Of what?" A chill raced down my skin.

"Just a photo I'm looking for a comment on."

"What photo?" My voice was stone cold, and it was more a demand than a question.

He held out the camera, the screen pointing at me. Emma and me kissing in the doorway of her flat the night after the pub quiz. Her face was mostly visible, while mine was primarily hidden. A child could guess it was me, though.

"How'd you get that?" I demanded.

"You mean despite the spell that you had cast to protect you?" He grinned. "I guess just enough of your face was hidden that it didn't work. I wasn't too hopeful when I shot the photos, but when I was going back through, I found that this one turned out."

That damned witch in London. She'd assured me this wouldn't happen.

"So, have you got a comment?"

"No."

"The woman tried to make me a deal. Don't you want to?"

"The woman?" My skin went cold.

"Emma. The one in the photo. She tried to make me a deal. Don't you want to try, too?"

A low roar started up in my head, and I was thrown back to the journalist who'd approached me after Katrina had sold my secrets.

Too good to be true.

I'd known it was the case. Emma was so perfect. No one could be that perfect. And I couldn't trust my own judgement when it came to women—that was clear enough.

"No comment," I said, my heart thundering so hard that I thought I could feel it against my ribs.

He grunted and turned away, climbing into a beat-up car. Before I could call him back to ask any questions, he was gone.

Fine.

I didn't need to ask any questions. I knew what had happened.

She tried to make me a deal. The photographer's words echoed in my head, so similar to the last time this had happened.

Of course she had tried to make a deal. This wasn't a real relationship, and it never had been.

But it had felt real.

Could she really have done this?

No, I needed to speak to her. To find out the details of what had happened. There had to be a good explanation, and I was jumping to conclusions. I couldn't let my own damage get in the way of something that could be great.

My phone buzzed, and I looked down to see a message from my aunt. *Emma is here. Where are you?*

We must have passed each other on the road.

I got into my car and drove back to the estate as quickly as I could, wanting to find Emma.

∾

Emma

HOLLY and I spent nearly an hour walking around the grounds, planning the ball. On the patio, Vivian and Madeline were still talking to the caterer. Harold had joined them, and the four were involved in an animated discussion that I wished I could hear.

"This place is incredible," Holly said.

"I know, pretty great, right?"

"I'll say. This ball is going to blow people's minds."

"I hope so." I turned to her.

"And what about the duke?" she asked. "How is that going?"

"I like him. A lot."

Holly grinned. "I thought so."

"Not sure if he likes me, though."

"Of course he does! You're amazing."

"That's not enough, you know." I looked down at Penelope, who had just arrived. She nodded her agreement.

"Well, he'd be a fool not to want you," Holly said, loyal as ever.

I shrugged. "We'll see."

"You fit in here," she said, looking at the people on the patio of the big house. "They really like you."

"Honestly, I want this life," I confessed, looking toward Vivian, Madeline, and Harold, who still stood on the steps that led up to the patio at the back of the big house. The camaraderie and love between them was everything I could want. Add Alaric to the mix, and it was perfect. "I mean, just look at it. Amazing."

Holly nodded, her gaze on the people I wished could be my family.

Incoming, Penelope said.

I looked up to see Alaric only a couple meters away. I hadn't heard him approach, but from the look on his face, something was seriously wrong. "Alaric? What is it?"

"You're a good actress, you know that?" he said, his voice harsh. "After all your protests that you weren't, it turns out that you were excellent."

Had he overheard something I'd just said and not liked it? But I hadn't said anything bad. "What do you mean?"

Anger flashed in his eyes, and I reeled back. He was mad at me. Like, really mad at me. Had he heard something in my conversation with Holly that he didn't like?

"What's wrong?" I said, my heart starting to pound.

"I thought you were too good to be true, and I was right." His tone made a shiver run down my spine. "We're done. This was never real, and I'm done pretending it could be."

"Uh—" I looked toward his grandmother, who stood on the steps leading up to the patio. She was too far away to hear, but she had a frown on her face as she watched us. I looked back at Alaric. "Your grandmother is watching."

"Stop using her as a cover. You don't care about her."

My jaw dropped. He *knew* how much I loved his grandmother. He had to. I'd told him about my childhood. Could he not tell that I loved his family?

No, I realized. He couldn't.

Because he didn't trust me. Not even a little bit, apparently.

"I guess I was wrong about you, too," I said, wanting to get the hell out of there. My heart felt like it was breaking, and it surprised me. My feelings for him had crept up on me, and now that he was revealing what he truly thought of me, they were making themselves known.

"I'll let you host the ball," he said, glancing at his grandmother. "And we'll keep up the charade. But no touching. And no speaking. We do this for my grandmother, then it's over."

"Fine with me," I said, spitting out the words.

"Good." He turned and left, his face hard as granite.

Well, shite.

I leaned back on my heels, blowing out a long, sad breath.

"That was...something," Holly said.

I looked at her, horrified to see her still standing there. As soon as I'd realized that something was up with Alaric, I'd forgot about Holly. But she'd witnessed it all.

"He's a bastard," she said.

"He is." And he'd dumped me like that in front of an audience. Iron bands tightened around my heart, and I felt tears prick my eyes. "I didn't see that coming."

"Neither did I." She shrugged. "Good riddance. He's clearly a jerk, and you're well rid of him."

I knew she was right, but I couldn't feel it in my heart. This had come out of the blue.

Maybe there had been a misunderstanding. Had the

paparazzo spoken to him, maybe? I had no idea, but I was going to find out.

"I'm getting out of here," I said. "I've got something I need to do."

"Want me to come?"

"I'd rather be alone, but thank you."

I'll come, Penelope said. *I insist. You might need backup.*

"Thank you." I reached down and picked her up, hugging her against my chest and burying my face in her fur. "I love you."

She wiggled so that she could look at me. *I will only get sappy this* one *time. But I love you, too. Now let's go find that bastard.*

~

ALARIC

I WALKED AWAY FROM EMMA, my head pounding. I'd come to talk to her to learn the truth about the paparazzo, sure there'd been a good explanation. And yet, as soon as I'd arrived, I'd found her looking at the house and saying how much she wanted this life.

Hearing that had thrown me back into the moment I'd discovered Katrina's deception, and it had cut like a blade. It was an almost identical situation, and I couldn't believe I'd been so stupid. She'd found her way into my heart—I'd let her in there, despite knowing it was a bad idea. And then this.

I felt like an idiot, thinking that she wanted me, when all she'd wanted were the trappings of my life. I should have learned my lesson with Katrina, and yet I hadn't.

But she'd been different than Katrina. Or so I'd thought. What I'd felt for her had been different—so much deeper and stronger. I'd thought I'd known her, but it was clear I hadn't.

It would be hell until the ball, seeing her around and being confronted with the horrible truth of the situation. If my grandmother weren't so excited about the ball, I'd cancel it.

I would just have to avoid Emma until then. Once the ball was over, I never had to see her again. But I hated how even that made my chest hurt.

How had I been so stupid?

Emma

IT TOOK us two hours to find the paparazzo, but we finally spotted his car outside of The Drunken Clam. It was fitting that he was hanging out in the pub where I'd first met Alaric and made an arse of myself.

Penelope followed me into the half-full pub, ignoring the stares of the patrons as she waddled up to the bar and hopped onto the seat next to the paparazzo who had harassed me. His beer was nearly empty, and he looked from it to me, his eyes widening. "Here already with a comment?"

"No."

Tell him I'll stink bomb him if he doesn't do exactly as you say.

"I'll handle the negotiations, thanks," I said.

"What?" he asked, his brow furrowing in confusion.

"Just talking to my familiar." I didn't bother sitting. "Did you say something to the duke about those photos? About me?"

"Yeah, why?"

"You said I had three days."

He shrugged. "You do. I'm just playing all angles."

"What did you tell him?"

"I don't know, the truth? Whatever you told me?"

"But I didn't say anything bad to you."

"Depends on your perspective."

None of this made any sense. Unless... "You told him I tried to make you a deal?"

"Yeah, 'cause you did."

"But did you tell him the nature of the deal?"

"I don't know." He threw back the last of his beer. "Have you got a comment or not?"

"Yeah. Go hex yourself." I turned and walked out of the pub, Penelope hot on my heels.

I didn't get to stink bomb him.

"It's the thought that counts." I walked toward the park across the road, my mind racing.

There was a thin strip of grass between Foxglove Lane and the sloped cliff that dropped into the sea about ten meters below. Very close to where I'd had my sandwich dinners with Alaric, in fact. Flowerbeds shaped like swirls bloomed in a rainbow around me, but I barely saw them as I plopped down onto a random bench and stared out at the waves below. That late in the afternoon, the sunlight sparkled on the water. It was actually even prettier when the tears filmed over my eyes, and I laughed as I wiped them away.

You don't seem so good.

"I don't feel so good."

But it's all clearly a miscommunication.

"Yep. That part is fine. What's not fine is that Alaric immediately assumed the worst of me. He didn't even trust me enough to ask me what had happened. He just assumed I'd sold him out and broke up with me." I laughed bitterly. "Not that we were ever together."

He was hurt.

"Maybe. But does that mean he gets to hurt me?" I shook my head. "I'm not interested in that. Anyway, he was probably just looking for an out. He never wanted a real relationship, or he would have mentioned it."

Maybe he hadn't got a chance.

I looked down at her. "Whose side are you on?"

Yours. But you're happy around him.

"I *was* happy around him. Now the idea of seeing him makes me sick. I was stupid to think this could work, and this is the proof." I drew in a shuddery breath, trying to get myself together. "But I'm not going to be stupid anymore. I'm going to focus on the ball, and I'm going to do such a good job that the coven makes me an official member. That's always been my goal, and I need to focus on it."

Well, I can't argue with that. There is a lot to do.

"Exactly. And Alaric can take a long walk off a short

broomstick. We weren't as close as I thought, and that's all there is to it. I'll get over it."

Good for you. She gave me a friendly punch with her little paw, but my own words echoed in my head.

I'll get over it.

Would I, though?

CHAPTER
TWENTY-EIGHT

Emma

I SPENT the next week in the coven workshop, living off takeout and sleeping in the big chair by the window. Obviously, I hadn't seen Alaric, and I'd only communicated with his family via text, explaining that I was busy with party prep. It was the truth, at least, if not all of it.

It had been a week packed with non-stop spell work and battery assembly. I'd also had to make a few revelation sticks for Vivian so that she could visit with Barnaby. Penelope had tried to go on strike several times, but she'd relented each time I'd bribed her with chips from Codswollop's.

There were still four days left before the festival, but we were behind. Holly and Penelope had done their best with the joy batteries, but I hadn't been much help because I'd been busy with other party prep. I ended every night with my magic totally exhausted, as did they.

299

It was time to ask for help.

Are you finally admitting it? Penelope asked.

I looked down at her. "Can you read my mind?"

No, but you look like you've been hit by a truck. Surely you know it's time to ask for help.

"You're right." I dragged a hand through my hair, which definitely needed a wash. "We've got almost all of the batteries assembled, thanks to your help. And Holly's, of course. But we don't have the magic we need to jumpstart them all. We need more witches."

Who will you ask?

I grinned. "I know just the person."

Well, maybe you should shower first.

She was probably right. I didn't know what I'd find on the street outside the shop. Paparazzi waiting for the duke's estranged girlfriend? Had that man published his story in the *Magic Mirror*?

He'd come to the building on the third day like he'd promised, but I'd refused to see him. There was nothing I could do, anyway. And since he'd spoken to Alaric, the duke could handle it.

I'd also refused to look out the window at Foxglove Lane and forbade anyone from giving me any updates. I hadn't wanted to think about it at all, and the idea that there might be photographers outside would totally mess with my head.

"Do I need to clean up in the bathroom here first?" I patted my head again. "Maybe tame this mess?"

Let me check. Penelope scampered to the window and looked out. *Coast is clear. Want me to head out first and keep it that way?*

She sounded like a furry little bodyguard, and I couldn't have loved her more for it.

"Thanks, mate. We'll head out together if you say it's clear."

Come on, then. She went to the stairs and hopped down one at a time. Fortunately, there was no one around to see me as I made the short run to my flat. It took a while to get fully cleaned up and presentable, but by the time I was ready, I felt a lot more normal. Maybe I should have been showering before this.

"Right," I said to Penelope. "Let's go rally the troops."

Alaric

I stared out the window of my office at the back of the house, watching as the preparation for the ball got fully underway. My grandmother was outside, directing the gardeners like a drill sergeant. She had them sprucing up the greenery and flowers as well as placing hundreds of lanterns throughout the space. They sat on posts and hung from trees and ropes.

The estate was starting to look truly beautiful, and it just made me angrier.

Angry with Emma, angry with myself.

Mostly angry at myself. Whenever I thought of her, all I felt was...hurt.

I want this life.

Her words echoed in my head, nearly a direct parallel to

what Katrina had said. She'd been looking at the house when she'd said it. So much for all her protestations of not liking it and wanting a normal life.

I barked a bitter laugh, but it didn't alleviate the tightness in my chest. I'd been wrong about her all along.

Still, the thought felt strange. Had I really been wrong about her? Had I jumped to conclusions?

No, it had been clear what I'd heard in the garden that day. Just a couple of sentences, but enough to make it obvious what she thought.

I pinched the bridge of my nose, an ache blooming in my head.

Everything should have been going well by now. The London witch had got me the spell for the paparazzo who was blackmailing me, and I'd used it. That threat was now over, and my grandmother was safe from that added trauma. It was what I'd been working for, so I should have been happy.

I'd even got the paparazzo who'd spoken to Emma to delete all of the photos of her and me. It had taken even more money, and the London witch was working on yet another silencing spell.

I sank into my chair.

Honestly, it was getting exhausting. I hated having my name in the papers, but trying to constantly manage it and keep things quiet was hell in its own way.

I should have just let the bastard run the pictures, but I found I couldn't put Emma through that. Even though she hadn't been what I'd wanted her to be, I didn't want her to suffer through that kind of scrutiny. She might want the big house and the title, but I believed her when she said she didn't like the public scrutiny.

Then why couldn't I believe her about the rest of it?

Did I need to?

I wanted to be with her, despite it all. That was the one thing that was driving me mad that week. I still wanted to be with her.

I was angry and hurt. Far more hurt than when Katrina had done something similar. It was the main reason I'd lost my mind when I'd heard her talking to her friend Holly.

But I wanted to get over it. I wanted to be with her.

"Alaric?" My grandmother's voice sounded from the doorway to my office, and I spun my chair to see her enter.

"How are you, Granny?"

"Fine, dear. You're a mess though." She pressed her lips together as she sat in the chair across from my desk. "What's going on?"

"Just busy with preparation for the ball."

"You haven't done anything for the ball. *And* I haven't seen Emma here all week."

"She's been busy, too."

"Hmm." She arched a brow, and I suddenly had the thought that she saw far more than she let on. "Trouble in paradise?"

Bloody hell. How did I answer that? Should I hint at problems to pave the way for our future public breakup?

"I see your mind working," she said. "Don't think you can fool me. I learned all your tricks when you were a boy."

"Perhaps I've become cleverer."

"You haven't." She sighed. "Especially if you've called things off with Emma, which I believe you have."

I frowned at her. "Why?"

"Because you look miserable. And guilty." She shrugged. "If it was just miserable, then I'd say she called it off. But I think it was you. Why did you do such a stupid thing?"

I couldn't confess to my grandmother without telling her all of it—Katrina, the press, the blackmail, and the lies. There was no way I would do that.

"Can we just leave it?" I asked.

"No, darling. And I think we should start with why her name isn't Katrina."

I blinked at my grandmother. "Ah—"

"Close your mouth, you look like a fish."

I snapped my mouth shut. "I never spoke of Katrina by name to you. I'm almost certain."

"True, you didn't. But there was a little article written about you when you attended the Protect the Bees benefit gala. She was mentioned by name, and I saw it."

"And you didn't say anything when I introduced my girl-friend as Emma?"

She shrugged and smiled. "I almost did, but I liked Emma, and I like a mystery. I wanted to figure out what you were up to on my own."

"Huh." Well, that was unexpected. "What did you determine?"

"That you didn't want to tell me you had broken it off with this Katrina woman and you were substituting Emma in her place. Though why, I'll never know."

"Because I thought you were dying," I said. "Or at least very ill."

She stared at me, aghast. "What? Why would you think that?"

"Because you sleep far later than you ever have and you still look tired sometimes. You also go to bed earlier. What was I supposed to think? That you were binge-watching gruesome programs late at night?"

She laughed, then blushed. "So you know about that, do you?"

"Emma told me. She didn't realize it was meant to be a secret." I sighed. "I'm sorry I've been such a snob that you didn't think you could tell me earlier."

She sighed as well. "I'll forgive you. If you'll watch an episode with me."

I winced. "I'd really rather not."

"You must."

"As long as it's not zombies."

"Don't tell me that my grandson is scared of zombies."

"Of course I am. It's only reasonable. Also, it's tragic. In those films, someone always has to shoot their zombie mum." It was the worst element in those films, having to kill someone you loved because otherwise, they would kill you. I didn't see how anyone could stand it.

Her eyes softened. "Oh, of course. You wouldn't like that, would you?"

"No. But I'll watch something with you. Just not zombies."

"It's a deal." She looked at me dead-on. "Now, what are you going to do about Emma?"

"Nothing. It's over, and that's for the best."

"Hardly. If it were for the best, you wouldn't be moping around here like such a sad sack of potatoes."

"I don't know what there is to do," I said. "She wants something different than I want."

"And what is that?"

"All of this." I waved my hands to indicate the house and land beyond. "The big house, the title, all of it."

"You don't want it?"

"It's not a matter of want for me. It is what it is."

"Then why is it a bad thing if she wants it if you have it?"

"What if she doesn't want me for me?" The words were quiet when they escaped, the heart of the fear that had been eating at me.

"Oh, my love. Of course she wants you."

"How can you know?"

"By the way she looks at you, you numpty." She frowned, her gaze going thoughtful. "Speaking of which, I've only ever seen her look at the formal part of the house with disdain. Are you sure she's all that interested in it? I got the impression she wasn't a fan."

"She's a good actress."

"Now, that's an unkind thing to say. And also patently false. She's a terrible actress, and Madeline will confirm it. We both love her, but she wears her feelings on her face and her thoughts in her eyes."

What if my grandmother was correct? What if I could have everything? Not just Emma, but an Emma who loved me instead of the title and the estate?

I blew out a breath. Probably not possible after what an

arse I'd been. But my grandmother was right, and I'd been wrong.

"Are you coming to your senses?" my grandmother asked. "You look like you might be."

"Maybe, but I'm not sure it matters. I was a right bastard to her."

"Hmm." She raised her eyebrows. "I think this means that a grand gesture is called for."

"I think you're right."

Emma

THE NEXT NIGHT, after everyone was finished with work, we gathered together in the workshop. Aria had brought her grandmother, Cici, along with her best friend, Tabitha, and Tabitha's eight-year-old daughter, Catrina. All were witches, and all were there to help us jumpstart the joy batteries.

I'd thought about asking some of the other apprentices, but they were such close friends with Lily that I thought they might not want to help. They'd do it to help the coven, but I didn't want to put them in an awkward spot unless it was totally necessary.

Anyway, the witches who had come to help were all incredibly powerful. We'd be fine.

"Before we start, I brought this!" Aria pulled a bottle of wine and a huge box of chocolates from her purse.

I smiled. "What's that for?"

"You, silly. You've looked a bit down in the dumps, so I asked Holly what was up. She mentioned your breakup."

"She shouldn't have mentioned it. I'm fine." I wasn't. "But thank you so much."

"You're not fine, because your eyes look sad," Catrina said.

"She's not wrong, dear," Cici said. She was a lovely older woman, with her white hair pulled back in a tidy chignon and an aura of power that would stop even the most powerful witch in their tracks. She'd run Seaside Spells for decades, and I'd liked her ever since I'd moved to town.

"All right. I am bummed. But I do appreciate the wine and chocolate. Those things always help."

"Let me pop it open," Aria said.

Catrina gave me a thoughtful look. "You know, if you like, I can give your ex a tail. Pick any animal you want. I'm quite talented."

I laughed at the girl's fierce expression. "I can see that. Remind me not to get on your bad side." I shook my head. "But no, he doesn't need a tail. He can make an ass of himself all on his own."

"That's the spirit, dear," Cici said. "Now, show us how to jumpstart these batteries. I see that there are quite a few here, and I imagine we'll need to come back if we want to finish them all. Might as well get started now."

"I can't tell you how much I appreciate that." I accepted a glass of wine from Aria and went to the table where we'd laid out the joy batteries. I picked one up and held it so they could see it. "We've assembled them all, but they need to be jumpstarted with a little of your magic. When you touch the battery, you're a conduit between it and the ether. Feed some magic into it until it glows a little, then move on to the next one."

"Is there room for a few more?" a voice said from the door.

I looked up to see Lily standing in the doorway. Behind her were the other apprentices. I frowned, confused. "What?"

"We're here to help," she said.

"Really?"

She glared. "Don't act so surprised."

"Well, I'm not surprised the others are here, though I don't know how they knew we needed help."

"I told them," Lily said.

"You did?"

"And I'm here to help, too." She crossed her arms over her chest. "If you need me."

"I do. I just thought you wanted me to—" I broke off, not liking how the rest of my sentence sounded.

"Fail?"

"Kinda, yeah." I looked at Holly to see if I was way off the mark, and she shook her head.

"You definitely gave that impression, Lily," she said.

"Okay, fine. I've been a bit prickly with you since you were chosen to host the ball. I apologize."

"Just since then?" I asked.

"Okay, before then, too. But you aren't so sweet, yourself."

"True." I frowned. "I'm sorry?"

"It would be better if it didn't sound like a question," she said.

Catrina nodded, her pigtails bouncing. "That's true. I've learned that the hard way."

I pinched my lips shut to repress the laugh. "I'm sorry, Lily. Truly. I'm just surprised, is all. I thought you hated me."

"Hated you?" She laughed. "That's ridiculous. You're my biggest competition here, but we're still a coven. That's like being family. And in a family, you always love each other, but you don't always have to like each other."

Warmth bloomed in my chest so unexpectedly that I grinned widely. "I like the sound of that."

"Me, too." She nodded. "So, I'm sorry for being a bit snippy with you, and we're here to help if you'll show us how."

"Of course. Come in." I reached for my glass of wine and handed it to her. Aria poured two other glasses, and Holly said she'd go down to the kitchen to see if there was any more wine in the fridge, since our bottle wouldn't go very far with so many helpers.

I showed the newcomers how to jumpstart the batteries, and we got to work. It was hard, but fun, and I felt like I was finally finding the home I'd been looking for.

CHAPTER
TWENTY-NINE

EMMA

THE DAY of the ball finally arrived, and I woke up equal parts excited and terrified.

And then I remembered that I'd forgot to get a dress. It was my first thought upon opening my eyes, and I cursed. A real curse, not just my usual *bum*.

"Penelope?" I asked.

Yes? She raised a sleepy head from the foot of the bed.

"Have you got an extra dress I can wear?"

You're joking, right?

"Sadly, no."

You could wear my bow, but if that's all you wore, I'm pretty sure the police would pick you up for indecent exposure.

"Good point." I squeezed my eyes shut and pinched the bridge of my nose. How had I forgot a dress? And it was a damned ball, so it needed to be a good dress. Where was I going to find a good dress at the last minute?

I rolled over and grabbed my phone from underneath the pillow next to me. Maybe Holly would have something. Lily definitely would, and as much as I didn't want to ask her for a favor, she'd been so helpful with assembling the joy batteries over the last few days that I knew our relationship was different now. I could ask her.

How embarrassing, though.

As soon as I turned on the phone, I saw a message from Madeline. I hadn't heard from her since Alaric had broken things off, and my heart thudded.

With slightly trembling hands, I pushed the buttons to pull up the message. As I read, I frowned. She wanted me to come over that morning. I texted her back, saying that I didn't have time because I needed to find a dress.

Her reply came back almost immediately.

THAT'S EXACTLY *why you need to come over, darling.*

I FROWNED. A dress?

If anyone would have one, it would be Madeline. That definitely solved my problem. But it meant I would have to go over to Alaric's house early. I might run into him. I didn't think I could handle that.

No. I wouldn't let him drive me away from the friends I'd made in his family. Just because he was being an idiot didn't mean I had to lose them, too. I'd just keep my chin up and walk in there like I belonged.

My shoulders sagged back into the bed. As much as I wanted to belong there, I didn't. But I did need a dress, and I couldn't turn Madeline down for anything, so I was going.

"Problem solved," I told Penelope. "Madeline has a dress for me."

Of course she does. That woman has everything.

"I bet she'll even have something sparkly for you to wear."

Penelope perked up. *You're right. I'm coming.*

I showered and dressed as quickly as I could. Everything had been delivered to Blackthorn Hall the night before, so there was nothing for me to bring over except myself and Penelope. We stopped by Margot's café to get almond croissants and coffee. Everyone inside was chattering excitedly about the upcoming ball, and I grinned.

"Any hints for us about what will be happening tonight?" Margot asked as she handed over the paper sack filled with croissants.

"You'll just have to come and see." I took the sack and grinned. "But don't forget to bring something important to you that connects you to someone you loved but lost, okay?"

She tapped her necklace, a simple golden locket. "Already have it. From my gran."

"Perfect." I picked up the tray of coffees, then headed for the door. "Can't wait to see you all there!"

Fortunately, the weather was bright and sunny as I headed to my car, Penelope at my side. The forecast predicted it would stay that way, which made things easier.

We could fix the weather with a spell, but that was difficult and would occupy the official witches during the ball. It would be better to not need to bother.

Penelope hopped up onto the passenger seat, then turned to me. *I'll hold the croissants.*

I grinned at her. "You will not. You'll eat them all before we can give any to Madeline and Vivian."

Penelope scowled, but she nodded. *True.*

"But you can have your coffee." I handed her the little paper cup of espresso, and she grabbed it eagerly with both front paws. I sipped mine as I drove, saving the croissants for our arrival.

I reached Blackthorn Hall without incident, and as I pulled up to the house, I gasped. It was magnificent. There were still hours left until the ball, but the catering company had already set up all the tables and chairs and a dance floor. I could only see part of it, since much of the party would be happening around back, but what I could see was beautiful. The flowers on the tables were magnificent, thanks to Aria, who had provided the centerpieces from the Enchanted Garden.

I parked the car in my usual spot and turned it off, then looked at Penelope. "Ready for this?"

Ready. She stood up on her hind legs and pressed her nose to the window, looking at the estate. *I'll stink bomb Alaric if you want me to.*

"No, but thank you."

Just keep it in mind.

I grinned, then climbed out of the car and reached for the bag of croissants I'd set on the backseat floorboard. Once I had the coffees and croissants, I approached the house, my heart thundering.

What if I saw Alaric?

Actually, I would definitely see Alaric. So that wasn't the question. How would I act?

Professional was the only option. This had started as a business arrangement and was ending as one. The mess in the middle had been my own fault for forgetting the rules.

Fortunately, Madeline met me at the door before I had to knock. She wore a huge grin as she welcomed me inside. "Come in. I'm so excited for you to see."

I raised the bag of croissants. "I brought treats."

"Oh, excellent. We'll be here a while."

"We will?"

"Oh, yes, darling. A ball takes ages to prepare for, and I've brought in the best hair and makeup people I know."

"Really?" I grinned, excitement rushing through me.

"Of course. This is a big day, and you've done an incredible job. We want to celebrate. I've invited your friends, too, so they'll be here later."

"Oh, that's lovely, thank you." I couldn't help myself. I threw my arms around her in a hug.

She laughed, then tightened her arms around me. When she drew back, she smiled. "I don't care what happens between you and Alaric. You and I will remain friends, agreed?"

I smiled and nodded, my throat tightening. "I'd like that."

"Now, come on, we need to go upstairs."

She led me up to a room I'd never seen. It was a beautifully decorated bedroom in shades of cream and pale blue. We passed through into a dressing room that was bigger than my entire flat. I gasped, spinning in a circle as I took in the entire space.

"This is magnificent," I breathed.

There were clothing racks on every wall, but not the normal kind. These were so fancy that I didn't have words for them, and there were several display cases that showed off gowns in their full glory. A small platform on the far side of the wall faced a three-paneled mirror. There were two chaise longues and a couch, along with freestanding sets of drawers made of beautiful golden wood. From the size of the drawers, they likely contained lingerie or jewelry.

"It's my darling," Madeline said. "Well, they're all my darlings." She gestured to the dresses. "I've invited your friends over to choose what they want to wear. They'll be fitted using magic, of course. But for you, I ordered a gown from Paris."

I gasped, turning to her. "You shouldn't have."

"Of course she should have." Vivian's voice sailed into the room before she did.

I turned to see her gliding in with her usual grace, wearing her favorite lined silk robe and carrying a medium-sized black box. She held it out. "And I've brought you this."

"Oh, you lucky witch," Madeline said. "She never lets me wear the family tiara."

"Tiara?" I asked.

Vivian arched a brow. "Of course. We are Blackthorn. Someone in the family wears the tiara to every ball. And you do too get to wear the tiara, Madeline. It's just that it's Emma's turn."

"But Alaric and I—"

"Shh." She waved that away. "You don't need to be with my grandson to be family."

Tears pricked my eyes, and my throat tightened almost unbearably. She approached me and wrapped me in a hug that felt like home, and I leaned into her.

"Thank you." My voice sounded strange because of the tears, but she didn't mention it. "For everything."

"No, thank you." She pulled back. "You've breathed life into this family again, and we love you for it."

"I love you all, too."

She smiled and looked down at the box. "Now, let's see how this looks on you."

I held my breath as she opened the box and revealed a delicate tiara made of gold and diamonds. It looked like twisted vines of tiny leaves, and I'd never seen anything so beautiful in my life.

"It's amazing," I whispered.

"It will look even better on you," she said. "We'll have the hair stylist create the perfect style to go with it."

"No matter how tonight goes, this day is going to be a dream," I said.

And it was. The gown that Madeline had got for me was a pale pink masterpiece. The silk bodice was adorned with intricate silvery embroidery and beadwork that shimmered like morning dew on rose petals. The skirt cascaded in layers of sheer silk, each layer designed to look like flower petals tipped in silver.

The hair stylists and makeup artists were set up in the huge bathroom, making it look like a movie set. And when my friends arrived—everyone from the coven, as well as Aria and her family—the party really began. There was champagne and chocolate and laughter and joy. Everyone found the perfect dress. Even Penelope had a diamond collar that would make anyone envious.

I wished I could commit the entire day to memory.

When I was finally dressed and made up, it was only an hour before the start of the ball. I was finished before everyone else since I needed to double-check the arrangements downstairs, but they would join me when the party started.

I found Madeline, who was still in one of the makeup chairs, the artist putting the final touches on her lips.

"Madeline, thank you so much."

"Of course, darling." She managed to speak while hardly moving her lips. It was clear this was not a new thing for her. "Check with Mother before you go down. She'll want you to make a grand entrance."

"What do you mean?"

The corners of her mouth tilted up in a little smile. "You'll see."

"All right then, Lady Mysterious. I'll see you at the ball."

She waggled her fingers in a cheerful goodbye, then turned her gaze back to the mirror.

I found Vivian across the bathroom, rising from the hair stylist's chair. She wore an elegant chignon accented with a diamond pin shaped like flowers. Her gown was a thick navy silk that made her blue eyes glow.

She gripped my hands. "Don't you look gorgeous, darling."

"You do, too. Barnaby won't know what hit him."

"Oh, he'll fall over when he sees me." She frowned. "If ghosts can fall over, that is."

"You'll find out." I grinned at her. "Madeline told me to see you before I went downstairs."

"Oh, yes. You're ready?"

"Ready as I'll ever be." And looking far better than I'd ever imagined I could.

"Good, wait here a moment. I'll come back and get you."

I did as she commanded, checking in with each of my friends to see how they were getting along with their outfits. Everyone looked amazing, each wearing gowns nicer than any of us had ever worn in our lives.

Finally, Vivian returned. "You can go now. I've got to check with Madeline about something, but I'll see you later."

"All right. I'm just supposed to go?"

"Yes. Head down the stairs."

"All right." The mystery was enough to pique my interest, for sure.

A huge sweeping arc of stairs led down to the main floor, just like the ones I'd seen in movies. Descending in a dress like this would be like something out of any girl's fantasies. Except in the fantasy, the handsome hero was waiting at the bottom.

I shoved the thought away and was determined to enjoy the moment, even if I was alone. I reached the top of the stairs and began to descend. I was halfway down when I spotted Alaric.

He stood at the base of the stairs, so handsome that he almost didn't look real. He was dressed for the ball in a glorious tuxedo, and his gaze was riveted to me.

"Alaric?" I asked, as if I didn't believe my eyes.

I almost didn't.

Because he didn't look mad at me, like he had the last time I'd seen him. He looked hopeful. And a bit worried. And like he'd never seen anyone more beautiful in his entire life. The expression on his face made me feel like a queen.

My heart thundered as I approached him, stopping a couple meters away. "What are you doing here? I didn't think you would come."

"I want to apologize." His voice was thick with sincerity.

"For what?"

Pain flashed in his eyes. "For being such a horrible beast to you. For not believing you, and for letting my own damage get in the way of the best thing that's ever happened to me." He drew in a breath. "You're the best person I've ever met, and every day with you has been the best day of my life. It seemed too good to be true, and I let my own fear and doubt get in the way. I hope you can forgive me."

The air rushed out of my lungs. "That was a pretty good apology."

The right corner of his mouth lifted up in a smile. "I worked hard on it."

"I can tell."

"I truly am sorry. You aren't Katrina, and I should have remembered that. I should have asked you what you meant when you said you wanted this life."

I frowned. "What?"

"That's what set me off. The paparazzo had come to me, and I was looking for you in order to find out what kind of deal you'd made. Then I heard you say you wanted this life, and you were looking at the house, and I was immediately back with Katrina, in the same situation." He shook his head, an expression of disgust on his face. "I'm so sorry. I should have asked you for clarification before jumping to conclusions."

"You should have." I smiled, and it felt a bit wobbly. "I was talking about your family. They were standing on the steps of the house. I love them."

I love you.

The words blasted into my mind, but I kept them to myself. I needed to see how the rest of this would go before I confessed to something like that.

"I realized that later. It just took me time. And a bit of a walloping from my grandmother."

"She knows about us?"

"She does. She always did. Or at least, she knew something was up, but she liked you enough to want to see where it went."

"Wow." Vivian would continue to surprise me, it seemed. "Is that all?"

He shook his head. "I have one more thing to show you. A gift. Then you can decide whether you'll forgive me."

I'd already decided, but I wanted to see what he had to show me. "Lead the way."

He held out his arm to me. "Don't feel like you have to accept it, though."

"Don't be silly. I'm sure I'll love whatever it is." I smiled at him as I slipped my arm through his, loving the connection with him. "Where are we going?"

"You'll see." He led me out of the house and around to the side lawn. We walked between a group of tables that had been set up near one of the bars. The mixologist was already there, perfecting cocktails that would change colors and release sparks of magical energy into the air. Vivian had found the bartender in St. Ives, of all places.

We passed the dance floor, which had been imbued with magic to cause time to slow down when the dancers wanted it to, allowing them to enjoy a special dance for a bit longer.

Then we left the party space behind, heading toward the woods that I'd first sneaked through in order to ask Alaric to let me host the ball there.

At the edge of the woods was a building I hadn't seen before. It looked like a normal house—at least, more normal than Blackthorn Hall. It was still very large, and absolutely gorgeous, with two stories built of pale gray stone. There were even rose vines climbing the walls.

"This wasn't here before, was it?" I looked up at him. "Or am I losing my memory?"

He smiled down at me. "No. It wasn't here before. Come look."

He took me to the front door, which had been painted a beautiful navy blue. He opened the door and gestured for me to step inside.

I did, entering a gorgeous open hall with a gleaming wooden floor and arched entrances on either side that led to two beautiful sitting rooms. In a trance, I walked toward the back of the house, where the kitchen of my dreams sat across from a dining area and family room. The space was huge, but it was the massive wall of windows and the French doors overlooking the back garden that were truly spectacular. They overlooked an expanse of grass that led up to a clear, babbling stream. Flowerbeds dotted the space, and on the other side of the stream, massive oaks marked the entrance to the woods. It looked like something out of a fairytale.

I turned to Alaric, my heart pounding. "This is amazing, but what is it?"

"It's yours, if you want it." He smiled and shrugged. "I'd live here, too, if you'd let me."

I laughed and threw my arms around his neck, joy bubbling up in my heart. I pulled back to look at him but didn't let go. "Of course I'd let you. But why? And *how*?"

"You said you wanted a normal life. And that you'd dreamed of a regular home since you were a child." He looked around. "It's not quite a regular home. A bit bigger. But it's more normal than Blackthorn Hall, and I built it for you."

"In a week?" Shock raced through me.

"Well, it took a lot of money, men, and magic." He looked up at the ceiling. "And there's absolutely nothing upstairs but drywall and plaster. But there will be."

I hugged him again, then pressed a kiss to his lips before pulling back and saying, "This is amazing. But what will happen to the big house?"

"Granny plans to move back, and I think Harold and Madeline will join her."

I grinned widely. "So they'll live right next door?"

"That's the plan."

I couldn't believe how amazing it all sounded. How had I got so lucky? This was all too amazing to be real.

But it was.

And so was Alaric.

He pulled back so that he could look at me. "I love you, Emma. I want to spend my life with you. I want to raise a family here, and whether that's five kids or just you, me, and Penelope, it will be perfect."

I grinned. "Maybe not five. But we'll talk about it."

"Thank you so much for forgiving me for being an absolute idiot."

I pressed my hands to his cheeks and looked into his eyes. "Of course I forgive you. I love you."

Joy lit his eyes, and he pressed his lips to mine in the most perfect kiss of all time.

No matter what happened at the ball or with my coven, life was already perfect.

THIRTY

ALARIC

SHE'D FORGIVEN ME.

I'd never been more grateful for anything in my life.

When she'd walked down those stairs looking like the princess from a fairytale, I'd been struck dumb. I'd never seen anyone so beautiful, and when I'd noticed the tiara on her head, I'd felt like it was a sign.

My mother had worn that same tiara to balls, and it was fitting that Emma would wear it. I smiled down at her, so happy that my soul felt like it could fly out of my chest.

"Your ball is about to start," I said.

"What if we just stayed here?" She smiled up at me, eyes glinting with joy.

"You've worked too hard to miss this, and the coven needs to see you shine. You'll be an official witch before the night is over, I'm sure of it."

"I don't care." She laughed. "Well, I do care. But not for the same reasons. I wanted to be made an official witch so that I would have a family. But they were already my family. Lily, of all people, made that clear a few days ago. Even if I failed here and lost my job because we didn't have enough joy for next year's spells, they'd still have loved me and helped me. I shouldn't have doubted that. And now I have you, too."

"True, you do. But you worked hard, and you deserve to be recognized for your efforts."

She grinned. "Good point. I do want to see how it's all going. There will be some fabulous events tonight. And I've got a surprise for you, too."

I arched a brow. "Oh, do you?"

"Yes. I do." She grabbed my arm and tugged. "Now come on. Let's go get a glass of champagne and toast to our future."

"I can't imagine a better one." I followed her out of the house and toward the party, which was just getting started.

Emma shot one glance over her shoulder at the house. "It really is perfect. Thank you."

"It'll be perfect once you're in it."

She grinned up at me, then turned to look at the guests beginning to trickle in from cars pulling up the drive. They were dressed in their finest, all with smiles on their faces, and I couldn't wait to see what Emma had planned for that night.

I caught sight of my grandmother and Madeline on the patio, overseeing the party with smiles on their faces. The band on the far end of the patio had started playing, and the magic filtered across the lawn. The sun was beginning to set, and the lanterns strung over the lawn were lighting up. Amongst the lanterns, the joy batteries were scattered, collecting the happiness from everyone in the crowd.

Emma flagged down a passing server and took two glasses of champagne, then handed one to me. "To our future," she said.

"To you, my love."

She smiled and pressed a kiss to my lips, then clinked her glass to mine and took a sip. "Oh, it's divine."

"Straight from the Blackthorn cellars."

She rolled her eyes. "What a life you live."

"You live it, too, now."

She shook her head and pointed to the house I'd built her. "I have a normal house." She smiled at me. "But you're right. Not a normal life. And I wouldn't want one, now that I know this is an option."

"Good." I pressed another kiss to her lips. "Shall we go get something to eat?"

"I'd love that. I can't wait to see what your grandmother and aunt have in store for us."

We climbed the stairs to the patio where the buffet tables had been set up, and I had to admit that my grandmother had outdone herself. There was every type of food I could imagine, along with ice sculptures that flowed as if they were alive. One was a pair of dancers, looking like living glass as they twirled on their silver platter.

All around, people ate and drank and talked. We filled our plates, joining a bar table where my grandmother and aunt stood with their drinks.

Madeline smiled at Emma. "You like the house?"

"I adore it." She smiled. "You knew about this?"

"It's hard to miss the most optimistic construction project on the planet when it's happening in your own garden. I'm amazed he completed it."

"I knew he would." My grandmother smiled. "And I'm so pleased to officially welcome you to the family."

"Although I stand by what I said at the door," Madeline added. "You'd be family with or without this one." She nudged my shoulder and grinned.

"Thank you." Emma smiled at them. "I love you both."

"And we love you." My grandmother hugged her.

We spent the next ten minutes in conversation with my family, during which I was unable to let go of my grip around Emma's waist. I never wanted to let her go.

"This is quite the party," Hazel said as she approached. The rest of the official witches were with her, and I recognized them all now.

"Do you like it?" Emma smiled hopefully.

"We're more than impressed," Hazel said. "The fairytale photo booth is a real hit." At my questioning look, she clarified. "Guests enter the booth and name a fairytale. Then they pose. The picture that comes out is them dressed in costumes from that tale, set on an appropriate background."

"It's a fantastic souvenir," Willow added, a smile on her face. "And the maze is a blast. The little surprises around every corner, and the enchanted statues! I just love them."

"But none of that compares with your big surprise," Hazel said. "You've truly outdone yourself, Emma. Those are memories that people will cherish forever."

I looked down at Emma, who glowed with pleasure, and asked, "Big surprise?"

She nodded up at me. "That's what I want to show you when we get a chance."

"I look forward to it."

"You two should go along and do that," Hazel said, before turning her attention entirely to Emma. "We'll announce this at the next coven meeting, but I want you to know now that you're going to be made an official witch. Congratulations, Emma. You deserve it."

Emma squealed and threw her arms around Hazel. "Oh, my gosh, thank you."

Hazel smiled and pulled back. "We're lucky to have you. Even if this ball hadn't been such a success, we'd still be lucky. You're a wonderful person, Emma, and an incredible witch. We'd have found a way to keep you because you're family, but I'm glad the ball is such a hit. Next year will be very successful because of all the work you've done here today."

"Thank you." Emma drew in a deep breath. "That means a lot to me."

"Good. Now go on and show your man the surprise."

Emma looked up at me. "Ready?"

"Ready."

We said our goodbyes to everyone. My grandmother accompanied us toward the surprise, saying that she needed to meet her date. As we neared the maze, I noticed that the garden surrounding it was filled with a ghostly blue glow. Drawing closer, I saw spirits—dozens of them, hugging and talking to party guests who held revelation sticks. Without a word, my grandmother drifted off to find Barnaby.

"What is this?" I asked. "Are we more haunted than I realized?"

"No." Emma smiled and shook her head. "This was my surprise. It was your grandmother, and our trip to visit the Marquis of Dale, that gave me the idea."

"You're going to have to clarify."

"I asked all of the guests to bring something that made them think of a lost loved one, just like Rupert's watch from his grandfather. Then I created hundreds of revelation sticks." She laughed. "It was a lot of work, and many of the local witches chipped in. The final key was finding a spell to imbue the sticks with a tiny bit of my magic and ability to communicate with the dead. So it's like I'm here, acting as a medium, even though I'm not really here."

"That's incredible." I couldn't believe what she'd accomplished. "I've never heard of such a thing."

"That's because it hasn't been done before." She grinned. "At least, not in this exact way. I had to cobble together quite a few spells, but it worked." The excitement in her voice filled me with joy.

I loved seeing her this happy.

"And my surprise for you, if you want it, is to let you speak to your mother." She pointed to the tiara on her head. "Your grandmother told me about this. I think it will help bring her forward."

The air rushed from my lungs. "That's possible?"

"I think so." She smiled. "I'll get you a revelation stick."

"I want you to be there."

"Really?"

I nodded. "I want you to meet her. If you're present, I won't need one of the sticks, will I?"

She shook her head. "I can do it without one—I should just be touching you. Are you ready?"

"As I'll ever be."

"All right." She drew in a deep breath, her magic filling the air. Since she wore the tiara, she didn't need to touch it with her hand. Instead, she gripped both my hands in hers. Her power flowed through me, and a shadowy form began to appear.

Moments later, my mother stood before me. A wide smile grew on her face. "Alaric? Is that you?"

I nodded, awe and happiness filling me. "Mother."

Emma released my hands but pressed her hand to my back so that I maintained the ability to see my mother.

My mother reached out her arms, and I hugged her. It was strange—like she was there, but not quite. Still, it felt as I remembered, the most amazing comfort and love.

She pulled back. "Oh, you've grown so handsome, my boy."

"You look as I remember. Beautiful."

She smiled. "I know you've worried about me, but you shouldn't. I don't remember what happened that night, and the afterworld is wonderful. I'm truly happy. And I'm so glad that you've had Vivian here for you. Please tell her I love her."

"Of course." I looked at Emma. "I want you to meet someone."

"Oh, I know who she is." My mother smiled. "There's quite a lot of talk about this one in the spirit world. I'm honored that you're going to be my daughter-in-law." She gasped and pressed a hand to her mouth. "I hope I didn't reveal something you don't already know..."

I smiled. "I'm going to ask her soon enough."

Emma laughed. "Let's not rush things. But yes, I think I'm going to be here for a while."

"Forever, I hope," I said.

"Forever." Emma smiled.

"I'll leave you two alone," my mother said. "But Emma will be able to connect us for future visits, won't you?"

Emma nodded. "I will. And it was wonderful to meet you, Your Grace."

"Oh, call me Maggie. Or Mum, if you want to. Eventually." She smiled and laughed. "I know it's only been five minutes, but I have a good feeling about this."

"Me, too," Emma said.

My mother turned to me. "I love you, Alaric, and I'll see you soon."

With that, she disappeared.

I turned to Emma, stunned. "You've brought my mother back."

She nodded. "I think that's my witchy gift." A little laugh escaped her. "I'd say it's a good one."

"The best one." I gestured to the people all around us. "Look how happy everyone is."

"I know. I'm so thrilled."

I turned to her, tilting her chin up so that her gaze met mine. "You're incredible, Emma Willowby. And I'm glad you're mine."

The smile that she gave me was so brilliant, it almost

blinded me. Overhead, starlight fireworks lit up the sky. They glittered like gold, hanging in the air without falling. Beneath their light, Emma was so beautiful, it defied words.

"I love you, Alaric. With all my heart."

"And I love you."

With the fireworks exploding overhead, I kissed her, knowing that the future would be brighter than anything I could have ever imagined.

ACKNOWLEDGMENTS

Thank you, Ben, for everything. There would be no books without you.

Thank you to Jena O'Connor and Ash Fitzsimmons for your excellent editing. Thank you to Susie and Aisha for your eagle eye with errors. The book is immensely better because of you!

ABOUT LINSEY

Before becoming a writer, Linsey Hall was a nautical archaeologist who studied shipwrecks from Hawaii and the Yukon to the UK and the Mediterranean. She credits fantasy and historical romances with her love of history and her career as an archaeologist. After a decade of tromping around the globe in search of old bits of stuff that people left lying about, she settled down and started penning her own romance novels. Her Dragon's Gift series draws upon her love of history and the paranormal elements that she can't help but include.

BONNIE
DOON
PRESS

Linsey@LinseyHall.com
www.LinseyHall.com
https://www.facebook.com/LinseyHallAuthor